A BEELINE TO MURDER

"A mystery featuring a lady cop turned farmer who can't help digging up clues? What fun!"
—*Joanne Fluke*

"Meera Lester's engaging debut, *A Beeline to Murder* offers beekeeping, organic gardening, pastry baking—and an engaging mystery. Crammed full of homey farming advice, beekeeping tips, and recipes, this debut cozy will be popular with readers who love G.A. McKevett or Joanne Fluke."—*Library Journal*

"Abby's a fun character—thanks for giving me the chance to meet her! Ex-cop Abby Mackenzie may have traded her badge for a garden hoe and a beekeeper's hood in Meera Lester's first Henny Penny Farmette Mystery, but danger and crime won't leave her alone. Beekeeping and garden tips, yummy recipes, and a darling dog named Sugar give this honey of a debut a special flavor that will leave readers buzzing happily."—**Leslie Budewitz,** two-time Agatha Award winning author of the Seattle Spice Shop Mysteries

"This fun cozy mystery brings a triple treat: a California wine country setting, a touch of romance with a handsome Frenchman and country hints and recipes from the writer's own farmette."—*Rhys Bowen, New York Times* bestselling author of the Molly Murphy and Royal Spyness mysteries

"Animal shelter volunteer Meera Lester combines careful attention to detail with her warm touch and abundant sense of humor to paint a perfect portrait of the vexations as well as the great joys of dog rescue. *A Beeline for Murder* is a must-read for anyone who loves animals, loves helping them, and enjoys a crime-fighting romp that blends rescue and romance with an irresistible woman-plus-pooch sleuth duo leading the way."
—***Katerina Lorenzatos Makris,*** editor of Spicy StoriesSaveLives.com, author of The Island Secrets Mysteries, and co-author of *Your Adopted Dog: Everything You Need to Know About Rescuing and Caring for a Best Friend in Need*

"Farming tips and murder vie for the reader's attention in Lester's appealing debut cozy, set in the California wine country . . . Recipes, including one for doggy treats, appear through-out."—***Publishers Weekly***

"If you love mysteries, and dogs, and food, this one's for you. We learn about bees and how and why they swarm, and enjoy delightful farming tips and recipes. And, of course, there's a dog - the wonderful Sugar. If you're a mystery buff, don't miss this charming, cozy series. A treat!"—***Hudson Valley News***

Also by Meera Lester

The Henny Penny Farmette Mystery Series

A Beeline to Murder

The Murder of a Queen Bee

A Hive of Homicides

Meera Lester

KENSINGTON BOOKS
www.kensingtonbooks.com

KENSINGTON BOOKS are published by

Kensington Publishing Corp.
119 West 40th Street
New York, NY 10018

ISBN-13: 978-1-61773-919-4
ISBN-10: 1-61773-919-7
First Kensington Hardcover Edition: October 2017
First Kensington Mass Market Edition: November 2018

eISBN-13: 978-1-61773-918-7
eISBN-10: 1-61773-918-9
Kensington Electronic Edition: October 2017

10 9 8 7 6 5 4 3 2 1

Printed in the United States of America

I dedicate this book to all the readers of the Henny Penny Farmette mysteries, with my appreciation for your continued loyalty and support.

Chapter 1

The *Varroa destructor* parasite is a true
bloodsucker, a mite that attaches itself
to a honeybee's body and feeds on the
hemolymph.

—*Henny Penny Farmette Almanac*

The steady drumming of rain had slowed to a
light sprinkle as Abigail Mackenzie navigated
her Jeep past Main Street shops decorated with
vampires, witches, goblins, and other spooky mo-
tifs. It was the week before Halloween. She hung a
left turn toward the Church of the Holy Names.
Parking behind the priest's cottage, Abby glanced
at the dash clock. Three thirty. Half an hour remained before the start of the ceremony, but it was
well past the time for confessing the truth.

She'd had plenty of opportunities to tell Paola
Varela about how she felt. So why hadn't she summoned the courage to speak up before now? Tell
her friend the truth. But she hadn't. Not at the
Wednesday night baking classes at the Kitchen Gad-
get Shop, where the two had become fast friends.

Or at the Labor Day picnic in the downtown park where civic leaders held the holiday tree lighting in December and the Shakespeare festival in June. She'd even hesitated to bring up the subject at the Columbus Day parade, where they had volunteered to flip pancakes in the food tent. And what could she say, anyway? It wasn't her place to criticize Paola's decision to renew her marriage vows with her husband, Jake, even if his infidelities had become common knowledge around town. No, she'd kept silent. Now it was too late.

For Paola and Jake's wedding vow renewal ceremony, Abby had promised to lend Paola her grandmother's thin, well-worn band as something "borrowed." It seemed rather ironic, since Paola had an enviable diamond set in gold, which Jake had placed on her finger during their wedding seven years ago. But Paola had told Abby she wanted something that symbolized a long and happy marriage, in contrast to her own troubled one. Lending the ring was a way to show support for a friend Abby had come to look upon as the little sister she never had. Maybe the wrinkles in Paola and Jake's marriage would eventually smooth themselves out. Her friend deserved a bright future with the man she loved.

Glancing up into the rearview mirror before leaving the car, Abby spotted a worker cleaning up storm debris. Abby didn't recognize the man, who was bundled up against the cold, with a knit cap and upturned jacket collar, but surmised he was likely another fellow down on his luck. Father Joseph recruited helpers from halfway houses for ex-cons and recovering addicts to work on the church property. The men would do odd jobs and maintenance in exchange for a hot meal and a dollar or two in their pockets. The priest believed that anyone wanting to work deserved a job. This particular hapless man, Abby thought, looked to be in his late twenties or early thirties.

Looking more closely in the mirror, Abby flinched at the reflection of the swollen cheek beneath her left eye. Of all the stupid things she'd done since moving to the farmette, cleaning the bee fountain without donning her beekeeper's suit had to be the craziest. Even if the weather had turned cool and the bees were less active. Now, after two days, the bee sting under her left eye pooched out like a puff pastry. Donning sunglasses on a dark and rainy afternoon would look ridiculous. And bailing on her commitment to Paola was not an option.

After sliding out of the Jeep, Abby eased her raincoat's hood up and over her reddish-gold locks, which she'd braided and twisted into a bun at the nape of her neck. Cinching her coat tighter around her black silk dress, Abby thrust her hand into her coat pocket and felt for the ring that carried the vibe of a loving marriage that had lasted a lifetime. She hurried up the steps and slipped into the small chapel dedicated to Our Lady of Guadalupe, situated on the north side of the church proper. Silk-ribbon flowers adorned the chiffon that served as a backdrop for the icon. The scent of fresh roses permeated the small space. Silhouettes danced on the wall behind the flickering flames of the devotional candles as the door closed behind Abby. The chapel—with its single bench—afforded more privacy than the cavernous Holy Names. Abby knew how her friend Paola favored that chapel when she needed spiritual solace.

Upon hearing Abby enter, Paola looked up, brightened, and stood to offer air kisses to Abby's cheeks. In her Argentine accent, Paola whispered, "Thanks to God, Abby, you have come. I could not do this without you."

"Of course you could," Abby replied. "But you don't have to."

"My nerves are a wreck," Paola said.

"I can see that." Abby clasped Paola's fretful hands in hers. "You are renewing your vows with the man you love. So what's with the nerves?"

"Can you not guess?" Paola's brown eyes darkened under heavily mascaraed lashes. A faint line creased her forehead. "In my mother's time, a man like Jake would go to jail. But now, even in Argentina, when a man cheats on his wife, she endures the pain. Or she divorces. I don't want a divorce, Abby. I want our marriage to be good again. Is this possible?"

Abby released Paola's hands and looked at the younger woman with admiration. She couldn't fathom why Jake would seek affection from other women when he had an exotic Argentine beauty by his side. After sliding her hands back into her coat pocket, Abby sought and found her grandmother's ring. The slightly misshapen band had worn thin through forty years of marriage. Yet Abby could still sense its power to ground. Perhaps Paola would feel it, too. The younger woman desired a stable, secure, and happy life, the kind

Abby's grandparents had. The kind Abby wanted for herself.

"You said Jake had changed," said Abby. "That he's promised never to betray you again. You've been through couples counseling. The worst is behind you. Surely, there are no more secrets between the two of you now." Abby hoped she sounded more enthusiastic and reassuring than she felt.

They could hear the soloist humming strains of the old hymn "O Perfect Love" from the adjoining church.

Paola looked intently at Abby. "Do you think he would have been a different husband if he'd married an American woman? An educated lady who speaks better English than I do?"

"Don't be silly," Abby said, shaking her head. She had a niggling hunch that Jake had used these excuses in the heat of arguments to intimidate the impressionable, vulnerable Paola.

"I love him, Abby. I do, but I don't understand what he wants or why he acts the way he does." Her eyes searched Abby's. "Why is that?"

"I don't know." Abby forced a smile and sought a way to lighten the mood. *No woman should have to question a husband's love on the day she's renewing her marriage vows with him.* "You are barely twenty-seven, and you're asking a woman at least ten years your senior who has yet to be a bride?"

Paola's features relaxed. "You just haven't found the right man . . . but you will."

"Maybe." Abby touched her palm to Paola's shoulder. "After all you've been through, here you are, reassuring me."

Paola murmured, "Did you bring it?"

Abby extracted the ring from her pocket. "Here you go. Let's hope it blesses your union with Jake."

Paola slipped the thin band onto the first finger of her right hand. "Your *abuela* . . . grandmother . . . she had large fingers."

"Yes, she did." Abby chuckled. "And I have hands just like hers—all the better for kneading bread, making jam, and beekeeping," Abby said.

"I'll give it right back after the ceremony," said Paola. "I know the ring means a lot to you." She shifted her gaze from the ring to Abby. "Will you be able to read the verses with your cheek and eye so swollen?"

"Stop fretting. I'm fine. You just need to relax and be present with every beautiful moment that comes today."

"I suppose," said Paola. "God has turned Jake's heart back to me. That's what Father Joe says."

Abby leaned in and whispered, "How could your husband not adore you?"

Paola stretched out her hands and gazed upon the rings.

Abby considered the irony—the diamond-bejeweled band seemed more substantive and flashy than most, even as the marriage it symbolized had been withering. And the misshapen thin band that now encircled the middle finger of Paola's right hand had held Abby's grandparents' marriage together for a lifetime.

A tenor voice had joined the soprano.

"Showtime," said Abby, relieved that she didn't have to say things she might not believe—like that she was confident Jake was now fully committed. "See you inside," she said, bussing Paola's cheek.

After she'd left the chapel to cross the courtyard to the Holy Names Church, Abby encountered Jake.

"Is she ready?" he asked. His tone carried a hint of arrogant impatience, which Abby found offensive. At five feet nine, Jake wasn't a towering figure, but he did have a commanding presence, charisma, and the looks of a model, with large dark eyes, thick brows, and a chiseled face.

"She is," Abby said, noticing his longish dark locks slicked back into a ponytail. He had grown a goatee—perhaps at the behest of Paola—and wore a gray wool suit with a crisp white oxford shirt and a striped tie.

"Good. It's past time to begin. What happened to your eye?"

"Stung by a bee," Abby replied.

"Obviously, it found your face irresistible," said Jake. "I wouldn't mind being one of your bees." Grinning, he reached out to touch her other cheek. "I know how to sting a woman without damaging her."

Abby flinched and stepped back. Brushing away his hand, she drilled him with a stare. "You wouldn't if you knew what you'd have to give up."

He tilted his head slightly, as if assessing her. "Oh, and what would that be?"

"Your life."

He grinned. "Might be worth it."

Abby's cheeks grew warm, and she looked past Jake to see if Paola could have overheard their

conversation. To her dismay, Paola stood just behind Jake, her large eyes shimmering with tears.
Not knowing what to do next, Abby hastened to
the nearest side entrance into Holy Names. The
pencil-thin heels of her shoes clicked softly against
the marble floor as she entered the sanctuary. The
pianist and a violinist had replaced the singers.
From the first few measures, Abby recognized
Pachelbel's Canon in D.

After spotting Katerina Petrovsky, her best friend
and backup—even though Abby no longer served
on the police force—Abby slid into a pew beside
her. "I could wring that man's neck," Abby exclaimed
beneath her breath.

"What? Whose neck?" the blond, blue-eyed Kat
asked.

"Who else? Jake Winston." Abby narrowed her
eyes and blew air between her lips.

"Uh-oh. Trouble in paradise already?" asked
Kat, smoothing her short bobbed cut, which had
been moussed into waves. She turned her head to
locate Jake.

"Don't look," Abby whispered. "I'll explain
later." She opened her small clutch purse and removed the folded paper on which she'd copied
the verses that Paola had asked her to read. She
scanned the words a final time. Eventually, she
looked up and gazed around the room, taking
note of the many family members and friends present for the solemnizing of the Varela-Winston
vows.

Abby focused on calming herself by taking several slow, deep breaths. When she felt settled, she
looked toward the aisle. Jake walked past her,

headed to the front, where he took his place near Father Joseph. Paola followed on the arm of her brother Emilio, who worked as the chef at Jake's family winery. Emilio was the skinniest chef Abby had ever seen. Tall too. Maybe six feet. Longish black hair framed a tan face with thick brows and large dark eyes. He had full lips and an angular chin. Emilio took his seat next to his aged father, who needed two canes to walk because of a ranching accident in their homeland, and his prim white-haired mother. Jake and Paola stood stiff and silent in front of Father Joseph, waiting for the music to end.

"So I ask you," whispered Kat, "who but Paola could stroll in from a rainstorm as fresh as an Argentine orchid?"

"Indeed." Abby trained her gaze on Paola's belted, knee-length ivory knit with three-quarter-length sleeves. The dress accentuated her petite and perfectly formed figure. Her waist-long black hair had been tied and twisted into a chignon at the nape of her neck, its only adornment a red silk hibiscus. Noticing the Stuart Weitzman bright candy-colored pumps with narrow heels Paola had chosen to wear, Abby smiled. The two of them had selected those shoes together.

Straightening her spine against the back of the pew, Abby listened to the final strains of the music and gazed at Paola's stunning ensemble. The dress's ivory hue symbolized the seven-year marriage. Abby had suggested that some colorful shoes could make a statement. The right heels, she'd told Paola, could signify to everyone that Paola was going places, putting her individual stamp on the

world with her truffle business. Then they'd found
the chic boho heels with splashes of red, yellow,
and blue. Abby recalled how animated Paola had
become as she explained why she needed the
heels.

"Good fortune must be in the air," the sales-
woman had remarked. She'd explained that another woman had just purchased the same heels.
The woman and her husband were taking a cruise.
"A second honeymoon," the saleslady had told
them. Much deserved after all the hard work they'd
put in to take their Silicon Valley software company public, which had made them overnight mil-
lionaires. Paola's smile had widened, as if she had
been injected with a bolus of happiness.

Jake now faced Paola, whom he'd sworn to love,
honor, and cherish until death. Did he feel one
iota of guilt for the come-on he'd initiated with
Abby? He didn't show it. His gaze swept the room;
perhaps he was checking out the females present.

The priest spoke softly, apparently guiding the
couple, because Jake reached out and took Paola's
hands in his. He gazed into her eyes. Father
Joseph spoke again. Abby thought she caught the
words "God is smiling."

Father Joseph asked the two to reaffirm before
God and those assembled that they were recom-
mitting their lives to each other. Both said yes. At
the priest's prompting, Jake began to address
Paola. His promises sounded sincere. When it was
Paola's turn, her wan smile and questioning eyes
revealed all the anxiety she must be holding inside. In a barely perceptible voice, Paola began to
recite her vows.

Father Joseph said, "Love is kind. Love believes all things, endures all things, and forgives. Love is a refuge. Love is a comfort. Love never fails."

Jake's and Paola's expressions remained somber and stoic. Father Joseph called for a short period of silent reflection and then recited a prayer. He then called for the reading.

Abby whispered to Kat, "My cue." She rose, walked to the lectern, and settled herself, paper in hand. She began with the biblical verses from the book of Ecclesiastes and the Song of Songs by Solomon.

"My lover is for me a sachet of myrrh . . . a cluster of henna from the vineyards. . . ." Abby hesitated, not so much for dramatic impact as to calm herself against the rising anger she felt at Jake's behavior. "His body is a work of ivory covered with sapphires. . . . His mouth is sweetness itself."

Abby looked up to see Jake gazing at Paola in a strange way, as if he were seeing her for the first time. Or maybe he was imagining someone else. Paola regarded him with tenderness. They were no longer holding hands but were still facing the priest. Paola now slowly twisted Abby's grandmother's ring around her finger, as if it were a touchstone for happiness.

Buoyed by the glimmer of hope she detected in the couple's faces, Abby proceeded to read the next stanza, which addressed true love's union. "I belong to my lover and for me he yearns. . . . Set me as a seal on your heart." The next verses were taken from Proverbs. Paola had confessed to Abby that she wasn't entirely sure they should be included, but in the end, she had added them.

"Lying lips are an abomination to the Lord, but those who are truthful are his delight. . . . In the path of justice, there is life, but the abominable way leads to death." For some inexplicable reason, a cold shiver ran up Abby's spine as she finished reading the words. The site around the bee sting on her cheek began to itch.

As the music started up again, Abby tucked the paper of verses into her coat pocket, stepped down from the lectern platform, and walked back to her seat. She took a tissue from her purse and gently rubbed her itchy skin, eventually finding a modicum of relief. She decided to take an antihistamine as soon as the vow exchange ended, but for now she'd just have to endure the itchiness.

The priest spoke about the sanctity of marriage and Paola and Jake's renewed commitment to each other. He asked everyone to raise their hands toward the couple as he said a prayer and administered a final blessing. When it came time for the kiss, Jake took his wife into his arms, and at that moment the heavy church door creaked open.

Kat and Abby turned their heads at the same time to see who'd arrived so late. The stranger appeared to be in her early thirties. Highlighted blond tresses in a boyish cut accentuated her youthful features. She wore a dark coat dress and silver pendant earrings.

Abby searched out Eva and Luna, Paola's sisters, to see if they recognized the pretty stranger. They were occupied with shushing their rambunctious daughters, both preschoolers. Next, she sought Paola's mother and father, seated on the other side of the church. They had flown in from Argentina for the occasion. They sat beaming approvingly at their daughter and Jake. Okay, so they hadn't noticed the late arrival, either. Jake's parents were no-shows, remaining in Hawaii for their much-needed vacation after finishing the grape harvest. John Winston II, Jake's grandfather, who never ventured far from his beloved winery, sat alone in the first row, hunched over, perhaps absorbed in reading the missal. Abby stole another look at the woman, who'd slipped into a seat at the back of the church.

Kat leaned in and whispered, "You think our stranger belongs to the bride's party or the groom's?"

"My money is on Jake," Abby answered.

When the service had ended, Abby followed Kat out of her seat and down the center aisle. They fell in step behind others who followed the couple and the priest. The young woman apparently had left.

"I hope they have plenty of chilled bubbly, some great dance music, and some good-looking guys up at the winery," said Kat. "I'm ready to party. Mind if we take your Jeep?"

"Well, sure. But why not just call it like it is? You want me to be the designated driver."

"Well, of course I do," Kat replied with a sheepish grin. "Unless you can't see out of that eye," she said. "Riding with a one-eyed driver could be hazardous to my health."

"Really, Kat. Let me reassure you that I can see and drive perfectly well, thank you very much. So, let's go."

Abby walked in lockstep with Kat behind a statuesque platinum blonde with a butterfly tattoo on her neck, below her upswept do; a thin woman with chestnut-colored hair; and a twentysomething with a long yellow-blond braid. These three women fell in step behind others filing toward the church doors. Abby wondered how many of the attractive ladies present had come to see for themselves that the man they'd known as a charmer was out of the game for good. As a man and a woman argued, their voices rose above the din of friendly banter among the guests.

"Holy crap," said Abby. "Surely that's not Jake and Paola going at it already?"

Kat stretched up on her tiptoes in her suede ankle boots. "Can't see a darn thing."

Outside, on the church steps, they encountered the argument in full swing.

"You bastard. You killed her," shrieked the woman in the dark coat dress and silver earrings.

"You know better than that," bellowed Jake. "Your sister wrapped her car around a tree on Highway Nine. And let us not forget, she was twice over the limit."

"You broke her heart with your lies. You were never going to leave your wife. That ridiculous ceremony I just witnessed proves it." After turning to address Paola, the woman shrieked, "I pity you if you think it meant anything to him. He isn't going to change. And if you believe he is, you deserve each other."

"Go home, Gina," Jake told her.

"And what . . . ? Grieve?" Tears streaked Gina's

face. Her eyes had a smoldering, heavy-lidded look. She lunged at Jake. He threw his arms up in defense as she smacked him with her purse. "I hate you. Hate you," she screamed.

Emilio and the other men in his family pulled Gina away from Jake. Paola's sisters walked Paola backward into the sheltering huddle of her family. Tears swam in the dark eyes of the truffle maker. Her expression bore a tortured look.

A struggling Gina blubbered, "Your family celebrates? Celebrates? While mine grieves? You're evil, Jake Winston. Evil. You will pay for what you've done." After twisting free from the men's grips, she spat at Jake and ran off into the misting rain.

"Let her go," said Father Joseph.

"Whatever!" Jake stormed down the front steps and walked toward Paola's blue Ford Escort.

A hunk of jet-black hair fell from behind Emilio Varela's ear to eclipse his cheek as he hurried to embrace Paola. After the hug from her big brother, she retreated into the church with the priest, and Emilio addressed the guests.

"Listen up. We have chilled champagne and hot hors d'oeuvres, and to follow, a sit-down dinner with fine wine. It would be a shame to waste it. So what are we waiting for?" Emilio seemed comfortable taking charge and clearly desired to get everything back on track. He trotted to the Ford Escort, where Jake had taken refuge, and tapped on the window. The two men spoke briefly, and then Jake got out and went inside the church.

Kat leaned into Abby and said, "I'm so there for the party, but I suspect our guests of honor will be delayed. I'd love to be a fly on the wall to hear what Father Joe has to say about this state of affairs."

Abby rolled her eyes. "Affairs? Seriously, Kat? No pun intended, I'm sure."

Kat replied, "Of course not."

"We should be happy for them," said Abby as she reached into her purse for the car keys.

"Well, I am," said Kat.

"As much as I want to be happy for them, I can't help feeling that this marriage is still in trouble."

On the way to her Jeep with Kat, Abby realized how tidy the parking lot looked now that the gardener/handyman had cleaned it. But she found it more than a little disturbing that as she approached her car, the man was bent over with a flashlight, peering into her Jeep. Seeing her, the man clutched the black garbage bag near the tire, carried it to a mound of other bags piled for collection at the parking lot exit, and deposited it.

"Father Joseph believes in the dignity of work and the power of a second chance for everyone. He sets a good example." Thinking about it, Abby said, "You know, I could use a helping hand around the farmette. Someone prescreened, of course, but it could be a win-win."

"Or not," said Kat. "A priest believes in the innate goodness of all people." She climbed into the Jeep's passenger seat and shut the door. "Father Joseph has that higher power thing going for him to keep those guys in line. And if something bad did happen, the church stands only blocks away from the police station. That's not true for your farmette. Who but your chickens and bees would hear you calling for help if somebody assaulted you?"

How a Honeybee Queen Mates

The honeybee queen (*Apis mellifera*) is the only fertile female in a honeybee hive. She can lay one thousand eggs a day. Unfertilized eggs become males (drones); fertilized eggs become sterile females (worker bees) or new queens. Before a swarm (the way a colony grows its population), the workers feed larvae a special food so the larvae will become new queens. Prior to the virgin queens emerging, the old queen takes flight with approximately half of the workers to find a new home. Back in the hive, the new queens emerge. One or more may leave with some workers, and those that stay behind will sting and attack each other to the death until only one queen remains. That queen will take her virgin flight through the assembled drones outside of the hive. As she flies, she releases pheromones (scents to attract the males). As many as ten drones will mate with her in flight or die trying.

Chapter 2

When a male honeybee succeeds in
mating with a queen, he will die within
a few hours or days.

—*Henny Penny Farmette Almanac*

Abby followed Kat as she merged into the line with the other guests who were heading through the heavy plank doors of the Country Schoolhouse Winery on Rooster Flats Road. The interior offered a cozy, convivial atmosphere for the vow-renewal party, in contrast to the cold night beyond its walls. With its air redolent with aged oak, grape must, and potpourri, the room's focal point was the welcoming blaze in the massive stone fireplace. Here, the party would soon be in full swing.

A female staffer in a black pantsuit and white shirt stood a few feet from the door, offering flutes of bubbly from the huge tray she held. The flutes had been engraved with Jake's and Paola's names and the date. With her cheek still itching, Abby remembered the antihistamine tablets and retrieved one from her purse. After washing it down with a sip of sparkling wine, she strolled back to the warmth of the fireplace, where Kat soon joined her. It would be the perfect people-watching spot, since newcomers often gravitated to the opposite wall to admire the private collection of wines Jake and his family had amassed.

A floor-to-ceiling glass cabinet showcased the collection, which required a climate-controlled temperature. The cabinet base rested on a black-and-white patterned tile riser that found resonance in the floor that swept around the S-shaped tasting bar. The staff had removed the bar stools and had retracted the movable wall to create a large open space. They'd moved in dining tables festooned in autumn colors. All that remained was for the guests of honor to show and the sumptuous celebratory meal to begin. Abby knew her honey would be a surprise gift for the guests. Chef Emilio and his staff intended to put out the miniature jars of lavender honey, which Abby had attractively tied with cream-and-orange gingham ribbon. The jars would remain safely locked in the Jeep until the chef was ready for them.

"Fabulous renovation, don't you agree?" Kat said. "I hardly recognize this place. I heard Jake had to conjure some real mojo for the turn-around, but he's done it, hasn't he? Kind of surprising considering that this nineteen thirties winery was dying on the vine."

Abby sniffed. "Let's hope he can conjure a similar revival of his marriage."

"Hmm. Easier said than done. Anyhow, it takes two, doesn't it? I've heard he's been having mercurial mood swings, and that the wife isn't entirely faultless in the marriage. Not exactly a recipe for success, and yet here we are."

Abby set her glass down on the hearth and removed her coat. "None of us are perfect, Kat, but what specifically are you getting at?"

Kat said in a conspiratorial tone, "You don't think she comes here only to deliver her truffles, do you? I've heard she likes visiting the barrel room from time to time."

Abby arched a brow. "So she's got a friend in the barrel room. I'm sure she knows everyone who works here."

A young woman approached. "Would you like me to take your coats?" the woman asked. "That's my job tonight."

"Oh," said Abby. "That would be lovely."

The blue-eyed woman appeared to be in her early twenties and wore tights, a short black miniskirt, and a white angora sweater. She'd plaited her blond hair in a long braid. "I'm Hannah Thompson, the intern."

"Thompson. Any relation to the barrel room manager?" asked Abby. She exchanged a warning look with Kat, hoping to censor any further comments about the barrel room worker and Paola.

Hannah smiled. "As a matter of fact, my uncle Scott Thompson—he got me this internship."

Kat moistened her lips and gazed over the room in her thoughtful way, as she often did during awkward moments.

"Well, here you go," Abby said. She and Kat handed over their coats. "Lovely to meet you."

Hannah flashed a wide smile and took the coats.

"Yes," Kat chimed in. "Lovely."

With Hannah gone, Abby's gaze swept the room. She was searching to see if Chef Emilio was among them. Not seeing him, Abby leaned into Kat. "I promised to check in with Emilio as soon as I got here. The kitchen is this way. You coming?"

"Thought you would never ask," Kat said. "Guys who can cook are such a turn-on. At the Church of the Holy Names ceremony, I couldn't stop staring at him. Those eyes, that hair."

"Don't you mean the hair on the back of his head? Because that was pretty much what you could see after he'd taken his seat."

"My point exactly," said Kat. "You'll be a love and introduce me, won't you?" she said, walking with Abby to the kitchen. "My birthday is coming—the day before Halloween—and I can't think of a nicer present to give myself than a relationship with a gorgeous new man, especially one that can cook. Wouldn't you agree?"

"No question about it. Just don't show him your broomstick and black cat before he discovers all your other magic," Abby teased.

As they passed an antique sideboard, Abby noticed a basket of folded cards positioned near a crystal bowl of fragrant potpourri. After plucking a card with the winery logo prominently displayed, Abby peeked inside. Another company logo stood out—Chocolaté Artesano. A plastic sleeve stapled inside the folded card held four cocoa beans.

"Oh, this is nice," said Abby, stopping to appreciate the card. "Genius, in fact. Paola and Jake are using their vow-exchange party as a promo opportunity for his wines and her handmade truffles." Handing the card to Kat, Abby said, "You've got to give Jake his due. Probably his idea, but I think our girl Paola is a rising star."

Kat clearly wasn't interested. She was now obsessed about her appearance. "Do I need lipstick? I think I do. What I was wearing is now all over this flute. Give me a minute. I can't meet that gorgeous hunk of a chef looking like this."

"Seriously, Kat. He's not going to notice your lipstick. And besides, what happened to the firefighter you were going to marry last week?"

"So six minutes ago," said Kat. "He could make you hot in all kinds of places, but a chef could mix all that heat with a little sweet. And I have got a mouthful of sweet teeth."

"Trust me, he is working. He won't notice your flirting."

"Oh, he will. Men always do. You might be thinking about men in more imaginative ways, girlfriend, if you didn't go to bed with the chickens, get up with the rooster, and sleep with a dog every night."

"Well, at least Sugar doesn't snore . . . much. Fine. I'll be in the kitchen. The ladies' room is that way." Abby pointed toward the restroom at the far end of the wall.

Kat turned and hurried away.

After tucking the card into her purse, Abby strolled into a hallway and followed the sound of

dish clatter and animated voices. Once through a
swinging galley door, she was met with the tantaliz-
ing scents of the dinner being prepared—fresh
greens with jicama and Fuyu persimmon slices,
harvest pumpkin soup garnished with pepitas,
roasted duckling with merlot-chocolate sauce, a
timbale of wild rice with ancient grains, and as-
paragus spears. At Paola's behest, Emilio had es-
chewed the cultural dishes loved by his Argentine
family and instead had made choices that would
appeal to Jake's family and friends and their winery associates. But Abby felt pretty sure no one
was going to mind. As if on cue, her stomach
growled.

Waitstaff came and went. A kitchen worker
stood at a sink, washing stacks of pots, in an area
off to one side of the room, near a small swinging
door. Fresh produce covered an entire counter. At
other stations, kitchen staff appeared not to notice
Abby as they worked at a fever pitch to finish the
various food courses for the dinner.

Abby soon spotted the sous-chef at her station
and remarked, "Smells divine. I've been saving my
appetite all day for this meal."

Remaining silent, the woman reached for a plat-
ter. She wore a smaller version of the traditional
toque blanche, with her light hair pulled severely
back and secured in a white snood. The long
sleeves of her double-breasted jacket had been
rolled back to nearly her elbows. She kept her
head down, working, as Abby looked on.

"You can't be in here," barked the sous-chef, at
last looking up.

"I'm looking for Chef Emilio. Know where I might find him?"

The woman shrugged. She stopped slicing Fuyu persimmons long enough to jerk her thumb toward the back door.

Leaving the warmth and the savory scents of the kitchen, Abby opened the door and faced a blast of cold air as she stepped outside. *Need a coat. Would have to find Hannah. Oh, forget it.* Shivering, Abby crossed her arms over her chest for warmth. On the lookout for Emilio, she paced past two Dumpsters—one for refuse and the other labeled for recycling. She peered to the left, saw no movement at all. And why would there be? In that direction, the vineyard swept steeply uphill in neatly planted rows. The grapes had been harvested, but the vines had not yet been cut. Some protruded like ghostly arms from the guide wires. Fog threaded along the paths between the vines like fingers of smoke.

"Emilio," she called out, looking to her left and right. Trucks and cars in the lot behind the kitchen appeared as silhouettes. Walking among them, Abby heard a sudden loud pop. She might not be a cop anymore, but she knew a gunshot when she heard one.

Out of instinct, she lunged toward a truck for cover. A car's headlights caught her as she dove. The high heel on her shoe snapped, and she slid on the wet pavement into one of the truck's tires. Uphill, the car lights dimmed as the engine cranked over. The sedan rolled toward her. Abby crawled to the truck's front bumper. Clinging to the cold, wet metal, she hunched low. Not moving. Not breathing. Waiting. The driver seemed intent on finding her, rolling slowly past and pausing at the truck's tailgate. The engine idled. A flashlight beam through the passenger window bobbed around and stopped to rest on the spot she'd just left. Holding her breath, Abby froze. Could the driver see her? Her heart thrummed against her chest wall.

The flashlight went dark. The window rolled up. The car inched on. Abby crawled on all fours to the truck's rear and peered into the darkness and fog, attempting to get a look at the license plate before the fog hazed over it. She watched the older-model, light-colored sedan brake and turn left, but not before Abby spotted the broken or missing lens cover of the passenger side taillight. When the driver gunned the engine, the tires screeched onto the country road, and the car fishtailed into a getaway.

She exhaled a breath of relief. After blotting her bruised and bleeding knees with her silk dress, Abby struggled to stand upright. She found her purse, and clutching it, she limped toward the incline—in the direction of the shot. She moved as stealthily as possible with her broken heel, not daring to call out Emilio's name. . . . There might be another shooter. It was unlikely, but then again . . . Who or what had the perp been targeting?

Parked beneath the pale light of a pole lamp, Abby spotted a car with the driver's side door open. A *Ford Escort. Paola's?* The hair stood up on the back of Abby's neck. Adrenaline rushed through her. Her hobbling gave way to a limping run. She could see the driver slumped over the wheel. As Abby got closer, she realized that the driver was motionless, as if in a deep slumber. It was Jake. Her gaze moved to the passenger, crumpled forward, as if in a defensive position. The pole lamp splayed light into the car's interior, illuminating Paola's head, which was slumped in a weird position, the red hibiscus still perfectly pinned into her chignon.

Abby's heartbeat pounded. She stifled a cry. Choked back tears. *No time to cry. Think. Assess. What's happened here?* Abby had heard only one shot. Of that, she was certain. *One shot, two vics. Only one explanation. The bullet entered and exited Jake's head and struck Paola.* Abby felt for Jake's pulse. Found none. After hustling to the other side of the car, she opened the door with her wadded dress skirt. Reaching toward the dash and feeling for a pulse on Paola's wrist, Abby feared the worst. Then . . . *Oh, God in heaven, yes. A pulse. Weak and thready, but palpable.*

"Paola, can you hear me? It's Abby. Please, please hang on. I'm going to get help."

Abby's thoughts raced. *My phone? Where is it? Oh, no. Coat pocket. Hannah took it. Run.* Abby kicked off her heels and sucked in a sharp breath at the cold, wet sensation on the bottoms of her feet. With purse and shoes in hand, she sprinted barefoot on the frosty pavement back to the kitchen—breathing steam into the frigid night air like a life depended on it and knowing it did.

Inside the kitchen, Abby dashed to the phone she had seen on the back wall, by the door. Trying not to fumble the receiver, she hastily tapped in the number of the emergency dispatch.

A female voice asked, "What's your emergency?"

Abby replied, "This is Abigail Mackenzie. One gunshot fired at the Country Schoolhouse Winery. Back lot. Two vics. Male dead, female alive, barely. Notify police of a one-eight-seven, and send an ambulance."

Jicama and Persimmon Salad

Ingredients:

1 small head romaine lettuce, leaves rinsed and patted dry

2 Fuyu persimmons

½ small jicama

3 tablespoons extra-virgin olive oil

1 tablespoon freshly squeezed lime juice

1 teaspoon honey

½ teaspoon kosher salt (or to taste)

¼ teaspoon freshly ground black pepper (or to taste)

¼ cup toasted pepitas (optional)

Directions:

Tear the lettuce leaves into bite-size pieces and place in a large salad bowl. Set aside.

Peel the persimmons and cut them into ½-inch half-moon slices. Next, peel the jicama and cut it into matchstick-sized pieces. Arrange the persimmon slices and the jicama matchsticks atop the reserved lettuce. Set the salad aside.

Combine in a small bowl the olive oil, lime juice, honey, salt, and pepper. Whisk vigorously until the dressing is well blended.

Drizzle the dressing over the reserved salad and toss it to coat evenly. Sprinkle the salad with the *pepitas*, if desired, and serve at once.

Serves 4

Chapter 3

Your dog will guard your house and
chickens but never your snack.

—*Henny Penny Farmette Almanac*

The whimpering of her darling dog Sugar—
who didn't understand why her owner was so
distressed—reminded Abby to snap out of her de-
spair any way she could. When she'd rescued
Sugar after the town's pastry chef met an untimely
demise, Abby hadn't fully understood how to be a
perfect dog parent. Still didn't. She reckoned it
would be a lifelong learning endeavor. But even
so, she took a therapeutic comfort in the dog's com-
panionship as she fed Sugar a treat and munched
on a piece of dark chocolate, as if it could shift her
hormones into feel-better mode.

She hadn't slept after being questioned by the
police. She'd driven Kat home and returned to the
farmette and crawled into bed and stayed there
well after sunup, despite not being able to sleep.
Mid-morning, tired and bleary eyed, Abby made
her way to her garden. Behind the last corn row,

she picked a bunch of late-blooming sunflowers and put them in a cobalt-blue vase. She took the arrangement to the hospital intensive care unit, hoping to see Paola. The ICU supervisor explained that visitation was limited to immediate family only—two at a time, and then, only five minutes of each hour. Furthermore, flowers and live plants were not permitted. Abby sank into a chair in the empty waiting room. Holding the vase of blooms in her lap, she closed her eyes and pondered the intangible and yet impenetrable wall that now existed between her and Paola.

Abby prayed for Paola's speedy recovery. Not only because her friend deserved a beautiful life—certainly that—but also because Abby hoped Paola would be able to bring absolute clarity to what had happened the night before. Initially, Abby had felt sure about what she'd seen and heard, but later, she hadn't been as positive. At times during the night, she had felt so muddled of mind that she wondered if she hadn't imagined some of the details.

The arrival of the elevator brought Abby to a wide-eyed attention. She watched as a nurse hurried inside the carriage and pushed a button. The doors closed. Alone again, Abby toyed with the idea of investigating Jake's death on her own. No one could know, of course, not even Kat. Chief Bob Allen had made it clear that if Kat did any more favors for Abby, it could mean losing her job. And if discovered, Abby, too, had plenty to lose, including her friendships with the coroner and the cops she'd once worked with who were still on the force. The chief would not tolerate anyone meddling in an active murder investigation. End of story.

The next day, Abby again drove to the hospital, believing that she would be allowed in to see Paola with Luna, who visited Paola every day. Even if Paola could not respond, she could hear and perhaps recognize Abby's voice as Abby whispered words of comfort and prayers for healing. But the nursing staff remained firm about adhering to the established protocols, and Luna had arrived with Eva. The nursing staff knew they were sisters. Even when Luna tried to persuade the nursing staff that Abby was more of a sister to Paola than a friend, the nursing supervisor remained unconvinced that it was reason enough to break the rules. On the third day after the murder, Abby asked Luna to keep her informed about Paola's progress via a daily phone call, and Luna agreed.

For the rest of the week, Abby spent as many daylight hours as possible working around the farmette. The murder dominated her thoughts as she planted bunching onions, radishes, and chives, along with some leafy lettuces and spinach in cold frames. Uncertain of how she would use river rock in her landscape, she restacked the pile under the elm tree in front of her house. And she clipped away the wild side shoots of the Japanese wisteria that were taking over the side gate trellis. Always, her mind returned to questions about who had a motive to kill Jake and critically injure Paola. Abby believed that seeing Paola could help reduce the anxiety she felt daily, but a visit to her friend wouldn't happen until she was out of the ICU and into a step-down unit. *Soldier on*, Abby kept reminding herself.

The narrative of Jake and Paola's married life might have been tempestuous, but it didn't support a case of murder-suicide, and the police had found no gun at the scene. Every question Abby conceived returned in a circular fashion. Who had a motive to murder Jake, and was he even the primary target? Did the killer know Jake would be driving Paola's car that night? Had the murderer intended to kill Paola? Had Paola offended a town merchant in that dispute over rental space she wanted for a truffle shop? Could that have driven someone to murder? Could the killer have shot Jake before realizing that Paola wasn't driving her car? How had the killer convinced Jake to lower the window on such a cold, foggy night? Did the killer know Jake? Or Paola? As Abby knew, Paola didn't have an enemy in the world, so why would anyone want to hurt her? None of it made any sense.

By Halloween, seven days after the murder, Abby had grown impatient to find out how Paola was progressing physically. She telephoned Luna and learned that Paola was in stable condition but that the doctors were keeping her in a medically induced coma to allow the swelling to subside. Luna told Abby that it could be weeks before her sister would regain consciousness—and then someone would have to tell Paola about Jake's death.

Abby cringed at the thought of Paola trying to process the reality of what had happened, even as the poor woman was trying to recover and heal. Still, the cops would need to know if she saw the killer and who might have wanted to harm her and Jake. In the meantime, the knowledge that Katerina Petrovsky and Sergeant Otto Nowicki were on the case gave Abby some comfort. Those two, along with Lieutenant Sinclair, who was a new officer, and Chief Bob Allen, would be casting a wide net. Nettie, the CSI technician, and Bernie de la Cruz in the evidence room might also help with the case. Jake's killer wouldn't be on the loose for long.

Eager to resume her normal life, Abby decided to spend the day in town. The swelling beneath her eye had gone away. She dressed in one of her many plaid flannel shirts and jeans. She tugged on lug boots and slipped into an old leather jacket she'd bought several seasons ago at Twice Around Markdowns. On the way out, she wrapped a scarf around her neck and grabbed her daypack. After driving into Las Flores, she parked her Jeep on Main Street and dashed into Edna Mae's antique store and quilt shop.

The scents of autumn potpourri, cinnamon, and apple cider permeated the brightly lit interior. Under her arm, Abby carried a cardboard box with an orange lid that contained an unfinished quilt from Edna Mae. Abby also had tucked into the pocket of her leather aviator jacket an eight-ounce jar of her Henny Penny Farmette trademark honey.

"I owe you this for the quilt pieces," Abby said, pulling the jar from her pocket.

The big-boned woman, well past middle age, looked up from the spools of thread she had been organizing on a Peg-Board. "Well, thanks, Abby. I hope you didn't make a special trip into town just to bring it?"

"No, not really. Now that the weather's turned nice again, I thought I would run some errands on this lovely Halloween day. You know, like check my post office box, see if there's any work for me at the DA's office, and get my honey deliveries back on schedule. This jar comes from the fall harvest, so it's darker in color and earthier in taste. I hope you like it."

"Well, of course I will," said Edna Mae. She gave Abby her full attention. "So how's the quilting coming along, dear?"

Abby rolled her eyes. "I wish I could say it's coming along, but that wouldn't be the truth. . . . Something's gone very wrong with the pattern." She frowned. "And I'm not sure piecework suits me."

Surprise lit the bright blue eyes peering from behind the wire-rimmed spectacles. "Oh, for goodness' sake, let me see what you've done."

Abby set the jar of honey aside on the glass countertop next to the register and opened the orange-lidded box.

Edna Mae examined the blocked pieces that were sewn together. "Oh, dear, dear. I see it. Your attention wandered right here." A twisted, arthritic finger, its wrinkled knuckle swollen into deformity, pointed at a row of squares where the pattern clearly had changed. "But it can be fixed,"

Edna Mae said in an optimistic tone. She picked up the large square and flipped it over. Then, shaking her head, she returned the piece to its right side.

"How?" Abby exhaled a long, deep breath. "Let me guess. I have to start over?"

"Well, yes, dear, you have to reestablish the pattern."

Edna Mae reached into the box, beneath folded pieces of whole cloth and a pile of fabric squares, as if feeling for something. Eventually, she pulled forth a paper with shaded boxes and a key. "Now, dear, were you following the diagram?"

"Not really. The truth is, I never noticed it."

"Never noticed it?" Edna Mae unfolded the paper and smoothed it on the counter. "That's so unlike you, Abby. You notice everything."

Abby thought of offering up an excuse to explain why she'd ruined the quilt pattern. *Jeez, I don't know. Maybe I was still obsessing over a murderer on the loose,* she mused silently. In spite of the congenial and friendly manner in which Edna Mae offered advice, Abby felt her face flush warm. Her heart raced. There was no reason for the apprehension she felt, but it was there all the same.

Looking directly into Edna Mae's bright, inquisitive eyes, Abby replied, "I guess I had murder on my mind."

"We all have, dear. That manifestation of evil has marred our lovely little town. It's just so terrible that you had to witness it. The whole downtown is talking about it." Edna Mae took a white hankie from inside her sweater sleeve and blotted it against her nose. She slipped the hankie back into her pocket. "Not me, of course, but lots of townsfolk are saying that Jake Winston deserved what happened to him. Sorry to say."

Abby felt her body tense. She quickly corrected Edna Mae about being an eyewitness. "I didn't see the shot being fired or the person who fired it. I heard it."

"But I thought you'd found the bodies."

"Well, yes, I did, but I wish I'd never seen them that way."

"I'm sure it was terrible for you." Edna Mae's energy shifted. Her tone softened. Reaching out an arthritic hand, she touched Abby's shoulder.

Abby flinched without understanding why, and Edna Mae withdrew her hand. "It's just wrong," said Abby. "Nobody has the right to snatch away another person's life. And Jake's reputation aside, he didn't deserve to die like some animal in a hunter's gun sight. Paola didn't deserve what happened to her. She's an innocent in all this."

"Some say she had a little something going with that barrel room worker. Surely, you've heard the talk, dear."

Abby's body tensed. "I don't believe it. That's just utter nonsense . . . gossip from people who have nothing else to gab about. Give me a break."

Edna Mae's shocked expression made Abby wish she could call back her words, start the conversation over. Her heart pounding like a hammer, Abby wanted to run straight out the door, but she managed through sheer will to remain rooted in place. *What's got ahold of you? Get a grip.*

The lines in Edna Mae's face etched themselves into a concerned expression. "Don't take this the wrong way, dear, but you talk like you might have a smidgen of post-traumatic stress. You're no longer on the force, now are you? You saw your friend Paola hanging to life by a thread. On the force, you could get some counseling. But now . . . I wonder, dear, is there anyone you can discuss this with? Talking can help, you know."

"Don't worry about it," said Abby, not meaning for the words to come out so forcefully. She didn't want to get into this subject with Edna Mae. The last thing she wanted to happen was for the locals to gossip about her mental state.

Edna Mae's lips thinned as she appeared to be thinking through a new tack. "Look, dear, I've got some cider heating in the back, on a hot plate. Shall we have a cup?"

"No, but thanks, anyway," said Abby. "I'm sorry for speaking so sharply. I really should go."

Edna Mae put her hand on Abby's arm. "Oh, no, dear. Not just yet. Please. I need to tell you something that might be relevant. I've told the police already. It's not hearsay. I saw it with my own eyes."

Abby dropped her defensiveness. She waited for Edna Mae to reveal some little detail that would likely have no relevance to anything but the gossip the antique shop owner had been hearing and repeating.

"That man, Jake Winston," said Edna Mae. "He came in here the day before he died."

"I'm listening." Abby stared intently at Edna Mae's bright blue eyes behind her wire-rimmed eyeglasses. "Did he say why he'd come to a shop of antiques and quilts?"

The bell jingled on the front door. Two senior citizen quilters strolled in. One wore a quilted vest over her sweater. The heavier of the two wore a lightweight coat and walked with a cane. They called out their good mornings to Edna Mae and headed to the other side of the store.

As the women began thumbing through the first round rack of quilted shams on hangers, Edna Mae leaned in closer to Abby and whispered conspiratorially, "He asked me to show his young friend some of my Amish quilts. They're collectibles, you know, and quite expensive. It cost me a lot to get them insured and shipped here."

Abby's antenna went on high alert. "Young friend, you say? A woman?"

"Yes, a woman. Jake's interior decorator, I think is how he introduced her. Although I must say, the lady didn't seem to know much about quilts."

"Did you catch her name?" Abby asked. Such details could be significant.

"Let me think. Dorothy, Deidre . . . No, it was Dori something."

"Purchase anything?"

"No. She wanted silk. I tried to tell her the quilts I carry are all made of colorfast cotton or lightweight wool. The quality and craftsmanship are superior. If she wants silk, I told her, visit a specialized bedding shop elsewhere in the county."

"Could you describe her?"

Edna Mae removed her wire-rimmed glasses and rubbed her eyes. "Lemme see. About five feet ten inches, or so . . . platinum-colored hair with dark roots. I'd say she was in her late twenties or early thirties. Oh, and that animal-print dress she wore wouldn't have required more than a yard of material to make. You could almost see her V-Secret."

Abby smiled. "That's funny."

An amused Edna Mae put her glasses back on and pointed to the diagram again. "This crisis will pass, Abby, so let the police do their job, and you get to work on this quilting pattern. It'll take your mind off that nasty business. Now, look. See how the whole thing increases to this point and then decreases starting in the very next row?" she said, tapping the paper. "That row there is exactly the midway point in your quilt. Use this legend as your guide, your blueprint. When you follow it correctly, you'll end up with a gorgeous quilt." She folded the pieces to put them away and then remembered something. "Wait a minute. I recall there's a picture of it in here somewhere." Rummaging through the box of fabric, she located a clear plastic bag with a folded sheet of newspaper inside. She pulled it out.

Abby watched Edna Mae unfold and spread the newspaper on the countertop. Next to a half-page ad picturing the quilt, the headline read OUR QUILT COLLECTION—BEYOND COMPARE. The slug line at the top noted that the date was Wednesday, March 24, 1993, and the paper was the *Kansas City Star*.

"Would you look at that?" said Edna Mae. "Can't you picture that quilt all finished and covering your bed?"

Abby nodded but wasn't so sure. Maybe the pattern would grow on her. Or not. She was still thinking about Dori.

Edna Mae refolded the paper and slipped it back into its plastic sleeve. "This box came from an estate sale in the Midwest. Quilters are not the type of people to stop in the middle of a project. That puzzles me."

Abby arched a brow. *Really? People move. Get sick. Lose interest. Die. Don't they?*

The older woman pushed back her glasses and pulled her sweater a little tighter around her buxom body. She leaned in to study the key for the diagrammed pattern. "It's fairly straightforward. There are only five variables of the squares—light green, dark green, light yellow, dark gold, and a floral print of all those colors. You'll need to pull the stitches out from here on." Edna Mae reached for a red pincushion and took a large pin with a yellow plastic head and marked the spot. "It's working a puzzle, isn't it? Five different pieces are rather like five suspects or five clues that you have to place correctly in your mystery for the proper solution to appear. And just like with a mystery, sometimes you have to start over at square one."

"Thanks," said Abby, thinking it wasn't that great of an analogy. "When you told the police about Jake and the woman, did they think it might be important to their case?"

"I don't know. They listened, wrote a note, and that was that." Edna Mae flashed a smile.

"Good that you reported it," said Abby. "I don't keep up with Officer Petrovsky and Sergeant Nowicki as much as I used to. As you know, I'm not a cop anymore. I'm a farmer lady."

"True," said Edna, putting the items back in the box. "If you have trouble with the pattern again, bring the quilt back. I'm happy to help."

After leaving Edna Mae's shop, Abby put the

quilt box back in her Jeep and strolled up the street and entered the Las Flores Police Department. At the glass partition, she asked to speak to Chief Bob Allen.

"He's out," said the fresh-faced uniformed officer behind the window.

"Then I'll talk to the guy heading up the investigation into the Jake Winston murder."

"Lieutenant Sinclair? Is he expecting you?"

"No."

"The nature of your business?" The woman drilled Abby with a stare.

Abby hoisted her daypack a little higher on her shoulder. "I have information for him about the murder."

"Right. I'll let the lieutenant know you're here. Name?"

"Abigail Mackenzie."

Seconds later, the latch on the door clicked, and the female officer held the door open and invited Abby into the same hallway she'd trod down countless times in years past on her way to the break room, the interrogation rooms, and the chief's office. Almost immediately, Sinclair appeared from the men's room down the hallway.

"Oh, Lieutenant," the fresh-faced officer called out. "Got a minute? Abigail Mackenzie here says she has information about your murder case."

"In here," Sinclair said. With his gruff tone, unshaven gray-streaked beard, and heavy-lidded eyes, he looked and sounded like a man who desperately needed sleep and was getting by on caffeine. He held open the door to the first interrogation room.

Abby walked in.

"Sit there," he commanded.

Abby slid into an institutional chair, aware that it was the seat most often occupied by those suspected of breaking the law rather than upholding it.

Sinclair, middle-aged and tall—standing at least a foot taller than Abby's five feet three inches—wore wrinkled gray dress slacks, a white oxford shirt, and a blue striped tie, its knot loosened. His light gray eyes and crew-cut gray hair gave him a weary, washed-out appearance, made worse by sallow circles beneath his eyes. To Abby's dismay, he closed an open file on the desk and slid some other manila folders across pictures and data sheets. If there were documents, images, or files relating to the Jake Winston murder investigation on his desk, he apparently wanted to make certain she didn't see them, at least not yet. "What do you have?"

"It might not be significant," said Abby. "But you'll be the judge of that."

He stared at her. Silent. Waiting.

She repeated the information that Edna Mae had told her. "Naturally, you'll want to get Edna Mae's statement firsthand rather than relying on hearsay."

"I know how to do my job, Ms. Mackenzie."

"Of course you do. I just meant—"

"Is that it?"

"Yes," said Abby, chalking up his ill temper to lack of sleep. Abby decided she'd ask him a question, anyway. "I was wondering if the killer left evidence at the scene, like a bullet casing or—"

"You can stop right there. What we know about this case is none of your business. Chief Bob Allen has briefed me on your service here. I've also heard that you don't seem to have a problem inserting yourself into an active investigation. I can't help it that you still have close friends in the department and somehow find out information before anyone else does, but that doesn't mean I like it. You made that call to dispatch in the nick of time to save your friend Paola Varela's life. That does not entitle you to special consideration. It certainly doesn't give you the right to learn insider information about this case. You've given us your statement. So I'll just say this once. Stay away from the Jake Winston murder case."

Abby sat in stunned silence.

He drilled her with a steely-eyed stare. "In general, I've found that when people take an undue interest in an active case, it generally means they have an ulterior motive or something to hide."

"Oh, *please.* Don't be ridiculous." Abby felt her pulse quicken. Her stomach knotted. She rose. He remained seated. She glared at him, wondering if she should just say what she was thinking. *You don't treat witnesses this way.* In a clipped tone, she said, "You're right about me not being a cop. But as an ex-cop, I know that alienating people around you who might be able to help solve the case, disregarding relevant information, and badgering a key witness are no way to launch a murder investigation." Surely he didn't already suspect that she intended to do her own secret investigation, or did he?

Abby jerked open the door and stormed down the hallway. She had no more time to waste on a tired cop who seemed intent on asserting his authority but doing it in a way more suggestive of having a chip on his shoulder and an attitude to go with it, rather than using a thoughtful, more professional approach. Maybe he was just having an off day. Or was tired. Or he was suspicious of her showing up with a possibly spurious detail from a third party.

Outside, Abby leaned against the streetlamp post. *You've dealt with Sinclair types before. Why let him get under your skin? And ditto for responding so sharply to Edna Mae.* Abby struggled for composure, trying to make sense of her overreaction. Back in the day, her fellow cops could always count on her to remain calm, clear eyed, and focused in any situation. Maybe Edna Mae was right. Maybe she ought to talk to someone about the reactionary feelings she seemed unable to control. Abby made a mental note to get checked out when she had more time and money. In the meantime, she would rely on her herbal remedies and teas to calm her frazzled nerves. And she'd find some paper and make an incident poster on which to list relevant facts, list the people in Jake's orbit, and create a timeline. As she uncovered more information, she'd add it to the poster and start making linkages. Taking action rather than doing nothing would help her face the darkness within that was robbing her of peace. Of that, she felt sure. And sooner or later, the killer's name would emerge.

After hoisting a case of honey from the passenger seat of her Jeep, Abby walked into the kitchen of Zazi's bistro and handed the chef the jars of honey with an invoice. After they'd settled up, she returned to her Jeep and drove to the post office to retrieve her business mail. And then it was on to the DA's office to see if she could pick up some part-time work over the holidays. After being told that the DA didn't have any new work for her and probably wouldn't have any until after the New Year, Abby left and steered a course to the pie shop.

"Here you go, Maisey. Six jars, eight ounces each." Abby set the carton on the counter. "This is a little earthier tasting than my spring honey," she explained. "That's because in the fall, my bees gathered pollen from mostly star thistle, eucalyptus blooms, and whatever else they can find in addition to the lavender. But a lot of my customers favor the autumn honey."

Maisey pulled a jar from the box and inspected it. "Oh, it's a lovely color. Six jars. Was that all I ordered? What was I thinking? Already the holiday pie orders are rolling in. Next chance you get, bring me another six, will you, Abby?"

"You got it." Abby grinned and presented the invoice. While Maisey wiped her hands on the apron covering her floral-print dress and then counted out the payment from the cash drawer, Abby admired the wide assortment of pies in the display case.

"Here you go. Sixty dollars." Maisey picked up a napkin holder that needed filling. "So, how have you been, Abby?"

Abby slipped the money into her blue zippered banking envelope and tucked the envelope back into her daypack. "Guess I can't complain."

"Now, you're not being entirely truthful, are

you?" Maisey's look challenged Abby to be more forthright.

"Okay, so I've been better," said Abby.

Narrowing her eyes and lowering her voice, Maisey put her hands on her hips, leaned in, and said, "We've all heard about the murder up at the Country Schoolhouse Winery. You found the victims. I forget who it was who told me one of those shot was your truffle-maker friend. So how can you trivialize it? Of course you can complain. That must have been horrific for you."

Feeling as though she were walking on an emotional tightrope, Abby tried unsuccessfully to push back tears. With her moist eyes shimmering, she looked at Maisey and said, "I'm not dealing with it very well. Maisey. I just want my old self back."

Maisey walked around and encircled Abby with her arms, embracing her like a mama bear enfolding her cub. "Well, where did she go, darling?"

Abby buried her face against Maisey's apron and mumbled, "I don't know. Honest to God, I don't know what's happening to me."

Six Facts about Honeybee Queens

1. A healthy bee colony will have roughly forty thousand to sixty thousand bees but only one queen.

2. A queen bee lives between three and four years and can lay a million eggs during her lifetime.

3. The queen mates a few days after she emerges from her birth cell.

4. She stores a lifetime of sperm in her body from her mating flight with drones.

5. A honeybee queen controls hive activity through chemical messages that dictate bee behavior.

6. If the queen dies, the worker bees will ensure the hive gets a new fertile queen by feeding a diet of royal jelly to a selected female worker.

Chapter 4

Hang near-empty frames of honey near
the hives for hungry bees to clean.

—*Henny Penny Farmette Almanac*

"Give me a minute, Abby," said Maisey. The proprietress strolled from the pie shop counter to the front door and flipped the sign to closed. "I swear, these old bones are creaking from the changes in the weather—fog and rain one day, sunny and warm the next. Let's sit a spell and catch up. Pie's on me." Maisey walked back behind the counter and brought out two white coffee mugs.

Abby's gaze swept the fifties malt shop decor, which Maisey kept scrubbed to a high shine. "I don't think pie is what I need, Maisey," said Abby. She dropped her daypack on the floor and climbed onto a worn red-leather stool at the counter. With Kat working long hours on the murder case, Abby had decided not to burden her with her at times seemingly irrational feelings. And even though

Maisey would be a sympathetic listener, Abby didn't much like talking about emotional stuff. To her, that was akin to exposing a nerve in a root canal. And, besides, her grandmother's voice was ever chiming at the back of her mind: *Be steady, my girl, and this, too, shall pass.* But it hadn't. And maybe it wouldn't.

Maisey poured coffee into Abby's mug. She put a slice of pie on standard white restaurant ware for Abby and slid a fork next to the plate. "Dive into that mile-high meringue there. You'll be right as rain in no time."

Abby picked up the fork and poked at the pie. "You sound like my grandmother."

"Honey, where I come from, there's nothing like pie to fix what's troubling you. And that's not meant as a platitude. It's just a low-country recipe for feeling better when nothing else is working." Maisey sat down on a stool next to Abby. Her contagious smile could have reassured a death row inmate that all would be right in the world as long as there was time for pie and coffee.

Abby pushed her fork into the soft golden peaks of meringue, cut down through the custard-type filling and the crust, and then lifted the pie-laden fork to her lips. "Tastes like lemon."

"You see," said Maisey. "That just goes to show you that you can't judge a thing from the surface. You've got to dig deeper. That there is vinegar pie."

"Really? Can't taste the vinegar."

"Of course not. You're not supposed to. That recipe has been in my family for generations." Maisey lifted the pot and poured herself a cup of coffee. "We always made raisin and vinegar pies for the wake after someone had passed on. The women in my family called them funeral pies."

"Lovely. I just wish I had more of an appetite." Abby set aside her fork. "I'm sorry, Maisey, but I can't eat more."

Maisey stirred two spoons of sugar into her coffee. After taking a long, slow sip, she put the mug back down and stared at Abby. "How long has this been going on? The not eating."

Oh, brother. Must we leap right into it? Abby sucked in a deep breath. She shifted her attention to the glass-enclosed pie display so she wouldn't have to see Maisey's eyes, her expression etched with concern. As Abby's thoughts flew to Paola, crumpled in the semi-dark car, next to her dead husband, a wave of nausea swept over her. "I suppose I lost it the night I found the two of them in the parking lot. It turned into a very long night. There was food—a lot of food—but I couldn't eat it. Anxiety and nausea got in the way. Still do."

"Talk to me, Abby. Tell me what's going on."

"I don't know where to begin." Already, her mind reeled with befuddlement, doubts, and fear.

"Why don't you begin with when these symptoms started?"

After blowing a small puff of air between her lips, Abby asked, "Maisey, have you been at someone's side while they're dying?"

Maisey nodded.

"Imagine the sheer terror of having someone point a gun at you and say, 'Time's up.' When it happens to someone you're close to, you try to make sense of it. You feel guilty that you weren't taken, too."

"Are you talking about your younger brother now or Jake Winston's murder?"

"Both, I guess. I know how horrible I felt when my brother died. I see Paola as a sister. Now she'll go through that terrible emptiness, the anger, and the guilt. It's all so senseless." Abby took a sip of coffee and stared at a tiny bubble in the white meringue.

"Abby, dear, all who are born will die, and the good Lord knows the exact moment when each child will return. You have to take comfort in that."

"If only everyone had faith as strong as yours. I think of Jake and Paola staring into the killer's face. The window was down on the driver's side. They were sitting in the car, getting ready to join the party. The killer wasn't about to let that happen. Was the shooting a punishment for Jake's cheating ways? I don't know. And what if Jake couldn't help himself, couldn't control his behavior? Don't know that, either."

"What do you mean by his lack of control?" Maisey raised a quizzical brow.

"What if something else explained why Jake behaved badly, like if he had a brain tumor? I've heard some types grow slowly and account for bizarre behaviors."

"Did his wife ever say Jake had one?"

"No. I was just trying to fathom why he changed from a loving husband to someone who wasn't."

"Who can say? These things happen. They're terrible when they do. Everyone gets hurt."

Abby shifted on the swivel stool. "He was gone when I got to him. She was bleeding from her wound. Probably believed she was dying, too. And I left her there in the dark to go for help."

"You gave her a chance at life," said Maisey. "Isn't it possible that you had your own fears to deal with and still you got her the help she needed?"

"Yes, but I wasn't facing certain death at that point. The killer had gone."

"But you didn't know that there weren't accomplices still at the scene, did you?"

"No."

"So any sane person would be frightened and traumatized. And yet you couldn't let yourself feel. You had to keep your wits about you to function, isn't that right?"

"I suppose." Abby massaged her neck muscles, which seemed tenser now that she was talking about the murder.

Maisey's fingers hugged her mug of hot coffee.

"I'm a mess now," Abby said. "When darkness sets in, so does anxiety." She tilted her head from side to side. "I lock the doors and windows before sunset, and then later, when I hear a noise, I recheck the doors. Sometimes, it's for the second or third time. And I worry that someone could be watching me through vertical slats of the blinds."

"Someone?" Maisey put down her mug and looked endearingly at Abby. "Darling, don't you mean Jake Winston's killer?"

Abby nodded. She plucked up one end of her scarf and held the fabric against her eyes, as though doing so could push back the tears that threatened to erupt.

"You poor, darling," Maisey said. "And you've always felt so safe on your farmette." She placed a large motherly hand on Abby's shoulder. "It kills me to see you suffering this way."

Abby leaned her face against Maisey's warm hand. "I've hesitated to talk to anyone about this. You'll keep it between us, won't you?"

"Yes. I won't breathe a word of it to anyone."

Choosing her words carefully, Abby said, "In a way, I feel responsible for what happened to Jake and Paola." Her voice cracked.

"No, Abby, there's no way. Jake Winston's death was not your fault." Maisey rose from the counter stool, leaned down, and hugged Abby. "Why on earth would you say such a thing?"

Abby sniffed hard against the threat of more tears. "If only I had been truthful with Paola. If I had told her my concerns about Jake, then maybe they would have put things off and got him checked out."

"We've all known men like that, Abby." Maisey traipsed behind the counter and looked at Abby. "I'd heard that they had some counseling with the priest before getting back together. That right?"

"Oh, they did, but Jake missed several sessions. And Father Joseph isn't a trained mental health professional."

"Well, maybe your friend Paola chose to see the best in her husband," said Maisey. "Maybe she forgave his bad behavior and focused on the good between them."

Abby chewed her lip. "Maybe."

"Listen, dear," Maisey said. "A wife may be willing to look the other way, but that doesn't mean she's blind. There are always signs."

"And he didn't seem to care about her finding out, or he was just oblivious. Only moments before they were to renew their vows," said Abby, "Jake hit on me. I wanted to slap him into Father Joe's rock garden."

"So, what did you do?"

"I walked into the church, leaving them to work it out."

Maisey stared at the counter, as though trying to take it all in.

"Bottom line, in all the time we spent doing things together, I listened to Paola talk about him. She loved him, so I said nothing. It might seem irrational, but it feels like I failed her." Abby reached down the counter for a dispenser with some white napkins. After pulling out one, she held it to her nose and sniffled into it. "If I'd just spoken my mind, maybe—"

"What? You think your friend would have canceled the wedding? And if she had canceled the ceremony, there would have been no murder?"

"Crossed my mind." Abby thought about her incident poster on the living room table, which had spokes from Jake to people in his orbit, and about how many times those individuals also connected with Father Joseph. It was entirely possible that the killer might have confessed. But Father Joseph, though he might have counseled the killer to turn himself in, would never break the seal of the confessional. So Abby had decided against trying to extract any information from him.

"Are you listening to me, Abby? No one could have foreseen that tragedy coming. Back in the day when you worked as a cop, you must have seen how bad boys behave. Did it ever make sense to you?"

"No."

"Some women can't resist bad boys. That's no one else's business. You have to get that through that noggin of yours that Jake's murder was not your fault."

Abby wadded the napkin and laid it near the pie plate. "His prowess with women might have been a blessing for him, but for her it had become a curse."

"Oh, my dear, it's far easier to stand on the outside and judge a marriage than to be on the inside, dealing with its hidden dynamics. With that said, I hear the sadness, the fear, and the guilt in your voice. But, my girl, when we face the hardest lessons in life, we suffer. I once heard a man say he didn't take pain pills, because the pain was teaching him something. If he avoided the pain, he could never get to the root of what was causing his suffering. The police will find Jake's killer. Let them do their job. And you focus on how to heal your suffering."

Rapping at the pie shop's front door caused Maisey to look up. "Well, someone doesn't believe the sign on the door means we're closed. I better go and see who that is," Maisey said, putting down her mug and ambling away.

Abby straightened her posture. She considered

what Maisey had said. The woman made it sound simple. Eat a piece of the pie, talk a little with a friend, face your darkness, and let it go. But if Maisey knew what Abby kept secret inside, what would she say then?

Maisey opened the door. "Well, good afternoon, Chief. What can I do for you?"

Chief? Abby's gaze shot up to the mirror angled overhead. Seeing Chief Bob Allen stroll in caused her stomach to clench.

"Got any banana cream left?" Chief Bob Allen asked. "Tonight the wife's hosting a quilting bee. That Schultz woman over at the antique shop was supposed to bring the pie by this time, but she claimed a store full of customers made leaving impossible. Wife sent me the SOS."

"I've got two left in the display case. Do you want both pies?"

"That'll work."

"Well, you better come to the counter while I box them up," said Maisey, heading back to where she and Abby had been sitting. Opening the display case and pulling out the two pies, Maisey said, "I'll bet Edna Mae's quilting business is booming with this burst of cold weather. Last year we had a heat wave around Halloween." From under the counter, Maisey pulled a couple of pre-folded boxes. She assembled them and placed a pie in each box.

Chief Bob Allen took a seat two stools down from Abby.

"Mackenzie," said the chief, looking over at her.

"Chief." Abby nodded and turned her gaze on

Maisey's dexterous fingers as she taped the partially open lids so as not to ruin the toasted peaks of meringue. When she'd finished, she slid the boxes in front of the chief and began writing out the sales slip.

"Have you found Jake Winston's killer yet?" Maisey asked. She handed him the bill.

"Nope," said the chief, his expression showing no emotion. "It's early." He looked up into the angled mirror and met Abby's gaze. She shifted her attention back to her coffee.

"I guess you know that none of us can rest until you've got the evildoer behind bars," Maisey said. She folded her heavy arms over the bib portion of her white apron.

"Yep." Chief Bob Allen reached into his pants pocket and pulled out a twenty-dollar bill. After handing it to Maisey and waiting for the change, he leaned in close to Abby.

"You know, Mackenzie, Lieutenant Sinclair tells me he's been going over your statement. Finds it more than a little curious that no one can vouch for your whereabouts when the two vics were shot."

"Yeah?" Abby looked directly at him. "My location for when the shot was fired is in my statement. And Officer Katerina Petrovsky was with me at the party."

"But she was not with you when Winston was killed. Sinclair tells me that no one can verify where Emilio Varela was, either, despite his statement that he was in the cellar. You two are friends, aren't you?"

The muscles in Abby's shoulders tensed again. Heat flushed her cheeks. "Yeah? So, what's your point?"

"You know how this works. Two people are missing from the party at precisely the moment when a fatal shot was fired. One or both of them are the last people to see the victim alive. That gets our attention."

Abby forced herself to stay calm. She drilled the chief with a cold stare. "I can't speak for where Emilio was. Check with the sous-chef. She was the one who pointed to the back door when I asked her if she knew where he had gone."

"Yeah, about that . . . The sous-chef says she didn't know the chef's whereabouts or why he'd left the kitchen when they were so busy. She claims she can hardly remember you but believed you'd returned to the party and joined the other guests."

"That woman pointed to the parking lot. That's precisely where I went. And like I said in my statement, I had cases of honey for Chef Emilio to give the guests."

"Well, try this on for size. Your former partner, Officer Petrovsky, said you and the Varela siblings were good friends, but you didn't think much of Jake Winston. It's a sentiment echoed by the Varela family. I can't understand why no one in that family liked the guy. He supported his wife—she didn't have to work—and he gave her brother Emilio that chef's job. It seems Emilio liked working there. He just didn't like working for Jake." The chief stroked his jaw.

Abby stewed in silence.

"So you can see why one could make the leap in logic," said the chief. "If you and Emilio got rid of Jake, it would end Emilio's misery and help your friend Paola out of a difficult marriage."

Abby felt an adrenaline rush. A wave of nausea. She swallowed the bilious taste seeping into the back of her throat. "You can't be serious. Emilio could quit working for Jake anytime he wanted to. As for Paola wanting out of the marriage, she didn't want out. And if she did, that's what divorce is for. She had just renewed her wedding vows with her husband. I don't know what your problem is, but your inferences are beyond ridiculous. I'm going to assume it's your idea of a joke, because if it isn't, it borders on harassment." Her heart thrummed. Abby gripped the counter's edge to steady her trembling hands.

"We're just having a friendly chat here, Mackenzie. No need to get so worked up." Chief Bob Allen straightened on the stool.

Abby shot a look at Maisey, who seemed equally surprised at the exchange. Abby rose. She reached for her daypack and hoisted it over her shoulder. "Thanks for everything, Maisey. It's getting late. I'd better go."

Maisey raised her hand, as if in blessing.

Abby wouldn't look at the chief. She flew out of the pie shop door. On the sidewalk, she stopped and then turned around. Remembering her grandmother's ring, she opened the door and called out to the chief.

"Paola wore my grandmother's ring when she was shot. I'd like that ring returned."

Chief Bob Allen rebalanced the pie boxes in his arms and strolled toward her. "Check with the hospital staff," he said. "Why would a newly reminted bride be wearing your grandmother's ring?"

"For good luck. What else?"

The chief chortled. "Well, *that* didn't work, did it?" he said.

Abby winced. *What is it about me that sets you off, or do you enjoy being mean-spirited?*

"Talk to Sinclair. It's his case." The chief pushed past her and walked away.

Abby marched off in the opposite direction. She located her Jeep and climbed inside. Gripping the steering wheel to calm her trembling, she leaned her head against her arm. The little girl inside her wanted to cry, but the grown-up Abby knew how to choke back tears until she could get to the farmette. *Don't react. Keep your mouth shut. Don't ever let them see you cry.* A life lesson she'd learned on the force.

Old-Fashioned Vinegar Pie

Ingredients:

Pie filling:
1½ cups granulated sugar
¼ cup unsalted butter, melted
4 large organic egg yolks (reserve the whites for
    the meringue)
1½ tablespoons white vinegar

1 teaspoon vanilla extract
3 tablespoons lemon zest (optional)
One unbaked 9-inch pie crust

Meringue:
4 large organic egg whites
¼ teaspoon cream of tartar
6 tablespoons granulated sugar

Directions:
Preheat the oven to 350°.

Prepare the pie filling. In the bowl of an electric mixer, cream together the sugar and butter. Add the eggs, vinegar, and vanilla, and mix well. Then stir in the lemon zest.

Pour the pie filling into the pie crust and bake for 50 to 55 minutes, or until the custard is firm. As the pie bakes, check the color of the crust. If it becomes too dark, place aluminum foil over the pie. Remove the pie from the oven and place it on a rack to cool. Allow it to cool completely before making the meringue.

Once the pie is cool, preheat the oven to 350° and prepare the meringue.

Place the egg whites in the bowl of an electric mixer with the whisk attachment. Add the cream of tartar. Beat the egg whites until peaks form. Using a dessert spoon, slowly add the sugar, beating between each addition, until the egg whites are stiff and the sugar has dissolved.

Spread the meringue over the top of the

cooled pie, making sure the meringue touches the crust all around. Bake until the meringue has turned a toasty brown, about 10 to 12 minutes. Allow the pie to cool before serving.

Serves 4–6

Chapter 5

Animals know how to rid themselves of
pests: chickens throw off mites in dirt
baths, skunks spray, and bees attack.

—*Henny Penny Farmette Almanac*

Driving from town, Abby stewed in silence.
Chief Bob Allen had baited her. Irritated her
like he was an immature schoolboy yanking her
braid, and she'd bristled right on cue. Had she
learned nothing about him from serving on the
force? Either he felt threatened by her—God
knows why—or he enjoyed provoking her. She'd
never figured that part out, but his behavior always
seemed to put her in a bad light. He might not
even know he was pushing people's buttons. But
for her sanity, she would avoid entanglements and
confrontations with him in the future and would
always have a way out or a backup plan for responding to his curveballs. Of course, walking
away still seemed simplest.

Braking for a flock of wild turkeys crossing the
two-lane road she'd decided to take from town to

Farm Hill Road, Abby watched them meander in
the beams of her headlights. They seemed disoriented by the light, starting back in the direction
from whence they'd come and then turning the
other way. In a millisecond, a memory broke
through into Abby's consciousness. She recalled
shivering in her black silk dress the night of the
murder and a car's headlights flicking between
bright and dim. Then she remembered seeing a
runner in a knit cap and dark clothing.

Dear God, is it possible I've seen the killer? Abby's
heartbeat quickened. Long after the turkeys had
disappeared from the road, she remained motionless, with her foot on the brake, processing the
memory. She tried to make sense of it. If she'd
seen the killer, why couldn't she put a face with
that knit cap? A car slipped by in the other lane,
blasting its horn, shocking her out of her reverie.

She released the brake and eased her foot onto
the gas pedal. Shaking her head as if she could
shake off the shock, Abby settled in for the ride
home. The image of the runner dominated her
thoughts, despite the necessity for Abby to focus
on the road. Dense fog had wafted in from the Pa-
cific coastline. It crept over the mountain ridges.
Slinking down forested slopes around the environs
of Las Flores, the fog created a slow and treacher-
ous drive to the farmette. Hurrying was not an option. She flipped on the Jeep's heater and tapped
the classical music station for the vigilant drive
along the two-lane blacktop. At last, she spotted
her mailbox with the rooster on it.

The sound of gravel crunching under the Jeep's
tires brought a sense of security when Abby wheeled

into the driveway and pulled up in front of the house. A warm glow through the windows greeted her, thanks to the living room lamp on a timer. But hearing Sugar's bark was even more comforting.

Abby turned off the ignition, grabbed her daypack, and slid out of the Jeep. Sugar met her in the side yard and yipped until Abby walked in and latched the gate.

"What's going on, sweetie?" Allowing her gaze to sweep their surroundings, Abby asked, "All this fuss just because you miss me?" Feeling guilty for leaving Sugar alone all day, Abby dropped down to pet her pooch.

Sugar's tail wagged in a happy frenzy. The mixed-breed dog with the long whippet legs had become a bundle of moving parts. After Abby pulled away from the sloppy pooch kisses, she looked for the electrical cord on the patio floor. Sugar jumped up on her.

"We'll play after chores, okay?"

Abby tossed her pack on the patio table and walked to the exterior electrical plug on the wall next to the slider. Her habit was to plug in the heat lamp in the chicken house on the coldest nights. Her heritage chickens were hardy, and their house was insulated. There was the straw in the nesting boxes and ground corncob two inches deep over the wood floor. Leaning down, Abby retrieved from her patio floor the orange extension cord that stretched across the yard to the chicken house. After plugging it in, she checked to see if the heat lamp had gone on where the hens were now roosting. It had. Light splayed through the small windows into the vapor-enshrouded yard.

The place took on a ghostly effect as the fog nearly obscured the bare branches of the fruit trees.

After grabbing her daypack, Abby pulled open the slider and stepped into the kitchen and then made her way to her bedroom. She removed her wool cap and tossed it and the daypack on her bed. She found a ball on the floor and rolled it down the hall to the living room, hoping to divert Sugar's attention. Sugar watched it but didn't leave Abby's side.

"You are going to have to stay inside the house now. I'll be right back."

With Sugar barking and pawing at the slider, Abby returned outside and walked to the chicken house. Autumn scents filled the air—eucalyptus, decayed leaves, and wood smoke from the fireplace of a prickly elderly neighbor who lived northwest of her property. The old man refused to use his furnace, insisting in his military certitude that the energy companies were gouging him, and that he'd show them not everybody needed their services. The adage of cutting off your nose to spite your face entered Abby's thoughts. She wondered if Jake had done something like that to prove a point or provoke a killer.

At the chicken house, Abby located six eggs, all in the first nesting box. She carefully tucked two into each of her jacket pockets. Upon finding the feed canister and the waterer sufficiently full, she began the head count with Mystery, the black Giant Cochin. That hen had hunkered down in the third nesting box, looking like a feather boa with a beak. So Mystery was number one. Looking up, Abby surveyed the top bar. There she counted the two white leghorns, Tighty Whitey I and II. Next to them perched Orpy—the yellow Buff Orpington—the two Silver-Laced Wyandotte sisters, and the Black Sex Link hen, whose bottom vent feathers were always poopy. Beside her were Henrietta and Heloise, the two cute Mediterranean girls. Between them Houdini squatted on the roost. He ruled supreme over this harem. So nine hens and a rooster made ten. But there should be eleven chickens in all.

Missing was the Rhode Island Red layer Abby called Red, notorious for getting herself into trouble. When barely a pullet, Red had overturned a galvanized bucket, trapping herself beneath it until Abby found her two hours later. Now, as Abby leaned into the coop as far as possible, she hoped Red might be in the last nesting box. Spotting the hen snuggled against the back wall and hunkered down deep into the straw, Abby whispered, "And one more makes eleven." Red made a contented clucking sound. Abby closed the door and locked it.

A loud metallic sound cut through the silence, causing Abby to turn toward the source. The sound seemed to originate from near the stone house on the vacant land adjoining her property. Her thoughts ticked through possible causes of the noise. Minutes passed. Then another gust produced a metallic rustle. The old stone house, as Abby recalled, had a breezeway attaching it to a greenhouse. Corrugated metal sheets over rafters served as a makeshift roof for the breezeway. Likely a sheet of metal had worked away from rusting nails and had pulled loose.

Yes, that has to be it. But it is Halloween night. Some-

one could be back there. But to check, I'd need the flash-light, and it's in the house.

As she turned back toward the kitchen patio, twigs snapped a few feet behind her. Spinning around, Abby asked, "Who's there?" A chill raced up her spine.

No answer came.

Maybe it's just a raccoon. Or a bract of peppercorns dropping from the tree over the chicken run.

But as she peered into the fog-enshrouded woods, a man stepped forward.

Caught by surprise, Abby's heart raced. "Who are you? What are you doing back there?" She hoped her cop tone would intimidate the man. She'd left Sugar in the house. At least a chain-link fence stood between them. The stranger on the other side of the fence couldn't know if she was armed or not. "Answer me," said Abby, "or I'll call the cops."

"No need," said the stranger. "I'm poking around for a place to park my RV."

"Yeah? Well, I'm not buying that." Abby took her phone from her pocket. *Who chooses a dark and foggy night to look for space to park an RV?* She didn't recognize this guy, and for all she knew, he could be Jake's killer. This was not a good situation, and she needed to get out of there, like, yesterday.

"No, no. Now, hold on a minute. It probably sounds like I'm making this up, but I'm not. Call the owners. They are old friends of mine. They'll tell you." The man waded through the grass, which had come up since the rains began. He stopped walking toward her when he was about a foot from her on the other side of the sagging metal fence.

"You must be Abigail Mackenzie. I was told a lady farmer lives where you do. Almost always home. The owners said you would let me cut across your farmette to get back here if I couldn't get in any other way."

"So, how did you get in?" Abby demanded.

"I climbed over the metal entrance gate on the other side."

Abby sized him up. He wore a deer hunter's jacket, cargo pants, and an SF Giants ball cap.

"Last name's Brady. Folks just call me Henry. The RV is for my hunting trips. It won't be here all the time."

"Well, why would it be here at all?"

"My wife and I are divorcing."

Great. Abby didn't exactly get a warm, fuzzy feeling from Henry. And she sure didn't like the idea of him taking up residence in an RV on the back side of her property. This situation seemed downright weird. "You're not going to be living in it, are you?"

He chuckled. "Ah, no. I'm staying with friends while I look for a place large enough to accommodate all my mounted trophies." His voice sounded husky, like he had the thickened vocal cords of a middle-aged smoker.

"Trophies? Like what?" Abby wasn't a fan of hunting animals for sport. But more importantly, she wanted to keep him talking while she tried to figure out if he posed a threat to her or was just some rather odd character who had chosen Halloween night to inspect a friend's property.

"Elk, bear, moose. Some are full size, not just the heads." He seemed proud.

Abby cringed. *So, you kill for blood sport. Probably own a few guns.* She'd heard enough. "Why didn't you come out here during the daylight?"

"Who says I didn't? I've been here for a while, poking around in the old stone house. I guess you know someone's busted the lock on the back entrance door and there are bullet holes in those heavy sliding glass doors on the eastern side. I'll let the owners know they need to screw shut the doors and get a new padlock."

"Yeah," Abby said. "And as soon as possible." She didn't want to show her surprise or deep concern. She hadn't heard any shots fired back there. Not ever. But then again, she sometimes went to town, so it was possible there had been intruders. This new threat accelerated her rising anxiety.

"So if I park my RV on the concrete pad I found in the stand of oaks and oleander bushes over there, I think it'll be out of your view. You won't even know it's here."

Oh, trust me, I'll know. "So, you won't be parking it here tonight?"

"Nope. Got to get that gate unlocked and need a key for that. The owners aren't in town to give it to me." Henry rubbed his forehead beneath the bill of his cap. "Say, you don't happen to have a spare gate key, do you?"

"No. I don't. Look, usually I wouldn't mind chatting, but I hear my dog. I've got to go." Apprehension took over, and Abby spun toward her barking pooch. As soon as she got back to her house, she intended to text the property owners and get the lowdown on Henry. Maybe he had their permission, but if he didn't, they needed to know about it. He could be a frigging squatter, for goodness' sake.

"Sure," said Henry. "Nice to meet you."

Yeah. Her phone vibrated, but Abby wasn't about to answer it within earshot of this guy. The caller could wait until she had returned to the safety of the house. The phone kept vibrating. Stopped and then started again.

"Hang on, hang on," said Abby to no one in particular. "Whoever you are, you can wait." Inside the kitchen, Abby locked the patio door. She closed the vertical blinds at the slider and those at the garden window over her sink. After putting the eggs in the half-full carton in the fridge, Abby shrugged out of her jacket and checked her phone. She'd missed three text messages from Kat.

She slid her finger across Kat's contact number and soon heard Kat's familiar voice picking up. "So . . . what's with the text bombing?" Abby asked, not yet over her annoyance and apprehension with the RV man.

"Well, you weren't answering, and there's something I want to talk to you about."

"And I just got in. I had to lock up the chickens first. So what's up?"

"Okay, I'm still at work, so I'll make it quick," said Kat.

"I'm listening." Abby looked up and noticed a honeybee flitting against the overhead light. She grabbed the tea towel from the oven handle. Intent on knocking the honeybee to the floor so she could take it outside, she swung and missed, further agitating the bee. "Arghh! Hold on a minute, Kat. There's a frigging bee in the light soffit."

After laying aside the phone and positioning herself under the flitting insect, which seemed to favor the forward left corner, Abby flicked the towel and knocked the tiny creature to the floor. She scooped it up and deposited the bundle outside on the patio. Upon returning to the warmth of her kitchen, Abby locked the door. A sudden realization sent a shiver through her. On such a cold and foggy night, the bees would be inside their hive, trying to keep the queen warm. When she'd left for town, the sun had been out. The bees had been out then, too. She had locked the doors and windows, so how had a bee gotten into the house? Alarmed, Abby held the cell phone to her ear and started rechecking all the locked doors and windows. The RV guy, Henry Brady, had implied that he'd been around the back property during daylight. Had he been inside her house? Abby discounted the idea as quickly as it came, for surely Sugar would have taken the guy's leg off.

"Sorry. What were you saying, Kat?"

"Just that," said Kat, "my birthday might be over, but do you think we could still celebrate? I'm looking at the schedule. Today is Saturday. I thought we could grab a bite together next Sunday, on November eight. I'm due for a night off."

"You got my text yesterday, wishing you a happy birthday, didn't you?" Abby walked to the living room window to check the lock. It was secure.

"Yes, I did. But I can't believe I didn't even get a cookie from my coworkers. None of my peeps remembered except you. So here is my bright idea. I thought we could celebrate together, even if it is after the fact. And you owe me for not introducing me to Chef Emilio, although I'm not so sure I'm interested anymore, now that I've already met him in the interview room and Sinclair has put him under the microscope."

"He's your suspect?" Abby knew her tone sounded incredulous. Her sixth sense told her they had the wrong guy. The rest of the community knew the immigrant Varela family to be industrious, law-abiding, and tax-paying citizens with high moral values. They were active in the church and volunteered for various community organizations. Lieutenant Sinclair was new to Las Flores. He didn't know that about the Varelas. He didn't know the character of Emilio Varela.

Kat cleared her throat. "I told the lieutenant we needed to cast a wider net, but Sinclair says we can't rule him out. He has a motive and possibly the opportunity, since no one has vouched for Emilio's whereabouts during the shooting. You didn't see him in the parking lot, did you?"

"I would have said if I had." Abby's mind was spinning. "So Sinclair believes not liking your brother-in-law is a motive. It seems ludicrous to me. Did you find a weapon? I guess you didn't."

"Emilio owns one. Claims it was stolen."

Abby approached the guest bedroom. "I could have told you that. It was stolen right around the time Paola and I took that cooking class several months ago." Abby checked the last window. It had been pulled back a half a foot. The screen was missing. *That's weird. I don't remember leaving that window open. But if I did, why did the screen fall off?*

Abby tuned out Kat as she considered whether or not the opening was big enough for a person like the RV guy to fit through. Deciding it wasn't, she reckoned Sugar might have gotten rambunctious and pawed the screen, unseating it. Regardless, she made a mental note to check the ground under the window in the morning. Shaking off her heebie-jeebies, Abby closed and locked the window.

"Right. So, we've let Emilio go," said Kat. "But Sinclair asked him to voluntarily submit a hair sample."

"Why? Did you find hair at the crime scene?" Abby asked.

"The cap that the canine handler with the sheriff's department found might have hair in it. The deputy's dog alerted on the object a little uphill from the murder scene. Didn't belong to anyone at the party, and none of the staff claimed it. Could be the killer's."

"It was a knit cap, right?"

Kat's tone became quizzical. "Is that an assumption you're making? Or, did you see it and forget to mention it?"

"Well, about that," Abby said, collapsing on her sofa. "Listen Kat, there's something I want to—"

Kat cut her off. "Let's finish up with my birthday request before we move into a conversation about something else, what say we meet up on Saturday night? Early, but after sunset. Say, six?"

Abby didn't push Kat into a conversation about her struggles with sleeping and the anxiety that she felt nearly all the time now. "That's fine. Where shall we meet?"

"The Root Cellar. There's a new headwaiter.

The dispatchers can't stop talking about him. He's cute. They think I should check him out."

"Of course they do," Abby said. "He's cute. You're cute. Why not?"

In a voice intensely animated, Kat added, "I know how hard you are working to make a go of that farmette, so you'll be my dinner date. I'll pay for both of us. Agreed?"

"No, Kat. I don't agree. There's no way. It's your birthday. I'm not that broke."

"So we'll split the bill. End of story," said Kat. "What was it you were going to tell me about the knit cap?"

"Well, I think I may be recalling—"

"Ah, jeez, Abby, wouldn't you know? Now I'm being summoned." Kat muffled her cell and called back to someone in her office. "Be right there."

"But, Kat, this is important—"

"It's the lieutenant, so I can't say no. See you Saturday," Kat said.

No sooner had Kat clicked off and Abby had made a cup of tea and grabbed her poster paper and picked up her felt-tip pens to work on her incident poster than Sugar began a high-pitched alarm barking. She sprinted to the front door as a knock sounded.

Abby tensed. She turned her incident poster facedown on the table and set aside the pens. After reaching for her grandmother's yellowware mixing bowl with hand-painted chickens around the rim and filled with candy, she padded in her stocking feet to the front door, with the bowl ensconced in her arm. With trepidation, she placed her hand against the lock. Since she'd moved to the place, she had never once had children knocking on her door on Halloween night. Her farmette was a bit too far from the main action in town. But there was always a first time.

"Please, Abby, can we come in?" called a soft voice on the other side of the door.

Recognizing Luna's voice, Abby flipped on the outside light and pushed back the dead bolt. She turned the knob and pushed open the screen door. The Varela sisters, Luna and Eva, stood on the front porch, under the soft glow of the porch light.

"Come in, ladies." Their troubled expressions told Abby something was very wrong. Setting the bowl back on the table, she asked, "What's happened?"

Tips for Protecting Chickens during Cold Weather

When the night wind howls and daytime temperatures plunge to bone-chilling cold, make sure you have some extra buckets for water on hand. If the water in the chicken water dispenser is likely to freeze, set out a bucket of warm water. Keep your chickens healthy and happy during cold weather with these other tips.

1. Hang a warming lamp in the chicken house (set a timer so that the lamp goes on an hour after sunset and off an hour

before daylight) when the weather turns freezing.

2. Leave the windows slightly cracked open, even on cold nights. Ventilation restriction can result in health problems for chickens due to ammonia buildup in their house.

3. Keep the chickens moving. Throw a layer of loose hay or straw in their run and toss scratch grains on the ground morning and evening to encourage exercise, which will warm them.

4. Ensure the feeder gets filled in the evening so the chickens can eat well before they roost.

5. Offer chickens scratch grains along with their regular feed to keep them busy, so they aren't pecking on each other, but consider scratch grains as their cotton candy—and no substitute for crumble or pellet food.

6. Don't let the feeder or the waterer go empty in winter.

Chapter 6

If you don't know which way the wind is
blowing, ask a farmer.

—*Henny Penny Farmette Almanac*

The raven-haired, dark-eyed Varela sisters—
their youthful faces etched with worry—
strolled into Abby's living room. Abby locked the
door behind them. Luna, the youngest sister,
barely twenty-three, wore a black rain jacket over
dark stretch pants and flats. Eva was the middle sister in the family, between Luna and Paola. Their
worried expressions conveyed distress. Abby greeted
them with a welcoming smile. Had there been a
change in Paola's condition? Or a break in the case?

Sugar's ear-piercing yips alarmed the women,
who cowered even after Abby had welcomed them
into her home.

"Please don't worry about my dog. She won't
bite. She knows Paola, but not you, and she is curious, that's all." Making a sweeping gesture with
her hand toward the dining room table, Abby said,

"Have a seat. I'll make us some tea." She filled three mugs from the spigot that delivered instant hot water from the unit she'd installed under the sink, inside the cabinet. "Have you already taken your toddlers trick-or-treating?"

"No," said Luna. "Maybe next year. They're still too young."

Abby took a tray from the lower cabinet where she kept her baking sheets and put the three mugs she'd filled on it. After taking down the honey jar and fishing out spoons from the silverware caddy, she placed those items on the tray and carried it to the dining room table. Then she reached for a large tin of handpicked organic herbal teas imported from a British tea shop and placed the tin on the table, next to the tray. "Help yourself," she said. "Tell me about Paola. Any change?"

Luna said, "Not that we can tell."

Pushing back into her chair, Eva quietly uttered in Spanish, "Es un gran problema."

With a drawn expression, Luna looked at Abby and said, "Yes, big problem. We've come to you because we need your help."

Abby's thoughts flew to Paola. She knew the neurosurgeons had put Paola in a medically induced coma. From what she knew from working on the force with victims in the past, an acute injury to the head through blunt force trauma could result in a subdural hematoma, or bleeding under the skull. To prevent increased intracranial pressure caused by swelling and bleeding, doctors would drill burr holes or surgically remove a temporary flap of bone and then later reattach the

bone piece they'd removed. The bone-flap proce-
dure gave the Varela family hope that Paola would
recover, but to what degree, no one could say.

"Problem with what? What's going on?" Abby
asked.

Eva blurted out in Spanish, "Emilio va a ser ar-
restado por la policía." Tears swam in her eyes.

"Emilio? Sorry . . . what?" Abby frowned, even
though she felt relieved that the problem didn't
concern Paola.

"I'll explain," said Luna, whose command of
English exceeded Eva's.

Abby glanced over at Eva. Her eyes now shimmered with tears. The reserved young woman
wiped a palm across her cheek to brush away a tear
rolling down and dug in her oversize shoulder bag
until she had tugged out a tissue.

Facing Abby, Luna said in a quavering voice,
"The police are going to arrest Emilio."

"Why?" asked Abby, trying not to react, despite
her anxiety. Her body tensed.

"Porque el ha sido interrogado dos veces," said
Eva, using the tissue to blot her tears.

Abby waited for the translation.

"Already, the police have taken him away twice
to ask questions," Luna said.

Eva tried to muffle her sniffles, prompting Luna
to place a consoling palm on Eva's knee and speak
in a tender, sisterly tone. "Mi hermana, tranquila."
Turning back to Abby, Luna said, "Like Eva, our
mother cries and prays the rosary, while our father
paces on his canes and asks if we should get a
lawyer. Your police have taken away our peace. Our

parents must return soon to Argentina, but they
fear losing Paola and now Emilio, too."

Abby drew in a sharp breath and let it go. "I'm
sorry that the actions of the LFPD are causing
worry for your family." Her words reflected the
heaviness of her heart. "It's possible they just need
to clarify inconsistencies in Emilio's previous statements. Innocent people have nothing to fear
when they tell the truth."

"But Emilio . . . he has told the truth. Our
brother would never make our sister Paola a widow."

Abby wound an errant clump of reddish-gold
hair around her finger and then tucked it back
into the elastic band restraining her messy, lop-
sided bun. How lucky Emilio was to have such
loyal and trusting sisters and parents who believed
in him. But they needed her help. *But to do what?*

Sniffing again, Eva said in a husky tone, "Pero la
policía lo ha estado siguiendo."

Luna studied the packet of tea she had chosen.
It contained green tea, rose petals, and pomegranate.

"What's Eva saying?" Abby shifted her position
on her hard 1929 Duncan Phyfe chair, the cushion
of which needed replacing.

"The police are following him," said a stone-
faced Luna.

"Why?" Abby asked. When Luna didn't answer,
Abby said, "Well, there has to be a logical explanation." She pushed the tin of assorted teas toward
Eva and got up to fetch a loaf of pumpkin-walnut
bread. Tailing a person of interest or a suspect was
an age-old tactic. The ploy sometimes resulted in

turning up the heat on a suspect. The guy gets stressed. Makes mistakes. Talks too much. Or visits people or places that can yield further information with relevance to the case.

"Did Emilio tell you this?" asked Abby, carrying napkins and slices of pumpkin-walnut bread to the table.

"Yes," said Luna.

"And the person following him is a cop?"

Luna nodded. "He recognized the officer from the station."

Abby selected a packet of hibiscus tea with an infusion of apple, raspberry, and black currant. After tearing open the packet, she pulled out the tea bag and dunked it repeatedly in her mug of boiling water. Which Las Flores cop, she wondered, had been tailing Emilio? The police department was small and perpetually understaffed. But then again, what did it matter? She needed to assuage the women's fear. But how? She could echo their father's advice and tell them to get a lawyer for Emilio. Or recommend he take a polygraph. The former was his legal right and would stop the police from talking with him without his counsel present. The latter could help the cops eliminate him as a suspect and end the family's misery. However, if the examiner found any of Emilio's answers to be deceptive, it would bring intense scrutiny upon him.

Luna drilled Abby with her enormous eyes. "Emilio insists he's done no wrong. He's mad that the police have focused on him, while the real killer goes free. Maybe you could find out if there are other suspects the police could investigate. And you could talk to Emilio. He might tell you things he refuses to tell our family." Luna reached for Eva's hand. Both sisters stared at Abby, united in their request for help.

Abby considered the irony. She was going to be looking into this case, anyway. Now the Varela sisters had given her a new impetus. Still, she fretted in a tense silence over the words *He might tell you things he refuses to tell our family. What things?* And were these "things" known to Chief Bob Allen? Was that why he wanted to keep close tabs on Emilio and was willing to pay for surveillance? The chief was the same man who'd insisted his officers pay their own uniform dry cleaning bills to save the department money. Alternatively, perhaps sweating out Emilio was Lieutenant Sinclair's idea. Regardless, Emilio was under a cloud of suspicion. And in a small town like Las Flores, the gossip mill would soon get wind of this development.

"Has Emilio taken a lie-detector test?" asked Abby. She gestured toward the pumpkin-walnut bread, which neither woman had yet touched.

"No." Luna looked at Eva as if for confirmation that their brother hadn't confided something different to Eva. Luna shrugged. "Do you think he should?" Luna asked.

"Well, it couldn't hurt," Abby said. She thought about how to explain the benefit and also the risk. Tearing off a corner of a bread slice, she said, "Passing the polygraph means the police can eliminate him as a suspect. But he must *not* be deceptive in any way. Do you understand? Things could get worse for him if he lies." Abby ate the small piece of bread and then sipped a little of her tea to wash it down.

Eva released Luna's hand to dab the corners of her eyes with the tissue. Tucking the tissue back into her purse, Eva eased out of her chair. She stood and adjusted her purse straps over her shoulder. Luna stood, as well. Sugar bounded toward them, yipping.

When Abby rose and called the dog's name, Sugar made eye contact with her. In a firm but up-beat voice, Abby said, "Quiet." Sugar maintained quiet, but not for long. Abby knew it was something they'd have to keep working on—she was far from the perfect doggy parent. Still, Sugar had not barked for several seconds. It was a start. She gave Sugar a stinky liver treat from the fridge as a reward.

Addressing the sisters, Abby said, "Sorry about that. Sugar gets alarmed at sudden movement, even by me. This whole murder business has me on edge. I'm sure it does you, too."

Luna nodded and followed her sister to the door. Before walking out, she turned and faced Abby. "Please promise me that you'll talk to Emilio. Before it's too late."

Abby hesitated. "I suppose. If you think it will help. But, Luna . . . ," said Abby, placing her hand on Luna's arm. "What aren't you telling me?"

Luna shrugged. "I can't tell you what I don't know. Speak to my brother."

Abby slipped into her cop mode. "I have to be clear about one thing, Luna. We're friends because we all love Paola. That said, you don't know me very well, and I don't know you—not truly. Nor Eva or Emilio, for that matter. What I'm trying to say is that your brother already feels antagonized by the cops. He might view me as another outsider trying to interfere in what must feel to him like a terrible nightmare. If you can tell me anything that would help me, now is the time."

"I understand," said Luna. "Eva and I believe Emilio is protecting someone. But we have no proof. It's just intuition. Please, Abby, find out what he is hiding for the sake of our parents and Paola. At times, Emilio can be his own worst enemy."

Abby managed a weak smile. Luna had become a tenacious little bulldog who felt honor bound to protect her family. She was not going to give up. "Okay," said Abby. She opened the door, and Eva walked out onto the porch. Luna held back. She threw her arms around Abby, whispering, "Thank you, *mi hermana*." And then she hurried off into the night with her sister.

Mi hermana—my sister. To Abby, it had sounded warm and genuine, not contrived. And it had been wrapped in the sweetness of human touch. Abby had needed Luna's hug. It had been an emotionally trying day. And now she would make a star on her incident poster, next to Emilio's name, along with a note to find out whom he might be protecting. Before she went to bed, she tapped a text to the woman listed in her phone contacts as the heir to the property behind her farmette. **Do you know Henry Brady? He's intending to park his RV on your land. Does he have your permission to do that?**

The terse reply came quickly. **Yes and yes. Old school chum.**

Great. Realizing she had no control over the situation, Abby resigned herself to it.

Long after the Varela sisters had left, Abby curled up under a comforter, her body snuggled in warmth. But her mind was as restless as a blustery storm. For a long while, she listened to the sounds outside her window—the clanging of chimes in the wind, the patter of a raccoon's paws as the forager sniffed out dried figs that had fallen on her roof, and the mournful bawling of a calf separated from its mother on neighbor Lucas Crawford's ranch. Even farther away, the whistle of a distant train, which grew so faint that at last she could no longer hear it. From the day she'd bought the farmette, she had relished the solitude of evenings here, where she lived close to nature. But since the murder, the familiar sounds of the night also brought a measure of anxiety. She now lived on the edge of something she didn't understand, at the mercy of a new kind of vulnerability.

Lying in the dark, Abby thought of Jake, his chiseled features marred by a bullet. Though she'd never spoken of it to anyone, Jake had always reminded her of someone else—Ian Weir, a man she'd met during her twenties. With his dark curls and appealing facial structure, Ian possessed a philosopher's tongue and a poet's soul. She had noticed him during the wedding of a college friend and had been immediately smitten. For the next year, they'd been each other's best friend. And then, when he'd popped the question, she'd said yes. But their union wasn't meant to be. Ian

had debilitating headaches, which doctors diag-
nosed as a rare, aggressive form of cancer. When
he passed away, he took with him the best part of
Abby—the ability to love with wild abandon. It had
made her cautious and reluctant to open her
heart to a man that way again.

Seeing Jake that first time had been like seeing
a ghost returned from the grave. It had been a
shock. She'd stolen glances at Jake all evening, unable to get past the physical similarity between him
and Ian. The niggling attraction had filled her
with guilt. The discomfort had become so great
that Abby had avoided all contact with Jake, even
as she enjoyed the blossoming of her friendship
with Paola.

The end of Ian's life came after there had already been much brokenness in Abby's. Three
times her mother had married. Two of those mar-
riages had ended in divorce, and one had been in
trouble when her mother died of a heart attack.
Abby became a motherless child whose father had
left for parts unknown. Her maternal grandparents took in Abby and her younger brother and
raised them. Years later, over winter break, her
brother was killed. And then Ian passed away. The
losses in her life had been tremendous, exerting a
profound emotional wounding that Abby feared
would never heal. Now, as she reflected on those
losses and on Jake and Paola's tragedy, her spirits
plunged into an abyss of sadness and heartache. A
mournful cry rose from deep inside her and
found its way out and into the down filling of her
comforter.

After she'd exhausted her tears, Abby sank into

an inner landscape devoid of light or comfort. The weight of her bedcovers felt as heavy as grief. She eased her foot out into the cold air of the bedroom. Just as quickly, the chill sent her foot back under. She curled into the fetal position. With sleep elusive, her thoughts drifted again, seizing upon the image of the knit cap on the head of Jake's killer, the earlier encounter with the RV owner, and the unexpected visit from the worried Varela sisters. *Sleep. I need it to think straight.* As she lay alone in the dark, Abby's only comfort was the snoring four-footed mound of fur next to her right hip and the gun in the bedside-table drawer. Sleep, if it came at all, likely would not be restful.

A hen's repeated loud cackles woke Abby. Already the sun's rays splayed across her bed and along the wall. She rolled over and faced the clock. Half past ten. Alarmed at the lateness, she heaved back the covers, sat up, and lumbered toward the shower. After drying off, she slid her arms and head into a cream-colored turtleneck. Next, she shimmied into a freshly washed pair of boot-cut jeans and shrugged on a mulberry-hued flannel shirt. After pulling on thick socks and stepping into her work boots, she assessed her image in the mirror. She liked what she saw except for her wild mane. After carefully plaiting her hair and securing it with an elastic band, she again evaluated her appearance. She looked like the lady farmer she was—not a plainclothes detective, investigator, or cop. Abby calculated that her nonthreatening appearance—especially if she opted for the clean-scrubbed look and lip gloss instead of makeup—would serve her well for questioning Emilio.

Dashing into the kitchen to reheat the coffee in the pot, which had already clicked off, Abby realized she had moved a little too fast, because Sugar went into a frenzied yipping session. Taking a slower approach, Abby poured dry food into the dog dish and set out fresh water. She retrieved her cup of coffee from the beeping microwave. While Sugar ate, Abby slipped out through the patio slider to unlatch the gate to the chicken run.

At the fence, her gaze flew to the property behind the chain links. *No Henry. No RV. Hallelujah!* She almost felt like doing a little jig. With the dog fed and the chickens out, Abby turned her attention to the apiary and the bees. In late fall and winter, a colony could die off, with the only sign being no activity, as was often the case on frigid and wet days. But today sunlight had warmed the hive entrances, and there was plenty of visible bee traffic. A small measure of contentment spread over her as she sipped her coffee and surveyed her surroundings.

Her farmette trees had lost their leaves. The grapevines needed cutting back, and the vegetable garden required composting and a final tilling before being left to rest. Her land was morphing into a winter landscape, making clear which outdoor projects still awaited completion. There were many. When she'd bought the place, she hadn't realized that it likely would take years to transform the land and rebuild the house into a modest dream home. Still, if she could no longer do police work because of the multiple surgeries on her shooting-hand thumb, which hadn't properly stabilized it, she would happily choose the farm life over the daily grind of a desk job. She took a swallow of her coffee and tossed the rest toward the base of an apple tree.

Back in the kitchen, Abby decided to set up a meeting time with Emilio. She located her cell phone on the charger and dialed the winery. But as soon as she'd dialed the number, her intuition told her to click off the call. An unannounced face-to-face would be better. If he was lying about anything, she'd see the signs.

Herb Tea for a Restful Sleep

Use herbs such as chamomile, hops, lady's slipper, lemon balm, passionflower, peppermint leaves, skullcap, Saint-John's-wort, and valerian root to create soothing teas and infusions when you want to banish anxiety, soothe frazzled nerves, and induce sleep.

Here's a simple four-part mixture for a good night's sleep. Combine the following herbs in equal parts: lemon balm, lady's slipper, skullcap, and valerian. Thoroughly mix together the herbs. Place one ounce of herbs in two cups of boiling water in a pot and steep for 20 minutes. Strain and enjoy.

*Note: Check with your doctor if you haven't used herbs before. While herbs have been used safely for thousands of years, some should not be used during pregnancy, and some can cause an allergic reaction, which should be treated as a medical emergency.

Chapter 7

Vineyards and farms are quiet places
until the birds arrive at first light.

—*Henny Penny Farmette Almanac*

At the Country Schoolhouse Winery, Abby chose to park under the decades-old sprawling oak. Just being near a tree, any tree, often soothed her spirit when she felt troubled, as she did today on this first visit to the winery since the murder. The gnarled scaffolding on this ancient oak was dramatic, and the sounds of birds chirping amid the nearly bare branches heartened her. Her gaze swept across the parking lot, past a dozen or so cars, uphill to the vineyard, where sunbeams lit the vermilion, green, and gold leaves on the vines. Red-winged blackbirds with conical bills and broad shoulders flitted along the paths and alighted on posts. Abby watched their erratic movements and then looked over at the winery's kitchen door. Dark images came flooding back into her psyche.

Her body tensed. With a self-reminder to hold it together, Abby resolved to focus on the positive impressions she'd absorbed that night—the crackling fireplace and pleasant tasting room. Both were elements of the warm refuge from the cold rain. She'd shared friendly banter with Kat and Hannah, the young intern, and had inhaled the seductive scents wafting from the kitchen when she'd gone in search of Emilio. The sous-chef had been expertly slicing orange Fuyu persimmons with a sharp knife. Abby's inquiry about Chef Emilio's whereabouts that night had intruded on the woman's focus and rhythm. She'd jerked her thumb in the direction of the parking lot. And that was where Abby had gone.

In spite of her efforts, unpleasant memories came flooding back. Abby's eyes fluttered closed, and her thoughts returned to the kitchen. Hadn't a male dishwasher been washing stacks of pots in the corner above the sink? Yes. Abby could see him in her mind's eye. He was wearing a knee-length apron over baggy cargo pants and was sporting a stringy ponytail that reached halfway down his back. And then she'd stepped out into the darkness.

In her mind's eye, she could also see the thin, misshapen band on Paola's finger. The couple hadn't gotten out of the car. But she had been out there walking and hadn't seen Jake and Paola drive in. So they must have arrived moments earlier. Maybe they'd been sitting and talking. Why had Jake lowered the car window? Perhaps to speak with the killer? Why? Did they know each other? Perhaps only one person knew the answer to that question, but she lay in a hospital bed, still in a coma.

Abby felt distressed. Maybe coming back to the scene of the crime wasn't such a good idea. But then again, the memory of the dishwasher being present in that kitchen had surfaced. What else had she blocked out? Her heartbeat loped ahead at a dizzying speed. Her face felt flushed. Her mouth went as dry as a cotton ball. Perhaps she shouldn't put off seeking professional help— someone who could clarify what was happening to her. She opened her eyes. At the winery's kitchen door, a sudden movement wrested her attention from the stress she felt to the situation at hand. Emilio had just darted out to toss a garbage bag into the Dumpster. With his longish dark hair, wide brows, and chiseled features, he had the handsome look of a polo player. He likely could have found work as an actor or a model, had it not been for his passion for cooking. She watched him walk back inside.

Abby cracked the windows of her Jeep for Sugar. She pulled the key from the ignition and turned to give her pooch a pep talk. "Listen up, Sugar Pie. I'm counting on you as my backup on this mission. Don't sound the alarm unless we need it. I promise to be back soon with a treat for my good little girl." The dog was having none of the sweet talk. She gave voice to her protestation through her incessant barking. "Oh, Lordy, do we need dog training," Abby said. "But right now I've got a suspect to eliminate."

Clutching her daypack, Abby exited the Jeep and locked it. She tossed her daypack over her shoulder and gripped the straps tightly, as though they provided her security in a situation of uncertainty. It was a silly compulsion, one among several of late that she didn't understand—the anxiety that increased at nightfall, the chronic insomnia, and the nightmares if she did by chance drift off. Still, she felt compelled to keep her word to Emilio's sisters. She would try to find out what he might be withholding from his family and to help him do what was needed to clear his name.

After strolling a short distance, she spotted the chef reemerging from the kitchen. Dressed in sneakers, jeans, and a turtleneck, he carried a chef shirt in a dry cleaner's bag in one hand and balanced a banker's box against his hip with the other. Watching his long, lean frame stride to his 2005 silver Buick Regal, Abby tightened her grip on the daypack straps and kept walking. He dropped the banker's box on the ground before yanking open the passenger door to his vehicle. Emilio hung the shirt behind the driver's seat and then hustled back to retrieve the banker's box. But instead of picking it up, he hit the trunk with the side of his fist and then stood with both hands, fingers spread, on the car's rear end. He clearly was in a mood.

Abby threaded her way through the cars but halted mid-step when she saw Hannah racing from the kitchen after Emilio, her long blond hair bouncing around her shoulders as she carried a rectangular case with a buckled strap at either end.

"Wait up, Emilio. You forgot these," she said, proffering at arm's length a cowhide culinary case of the type that chefs used to transport their expensive knives.

Abby's antenna went up. Why had Emilio forgotten his knives? What was going on here? Standing between cars several rows back from Emilio's four-door sedan, Abby waited and watched. The couple talked, but Abby couldn't make out the words. Still, it didn't take a Ph.D. in behavior analysis to know that when Hannah threw her arms around him, she was consoling him over something. Emilio responded by lowering his cheek against her neck. Without warning, a shout erupted from the Dumpster area.

"It ain't over, Varela," Scott Thompson's voice boomed. He marched to within a few feet of Emilio. "Get back inside, Hannah. Now."

Hannah made a move toward her uncle and placed her hand on his arm, apparently in an attempt to calm him. Scott jerked his arm from her grasp. Without following his command, Hannah backed away for safety's sake. A dozen winery workers who'd spilled out into the lot to watch the fracas joined her.

Abby froze, holding tightly to the daypack straps. The quiet *tchup-tchup-whee, tchup- tchup-whee* of a flock of common blackbirds perched on the highest branches of the oak over the Jeep became shrill. Their wings made a deafening noise as they flapped in ascension. The birds flew toward the vineyard. Emilio looked up at them. Then over at Abby, still yards away. He didn't acknowledge her. Instead, he grabbed the banker's box and the knife case, stored them in the trunk, and, slamming it shut, turned to face his adversary. Motioning with his fingers, Emilio made a "Bring it on" gesture.

"You'd sell out your mother in a heartbeat," shouted Scott. When he was within a foot of the chef, he lunged forward with a looping haymaker. Emilio ducked and threw back a straight punch that hooked to the right. The blow brought Scott to his knees with a muffled "My God. You busted my nose. My effing back. Somebody help me up."

Abby watched as workers helped Scott to his feet. She searched out Emilio and saw him holding his fist to his chest, as if doing so would ease the pain he must be feeling. After ducking into his car, Emilio backed it up and drove away. As he did, Abby heard the siren of a patrol car advancing. Someone had called the cops. As a cruiser rolled into the lot with its light bar flashing and siren wailing, Sugar barked and pawed the window glass. Abby showed Sugar an upraised hand, a signal she'd been teaching Sugar to stop barking but, as usual, it didn't work. Abby thought about going back and getting in her Jeep to leave but then she spotted Jake's father, Don Winston. He'd joined his winery staff out in the lot. Dressed in a dark suit, a white shirt, and a red silk power tie, he stood out in the crowd of mostly khaki- and jeans-clad workers.

Sergeant Otto Nowicki exited the cruiser from the driver's side, while a uniformed officer climbed out on the passenger side. Abby smiled at seeing Otto, true to habit, take a moment to hitch up his duty belt as he assessed the situation. Glancing around, Otto soon spotted her. She waved. He said something to his partner, who took out a notebook and made a beeline toward Don Winston.

Otto crossed the seventy feet or so of asphalt

that separated him from Abby. "Why am I not surprised to see you here, Abby? Shouldn't you be planting something back on the farmette?"

Abby chuckled. "I hate to break this to you, Otto, but it's the harvest season, not planting. I am eager to get through the holidays like everyone else and am hoping for a wet bare-root season."

He grinned and cocked his head from side to side, as if trying to stretch out a kink. "So why are you here?"

"Jake's sisters asked me to look in on Chef Emilio. They're worried that he's under a lot of pressure, not lessened any by the cops keeping tabs on him."

Otto raised a brow. "Now, you know I couldn't comment on that."

"Can't imagine why you'd be watching him."

"Oh, I think you do. You know as well as I do that the chef has friends and family in Argentina. Don't want him flying south like a Canadian goose until we get this murder case solved."

"Confiscate his passport. Tell him to stick around."

"We did that day one."

"An innocent man wouldn't run. His family says he didn't do it."

"Well, of course they say that. It's what families do."

"And I feel like the killer is still out there. It's not Emilio."

"You basing your opinion on facts or your sixth sense?"

She shrugged, knowing what he would say next.

"We let the evidence lead us, Abby. You know that.

Not our intuition. He's got the motive. He had the opportunity."

"Well, for that matter, there are a lot of people with motive—many of them angry husbands and boyfriends. From where I stand, it might even have been a professional hit. No jewelry was taken, no money. Looks like Jake could have been the target, and Paola, the collateral damage."

"Maybe. How do you know there was no money stolen?"

"Word got around that they had money and credit cards, but his wallet and her purse were intact. But let's talk about the gun that killed Jake. Have you found it?" Abby drilled Otto with a questioning look.

Removing his cap and rubbing a pudgy, pale hand over his nearly shaved head, he replied, "Not yet. But we know he owns a weapon."

"I heard someone stole his gun about three months ago."

"That may be, but he never reported it stolen, and that's a problem."

"Well, I know you aren't the type to zero in on a suspect because it's convenient. I hope Sinclair is being methodical, too. I know you all are looking at the finances of the winery and who inherits. I'm sure you've taken statements from everyone, but you might want to talk to Hannah again."

"Yeah? Why's that?"

"Call it a hunch. Hannah knows all the workers. She was here the night of the shooting, and her uncle just threw the first punch in the fight with Emilio—which is why you are here. And I'm here because Emilio's sisters have asked for my help. So let's make a deal. I'll encourage Emilio to cooperate, and I'll explain the benefits of taking the polygraph so you can eliminate him. In return, you promise not to suggest in any way to Sinclair that I'm sniffing around his case."

Otto hesitated. His jaw tensed.

"Look, Otto," said Abby, "Sinclair has warned me off, but Paola is like the little sister I never had. And the poor Varela parents—with one of their children in critical condition and the other under suspicion of murder—they are feeling pretty desperate."

He sniffed and adjusted the radio on his lapel. "You've gone soft, Abby." Then, cracking a grin, he asked, "Still got me on speed dial?"

Abby smiled. "You know I do."

"Watch your step, Abby . . . in case you're mistaken about this." He winked at her. "You know you were always my favorite on the force." He left Abby smiling as he sauntered off to join his partner.

With Emilio also gone, Abby decided to see if she could corner Don Winston. She strolled over to him. And soon she saw the opportunity to approach him when Otto and his partner walked back to the cruiser for a private talk.

"Mr. Winston, might I have a minute or two of your time?" Abby asked. "I mean when you finish with the police."

Winston scrutinized her. "And you are?"

"Abigail Mackenzie." She extended her hand. "Sorry for your loss. I'm a friend of Paola's."

"Hmm." He set his lips in a tight line but grasped her palm in a handshake.

"That fight between Emilio and Scott Thompson just now—what was that all about?"

"Two young bucks who have hot tempers, I'd say. They never could get along, and this isn't the time for divisiveness. Jake may have had the patience to control them, but I don't." He looked at her curiously. "Sorry, why have you come here this morning?"

Not wanting him to know her true purpose, Abby felt her face flush as she tried to come up with another plausible reason. "I assume you have a lost-and-found department. I thought I'd see if someone had found my earring. I lost it the night of the vow-exchange party, right after I'd given Hannah my coat. Perhaps she found it?" Abby prompted.

Donald Winston shrugged. "You'll have to ask her yourself. She's working in the tasting room, removing stock." He looked back at Otto, who had cocked his head to the side to use his shoulder-mounted radio. Winston added, "Or check with Brianna Cooper. The lost-and-found bin is in her office. Better hurry, though. It's her last day."

"Why is that?" Abby tried to sound innocent and charming, but Winston seemed immune.

His expression darkened. "We're outsourcing our graphics work from now on." His tone had an edge to it.

"May I ask why?"

He shot her a look that seemed to convey dismissal. "Excuse me," he said, "but I don't see that it's any of your business. I've got to deal with these officers so I can get back to work."

"Of course," said Abby. "But . . . one more question, please. What is the name of your winery's sous-chef?"

Winston drilled her with an inquisitive look and then frowned. "Why would you need to know that? Why is that your business?"

Abby pushed on without giving a direct answer to his question. "The sous-chef was the last person I saw the night of your son's passing. She was in the kitchen. She might remember if I was wearing both of my earrings before I went out into the parking lot."

"Oh, you're *that* Abigail Mackenzie, the person who found Jake."

"Yes."

"Dori Langston is our sous-chef." With that, Don Winston walked away. When he reached Otto, Abby heard him say, "I'd like to get back to work."

Otto nodded. "Sure."

Abby waited until Winston was gone and then strolled into the kitchen. Not seeing anyone, she headed to the tasting room, where she caught a glimpse of Hannah, who was about to leave through a side door.

"Wait up, Hannah." Abby tugged at the straps of her daypack and hurried over to the young woman. Seemingly, she'd caught Hannah by surprise. The young woman looked up at her, tears swimming in her blue eyes.

"Do we know each other?" Hannah sniffled as she set on the wine bar an armful of T-shirts and baseball caps bearing the winery logo.

"Ah, sweetie. I'm sorry to have startled you." Abby assumed the role of a supportive friend. "You look like you could use a hug right about now."

Abby's sympathy drew a torrent of tears from Hannah. Abby placed her arms around the young woman. "Ah. You poor thing. I wouldn't expect you to remember. We met the night of the vow-renewal party. Your boss told me I could find you here."

"My boss?" She pulled away from Abby's embrace and straightened, as if her whole body had tensed. "Why?"

"Not to worry," said Abby in a reassuring tone. "I was just inquiring about a lost item, and Don Winston told me to ask you."

"Oh," she said, her tone reflecting relief. She sniffed and wiped away the tears from her eyes with her fingertips. "We have to report to *that* Mr. Winston now."

"So he's at the helm, not the grandfather?" Abby asked. "I thought maybe the old man would take control."

Hannah hunched over the shirts and caps as a new round of tears threatened. "Too old, I guess. Jake's granddad used to come around a lot. We haven't seen him since Jake's death."

"I'm so sorry, Hannah." Abby dropped her day-pack on the bar and fished out a tissue. Handing it to the young woman, she said, "Seems kind of sudden to be making changes to the business. Has Don Winston already moved into an office here?"

Hannah nodded. "He's taken over Jake's and ordered us to box up all of Jake's things and moved them off-site."

"Seriously? How's morale?"

"Awful. Jake's dad isn't a people person."

"Really? What's he like?"

"I shouldn't say."

"It's just you and I talking here. It might feel good to vent, and I'm a good listener. I won't betray your confidence."

Hannah looked around to make sure no one was within earshot. "To me, he seems calculating and coldhearted. Don called a staff meeting and yelled when the sous-chef was late. Then he lashed into Brianna. And he told Emilio and my uncle Scott to leave. We all fear we might lose our jobs." Hannah began fingering the merchandise.

"Oh, dear," said Abby. "Let me help you with that." She gestured to the load under Hannah's hands.

"Thanks," Hannah said, following with several short sniffles. "It's got to go back to the stockroom."

"Well, I came to ask you if anyone has turned in a pearl earring. I lost it the night of the party. The last person I spoke with before going outside was the sous-chef. I'd like to ask her if she remembers seeing it."

Hannah frowned. "I haven't seen it, but I'll take you to Brianna's office to look in the bin if you want, and you can check with Dori in the kitchen. I need to stop in the supply room first."

Abby nodded and followed Hannah to a small room with industrial metal shelves stretching up the four walls. It looked like the records room of a police department, with a dozen boxes of records and merchandise, all labeled with colored felt-tip markers.

"This is where we keep all the stuff the winery sells. Mr. Winston says he doesn't believe we need to clutter the tasting room with lots of non-wine items. We're to display one of each thing and each size. Putting out a lot of merchandise, he told us, will just invite theft."

"I see his point," Abby said, taking notice of labels noting wine-themed glassware, kitchen cutting boards and utensils, table linens, apparel, hats, and bric-a-brac. "Seriously, there's a ton of stuff packed in this little room."

Looking wistful, as though recalling a treasured moment, Hannah said, "You know, Jake had planned to open a proper wine shop, but his dad was against it. Don wanted to streamline the operation. I guess Jake's dad will have his way now, and we'll ship this stuff back to the suppliers. With Brianna having to work from home now and the chef and Uncle Scott taking time off without pay, the rest of us have to work harder and longer hours. It isn't fair."

"Time off without pay . . . Is that why your uncle Scott and Emilio were fighting, sweetie?"

"Not really. Since clocking in this morning, Emilio and my uncle had been mouthing off at each other. Mr. Winston overheard them arguing before the staff meeting, when my uncle accused Emilio of sidling up to other winery owners in the area." She gazed directly at Abby. Her large eyes were swimming in tears. "Emilio dredged up a story about my uncle's drug use. He said Uncle

Scott is unfit to handle the safety of the barrel room. And later, he shouted that my uncle associates with some of the shady characters in town."

"Wow. Those are serious accusations," said Abby.

Hannah opened a box and slipped the caps into an empty plastic bag before closing the box and setting it back on its shelf.

Abby didn't want to add to Hannah's misery, but the young woman had piqued Abby's curiosity. "Does Scott use drugs?"

"I've never seen it," Hannah said, turning her attention to a stack of shirts that had to be returned to their boxes. Each had been wrapped in plastic and bore a price sticker.

"So, how did Mr. Winston react when he heard them arguing?"

"He ordered them to clean out their lockers and go home. He was going to take stock and let them know when they could come back to work, if at all. Of course, they blamed each other for the boss's action."

Abby fingered a French country table runner in the colors of sky blue and lemon and featuring French appellations of wine. "The holidays are almost here. If Mr. Winston is sending back these products to the manufacturer and he's laying off workers, how does he plan to generate revenue during the season?"

Hannah blotted her eyes with the tissue, tucked it into the sleeve of her sweater, and opened a large cardboard box. "I'm not sure. He's got to entice people to buy the wines. I thought Emilio could convince him to stick to the plan Emilio and Jake had plotted. But here we are, with everything up in the air and Don Winston cutting all non-essentials."

After filing shirts by size into the appropriate smaller boxes, she restocked them into the large cardboard box and sealed it. "Follow me to Brianna's office. It's this way."

Hannah led Abby from the supply room past two doors down the hallway. Brianna's office door stood partially open. "Brianna is not here. She's probably carting stuff to the car," Hannah said. "The lost-and-found bin is over there." She pointed to a banker's box in the corner. "If you don't mind, I've got to get back to the tasting room. Jake would let us work in peace, but his dad is always sneaking up and watching us. It's creepy, but whatever." She rolled her eyes. "Good luck finding your earring."

"I'll just do a quick check here and be on my way," said Abby. "Thank you, Hannah." She gave the young woman a quick hug. "It's just my opinion, Hannah, but Mr. Winston would be a fool to let you go."

Hannah flashed a weak smile. Smoothing her braid, she adjusted the soft collar of her angora sweater. "If you see Chef Emilio, tell him I'm on his side. My uncle deserved that bloody nose for suggesting Emilio was giving away trade secrets. He'd never do that."

With the possibility looming large that Brianna might return at any moment, Abby went to work. The room had a black filing cabinet with five drawers—two partially pulled out. A cursory glance in each of those drawers revealed little beyond folders of business documents. Abby hustled behind

Brianna's desk, a sleek Scandinavian piece of furniture. Miniature statues of Ares, the Greek god of war, and his sister Athena, the Greek goddess of wisdom and war, served as bookends to Brianna's collection of catalogs and graphic art volumes.

Glancing into the opened side drawers of Brianna's desk, Abby noted they held mostly office supplies, like paper clips and notepads. Then, noticing that the middle drawer stood slightly ajar, Abby spotted a Sig Sauer P229 pistol and numerous boxes of ammo. Her eyebrow shot up. She ruminated on what made Brianna tick. Why would she pack a gun at work? Why have so many boxes of ammo unless maybe she was doing target practice on her coffee breaks? And why would Jake have allowed that? It was just plain weird.

"Excuse me!" Brianna Cooper sounded infuriated. "Who are you? What are you doing here?"

Abby looked up at a thin-boned woman with penciled brows, pale eyes, and naked lips set in a straight line. Standing roughly five-ten, she wore her chestnut hair pulled into a tight bun. Abby sensed that this woman—who had lied to police about her boyfriend being with her the night of Jake's murder, when, in fact, he was returning from Oregon, where he ran in a marathon—was not going to be friendly and helpful.

"My name's Abigail Mackenzie. Mr. Winston told me the lost-and-found items were in this room. I'm looking for a small pearl stud I lost at the Varela-Winston vow-renewal party. Have you seen it?" Abby moved from behind the desk. She allowed her daypack to sweep the slightly open drawer, causing it to slide closed without a sound.

"You won't find it in my desk drawer," the woman said. "I think you'd better leave."

If you say so. *Gotta wonder, though, why you're packing a gun at work. Tends to raise a few questions, but I guess now isn't the time to ask them.* Abby backed away from the desk and strolled from the office. She found her way back to the kitchen and spotted the sous-chef in her toque—which was smaller than Emilio's—wiping down a work area.

Clearly, Dori Langston was the platinum-blond woman whom Edna Mae had described as Jake Winston's interior decorator. Surprised, Abby left the kitchen before the woman could see her. She walked out the back door and made a beeline to the Jeep, where Sugar waited for her. Only after Abby had reached the sprawling tree where wild birds still twittered did she feel a measure of relief from her mounting anxiety. She made a mental note to write down on her incident poster the details she'd learned during the visit, including Dori likely being the interior decorator; Scott possibly having a drug problem; Brianna keeping a gun and plenty of ammo with her at all times; and Emilio sidling up to the other wineries.

Tips on Feeding Wild Birds

- Fill a feeder with cracked corn and seed mix to attract red-winged blackbirds.

- Hang a mesh sock filled with Nyjer seeds to attract finches.

- Fill large saucers with mixtures of seeds that songbirds love and place them in the crotches of trees. As the seeds are scattered, let them grow to produce a crop of homegrown birdseed.

- Make a seed-and-nut suet ball with dried fruits (apples, for example), kernels of corn, peanuts, and suet, and hang it from a tree to attract nuthatches, woodpeckers, blue jays, mockingbirds, and other species of wild birds.

- Mix together millet, sunflower seeds, corn, wheat berries, dried worms, and white pine seeds in an old pie tin and set it in your garden for the ground feeders, like mourning doves.

Chapter 8

Honeybee pupae wait to chew through
their wax-capped cells until the color
of their compound eyes and bodies
darkens.

—*Henny Penny Farmette Almanac*

Abby focused on the two-lane road, while Sugar perched on the passenger seat, as if riding shotgun. They were taking the scenic way home from the winery. Troubling questions occupied Abby's mind, most of them having to do with what Hannah had confided. What had Scott meant by his accusation that Emilio was sidling up to other winery owners? And how did Emilio know Scott Thompson's drug use was making him unfit to handle the barrel room? And why had Dori Langston claimed to be an interior decorator? Why did Brianna keep a gun within easy reach? What did any of this have to do with Jake's death? Abby resolved to dig up the answers. And one thing she was very good at was digging.

Paola's impressions of Scott had been positive.

She had told Abby he was a good listener. And yet Abby had witnessed a darker side. What explained it? Maybe Scott sought job security by sidling up to his boss's wife. It wouldn't be the first time a man used a woman that way. Abby made a mental note to find out more about Scott when Paola regained consciousness. A sobering thought intruded. What if her lovely Argentine friend never woke up? A wave of sadness swept over Abby as she envisioned Paola lying helpless in a pentobarbital coma, with a skull flap removed to accommodate brain swelling. When and if she did awaken, Paola would have to tell the police what she witnessed that horrible night. Abby could only hope that a member of Paola's family would be there to hold her hand through that interview.

The hilly road twisted through stands of white birch, red-bark eucalyptus, and manzanita trees. Vineyards, their linear rows like leafy tiling patterns laid out in perfect symmetry, served as backdrops for white farmhouses and tall, open barns set back from the road. In some barns, Abby could see baled hay stacked in lofts under corrugated tin roofs. After the multiyear drought, farmers had raced the early onset of storms this year to harvest their hay fields. Most had put their hay up, but a few fields remained dotted with bales still to be transported.

Passing the old church that the Lutherans and later a sect of Buddhists had once occupied, Abby noticed strange angular pads on a cell phone tower antenna perched atop the building's roofline. Grimacing at the unappealing aesthetic, she recalled hearing a lot of debate from towns-people about congregations accepting money for a house of worship to be a conduit. Many believed that possible communications transmitted through the tower's antenna might not be in alignment with the spiritual beliefs and practices of churchgoers.

Abby eased off of the accelerator and let the road ahead unfold as her thoughts quietly drifted. But within seconds, her thoughts zipped into high alert. Her foot hit the brake pedal. Up ahead a drought-stressed western sycamore with mottled bark, dangling brown balls, and few remaining broad leaves collapsed in slow motion, with a heavy thud, over a horse trailer being towed by a pickup. Brakes screeched; horns blared. Abby's cell phone started ringing. Drivers began to attempt backing up. Some tried to pull off on the shoulder to maneuver away.

Abby glanced at her phone. *Seriously, Kat. Can't talk now.* Abby's heart raced like a runaway train. Her cell continued to ring, even as a siren wailed on approach behind her. *Must be Otto. He'd be monitoring the radio traffic and know if dispatch had put out a service call.*

Heart thumping and anxiety gnawing at her insides, Abby ignored the phone while she tried to figure a way out of the mess. Looking to her left, at a tree-lined, narrow gravel road, she recalled that it followed Las Flores Creek as it wound through the foothills past the Las Flores Regional Park. There the creek widened into a small lake, mostly visited by fishermen, bird-watchers, and hikers interested in following the numerous trails throughout the local wine region. Abby knew she could take the road and several others that connected to it and slowly make her way back to Farm Hill Road, about nine miles out.

In a split second, she backed up the Jeep and swung left. Even if it did take longer to get home, at least she wouldn't be stuck in this mess. After she'd rolled out of view down the two-lane gravel road, Abby pulled over and stopped in the shade of a tall pin oak, where she answered Kat's call.

"About time you picked up," said Kat.

"Sorry about that." Abby hit the speaker button on her cell. "I was dealing with traffic backed up behind a horse trailer." Breathing easier and feeling her anxiety lessening, Abby stared at a low-hanging branch, noticing the way the hue of its leaves shifted in places from sap green to verdigris.

"On Farm Hill Road?"

"No. I'm on Rooster Flats Road."

"The only thing of note on Rooster Flats Road is the winery. So why are you up there at this early hour?"

"To have a word with Emilio."

"And that would be what cell phones are for, girlfriend."

"Yeah, Kat. I get that. So what's up?"

"I wanted you to know first," said Kat. "Well, actually, Sinclair was first up in the loop, because the hospital called him. And then he told me."

"Oh, for goodness' sake, Kat. What? He told you what? Tell me already." Kat could be annoying sometimes, but now she had Abby's undivided attention.

"Paola's doctors are saying she is wiggling her toes on command."

"That's fabulous news."

"Sinclair's mood went positively buoyant. He's headed there now."

"Is her doctor okay with a cop questioning her? I mean, it's soon . . . too early, surely. She needs time to—"

"What? She's got to be interviewed, Abby."

"It's not that, but Sinclair will be asking her about her husband's murder. What could be more traumatic for a woman who's been through what she has?" Abby swallowed against a small lump that had formed in her throat. She felt unsettled. "Shouldn't Paola have a family member or at least Father Joe with her for that?"

"Well, if you are there with Emilio, couldn't you ask him to leave work to be with her?" asked Kat.

"As it turns out, he's not working today," said Abby. She quickly added, "But, look, it is possible one of her sisters might be with her already."

"Ah, not to worry, then. So I'll see you Saturday. My birthday dinner?"

"I haven't forgotten. But thanks for the heads-up." Abby clicked off the call.

Fifteen minutes later, Abby navigated a narrow, winding uphill stretch of the road. From the top, she enjoyed sweeping panoramic views of green valleys and the mountains beyond. Below, the regional park came into view. It sprawled over forty-five acres, encompassing rolling knolls, stretches of woods, and a crystal clear lake fed by Las Flores Creek. The lake's surface reflected the billowy white clouds dotting the sky. She could see the ranger station and a couple of vehicles parked near it. While the park might not have many week-day visitors during the rainy season—November through April—people came out during weekends and on holidays to see the ducks and other resident wildlife.

Abby negotiated the hill's descent, maneuvering carefully around curves, until the park entrance emerged again in her line of sight. Rolling past the unstaffed ticket kiosk, which did a brisk business during the summer months, when staffers collected parking fees, she maneuvered the Jeep next to the Buick Regal, one of two vehicles in the lot. Unless she was mistaken, that sedan belonged to Emilio. She glanced out the car window but could see no one inside the Regal. *So where are you, Emilio?*

After Sugar had bounded out of the Jeep to the ground, Abby snapped the leash to the dog collar and slammed shut the door. She hustled over to the Buick and peered in. Sure enough, a clean chef's shirt hung on a hook at the rear passenger window. After following Sugar's eager lead to the ranger station, Abby snooped around, but the place appeared empty. Perhaps the ranger had gone to the restroom.

Next, Abby walked past a row of picnic tables and barbecue pits that dotted the lake's edge. She and Sugar approached an area of tall green and golden reeds where someone had tied a blue rowboat to the dock. At the farthest end of the wooden structure, Emilio sat dangling his long, jeans-clad legs over the edge, near a stand of brown, fuzzy cattails. He seemed fixated on the smooth liftoff of a sandhill crane on the lake's far side.

"*Hola*, Emilio," Abby called out.

Emilio turned to look at her. His brooding expression registered surprise. "Abby, what brings you here?"

She volleyed the question back at him. "I could ask you the same thing."

He twisted his head, as if to work out a kink. "I often come here after work or on my days off. I think better in nature."

"I can see why. It's peaceful. We're not interrupting, are we?" She gave Sugar a pat on the head.

"Not at all. Come. Sit with me."

Abby strolled over to him and dropped down on the wooden surface. Sugar, a leash length away, set about sniffing the air, the dock, the reeds, cattails, and anything else she fancied, yipping now and again at a sudden movement in the rushes.

"Saw you at the winery, Abby. It didn't seem like a good situation to welcome you into." His deep-set dark eyes gazed out over the lake's edge, where a fish splashed out of the water.

"Well, I was there to see *you*. I didn't expect to witness that fight. Care to tell me what it was about?" Abby hoped he would feel like talking.

Emilio pushed a shock of jet-black hair behind his ear. Except for that section of hair, he'd secured the rest with an elastic band. "Things got a little heated at the staff meeting with our boss. Now that Jake's gone, he wants a strategy for the winery's future. Scott Thompson and I don't see eye to eye on that issue, so I guess you could say we butted heads."

"How so?"

"Scott used to listen. These days, though, he's just reactionary. He shot down every idea I mentioned without offering other options. So disrespectful."

"Well, what were you proposing?"

"More wine and food events. You know, tie them into the seasons of vineyards and wine making. Better not get me started on all the ways I think we could create special occasions for wine club members and the public. If our events involved music, we could cross-pollinate promo with the participating bands, and so much more."

To Abby, it seemed like a perfectly reasonable idea. Lots of other wineries in the region already offered events. Some united music from local bands and offerings from food trucks. Abby could see the payoff for Emilio, but how did Scott see that as a disadvantage? "Tell me how your idea would work."

"So, Abby, you know that all the local wineries do tastings now. But what if two or more wineries joined? Say we had a group participating in something like a port-of-call series of events."

"You mean like a cruise ship stopping at new destinations? So go on."

"Yes. Exactly. We could finish a season with an annual competition of some kind. Maybe it could be for the best food and wine pairing for that season in our region."

Abby smiled. Emilio certainly did not lack enthusiasm or ingenuity.

"Can't see why Scott wouldn't like that," said Abby.

"Me neither. I'd brought these ideas up to Jake, and he'd seemed open to them. But Scott objected to change. Thinks we should stay small and focus on great wine. And that part-timer Gary Lynch, who sometimes helps out doing odd jobs when his cousin Trevor Massey is doing a kitchen shift . . . Well, they are just three guys who haven't a clue how to think big."

"What would Scott get out of the winery sticking to the status quo?"

"Who knows? I used to like the guy, but he's been off the hook lately. Always complaining and shirking. Mood swings with no warning. He went ballistic when I brought up an idea about starting something like the Napa Valley Wine Train. I mean, there's already a small railroad that runs through the mountains beyond these foothills. Did you know that?"

Nodding, Abby said, "It doesn't go anywhere except up into the old-growth forest and back down." She could hear the enthusiasm in his voice and see how his eyes sparkled as he spoke about his passion. He was clearly a man with bold ideas, just like Jake had been. Abby watched an insect on the water's surface flitting and widening the ripples. "Well, I guess your new boss's response is what will matter in the end."

"And I had won him over until Scott started tearing apart every idea. Before Jake died, Scott had been panicking that he was going to get canned. So maybe Scott thinks the way to stay on the payroll is by not rocking the boat. He and that odd jobber Gary Lynch are awfully chummy. Makes you wonder what they have in common."

"What do you mean?" Abby leaned back on the

heels of her hands and looked over at Emilio. His expression darkened.

"I should leave it at that. I've said enough."

She should have anticipated that response. Emilio was ex-military and a crack shot, but not the type of person to criticize or judge others without good cause. But maybe if she hit the question directly on point, Emilio would answer in an equally forthright manner. "So, Emilio, I've heard about Scott's drug use. Maybe that accounts for his mood swings and combative behavior. Any truth to it?"

Emilio shot her an incredulous look, as though she expected him to engage in community gossip. His jaw tensed. He looked away.

By his silence, Abby realized that this was the brother that Paola had called her "moral compass." He was only thirty-five years old, but in many ways he seemed older and wiser. This character of creative imagination and strong moral compass was whom Paola believed Emilio to be, and whom Abby hoped him to be.

"May I ask a question of you, Emilio, about the night of the murder?"

He cupped a hand over his eyes momentarily, as though trying to make out the species of a hawk circling in the distance. He dropped his hand and gazed directly at Abby. "Sure."

"Where were you when Jake was killed?"

Emilio's jaw tensed. "Like I've told the police, I was in the wine cellar." He didn't blink.

"But no one saw you go down there." She looked over at Sugar, who'd stretched out for a snooze in the sun on the warm pier boards. Staring at the ripples in the lake, she asked, "Was anyone with you?"

He hesitated. "Why would there be?"

"Look, Emilio," said Abby. "I don't have a dog in this fight. It just so happens, I believe you are innocent. And unless you shock me with an admission that you murdered your brother-in-law, not much else you say would surprise me."

"Uh-huh."

"Here's what the police know. You had a motive. You owned a gun that shot a bullet of the same caliber as the one that killed Jake and that they fished out of Paola. No one can alibi you for the time Jake was murdered. And you drive an older-model sedan, like the killer's getaway car." Abby inhaled a deep breath. "Now I'll confess something to you. I believe you were with someone when your brother-in-law was killed. I also think that for whatever reason, you are protecting that person. Why?"

He plucked a broken cattail growing in the swale along the dock. After examining the brown, fuzzy flowering spike, he said, "Can I trust you, I mean, to keep silent about this?"

"Absolutely."

"Do you know Appleton Wines?"

Abby recalled the local winery's recent awards from some prestigious competitions. "I do."

"One of their daughters, Hailey . . . Well, we've got a lot in common. She's about my age and has had some culinary training, too. She believes my ideas fit with their family's vision for the future of Appleton."

"And this is connected to the murder how . . . ?"

He started to speak and then stopped himself.

Abby gave him time. She watched him chew his lower lip.

Eventually, he summoned the courage to speak. "The night of Jake and Paola's party, I invited her down to the cellar. There are some spectacular wines down there, wines even more rare than those displayed upstairs. We talked. She offered me a job. A good offer. One hard to pass up."

Abby felt the tension leave her body at the realization that Emilio had an alibi. "And?"

"I told her, 'No. At least, not now.' Look, Jake was exceptional at pissing people off. Especially me." Emilio sneezed into a bent elbow. He fished a handkerchief from his jeans pocket and blew his nose. Pushing his handkerchief into his pocket, he continued, "My employment contract runs for another six months. I believe the right thing to do is stay. Help the Winston family move forward, because this is a terrible thing to happen to a winery this time of year." Methodically plucking brown cattail fuzz and flicking pieces into the water, Emilio seemed resolute.

"Tell the police, Emilio. Take their polygraph. Clear your name."

He stared straight ahead. "Can't. My alibi is a woman in a contentious custody battle for her kids. If word gets out that she was in the cellar with me the night of the party and the murder, her husband's lawyers will crucify her in court. I can't be the cause of her losing her kids."

"The police kept everyone there that night. They must have asked her where she was when Jake was shot. Did she lie to them?"

"I don't know. Hailey couldn't very well tell the truth. Probably got her girlfriend to alibi her."

"I see. Lying to the police, Emilio, it's a bad—"

He threw up his hand. "Discussing this further is pointless. I know you used to be a cop, and maybe you feel like you have to defend them, but I don't trust them. And I gave Hailey my word."

"Your conspiracy with her stalls a legitimate investigation and allows a murderer to roam free. Who knows who the next victim might be? Emilio, help the cops find Jake's killer." Abby knew her tone reflected her impatience. She tried a final push. "Tell Hailey the truth—you could be facing a murder charge. She wouldn't want that."

He brushed the cattail fuzz from his jeans and said nothing.

Abby pressed him no further about Hailey, but it was as good a time as any to ask about Scott. "Would Scott Thompson have a reason to kill Jake?"

"I don't know. The guy is hooked on prescription drugs for a back injury. He complains about it all the time. Supposedly, he hurt it from a barrel-room accident before we had the place retrofitted for earthquakes. Scott's got debts, too. But kill Jake? Nah, I don't see how he'd profit from that."

"I'm surprised that with a bad back, he'd want to pick fights."

"Yeah, go figure."

Abby's brows furrowed. "What about Brianna Cooper? Did you know about the gun she has stashed in her desk at work?"

He nodded. "Yes. She brought it in after that vineyard owner shot his investor and then did himself in a couple of years ago. You remember that?"

"Yep. The media was all over it."

Emilio swatted at a gnat near his face. "There's something slightly off about Brianna, but then, she's a super-creative type. Likes her guns. Told us she lets off steam by visiting the shooting range at least once a month. "

"She and Jake get along?"

"Jake and Brianna sparked off each other for a while. If they had a fling, it didn't last too long. I heard Brianna tell Hannah that she had an insurance policy to make sure he never talked about it."

"Really? That sounds ominous." Abby's interest perked up. "Know what it was?"

Emilio closed his eyes and turned his face to the sun. His look conveyed weariness with the whole affair in general and perhaps her questions in particular. "No."

Abby flicked a thistle from her jeans. "Emilio, listen to me. Please. Ask Hailey Appleton to release you from your promise of keeping silent. You both have a legitimate alibi."

His jaw tensed. He said nothing.

Abby reckoned it was time to move on. "I've got some good news. Paola is wiggling her toes."

Emilio jerked upright. His expression brightened. "Really? Oh, thank God." He tossed the cattail into the water. "Why didn't you tell me sooner?" After scooting backward, he quickly climbed to his feet and pulled Abby upward.

"Think about what I said, Emilio. Talk to Hailey. It's time you put this behind you."

He engulfed her in a bear hug. Pulling away and still beaming, he said, "I'm not the shooter. Not me . . . So who is it, Abby?"

"I don't know. At least not yet. But one way or another, I'm going to find out." She looked him the eye. "Do me a favor, Emilio. Watch your step."

Tips about Honey and Its Uses

1. Honey is nearly twice as sweet as sugar.

2. Honey contains antioxidant and antimicrobial properties not found in sugar.

3. Honey has a water content, while sugar does not, and therefore, recipes may need adjusting if honey is substituted for sugar.

4. Honey must be accurately measured. If you coat a measuring cup with a spray oil before adding honey, it will be easier to pour out the honey.

5. Honey supplies abundant moisture to cakes and other baked goods.

6. Honey enhances and complements other flavors in a recipe.

7. Honey can be added to beverages, fruit, or yogurt to sweeten them; whisked with oil into salad dressings; mixed with seasonings for basting barbecued meats; or drizzled over pancakes, waffles, and hot biscuits.

8. Honey may be used in homemade soaps and bath washes.

Chapter 9

Living with uncertainty is a big part of a
farmer's life.

—*Henny Penny Farmette Almanac*

Mid-morning Friday, Abby leaned back in one of the chairs to her 1929 Duncan Phyfe dining-room set and rubbed her burning eyes. For the better part of two hours, she'd been staring at her incident poster, to which she'd just added Hailey Appleton's name as Emilio's alibi, pending verification. The incident poster wasn't exactly like the ones she once used at the LFPD. Her tabletop poster had holes where information was missing—in fact, lots of blanks to fill in. But she'd been a cop long enough to know the value of knowing what you knew and what you didn't, as well as to access quickly what you still needed to learn. She also understood that while a good investigator let the evidence lead her to the facts, a case sometimes got solved when a strong hunch paid off in spades. And she was relying more on hunches these days. It might be different if her cop friends were sharing, but they weren't.

The official investigation would have already assembled a master list of evidence collected at the scene, as well as the supplemental interviews with anyone who might have heard the shot or witnessed the car entering or leaving the winery parking lot. The official investigation would have copies of the itemized list of evidence recovered, such as fingerprints and other latent prints, blood/saliva, semen, hair, fibers. There would be victim photographs, crime-scene diagrams, pictures of vehicles and tire impressions, images of tool marks and shoe tracks, and anything else detectives considered relevant. The patrol officers who conducted a check of the neighborhood around the winery for any ear- and eyewitnesses would have provided supplemental narratives. The cops would likely have compiled a list of the license plates to all the vehicles in the winery's parking lot. And most importantly, the official investigation would have both the initial assessment by coroner Millie Jamison and the official autopsy report. Abby had none of what the official investigation had to unmask Jake's killer. But that didn't mean she was giving up. Far from it.

"Come on, Sugar. Let's get the mail. Maybe a new heritage seed catalog with lots of pictures will rejuvenate me." Abby put the leash on the dog. Traffic on Farm Hill Road was light most mornings, but Abby knew one crazy, inattentive driver could take out a deer, cow, or dog in a heartbeat.

She still had plenty to learn as a dog parent, but she would go to any length to keep Sugar safe.

Beneath the Thanksgiving circulars, junk mail, and catalogs in the mailbox, she found a twenty-dollar bill with a note attached to an empty egg carton. The money was a payment from a friend working in the emergency room of Las Flores Community Hospital. The message reminded her about the need for a Henny Penny Farmette flyer for the ER break room. With the holidays approaching, the timing was perfect for selling the remaining summer fruit jams and honey that Abby's flyer promoted.

Closing the mailbox, Abby considered her growing to-do list. She needed to find a suitable gift for Kat's birthday, since their dinner was tomorrow evening. And she'd promised Maisey an additional order of honey. With the pie shop located within a few blocks of the hospital, Abby could drop off Maisey's order and then swing by the hospital to get the flyer posted and to peek in on Paola. Thinking about the tasks before her, Abby realized that combining her errands into one trip to town today made the most sense.

With her mail in hand, she opened the side gate and unfastened the leash from Sugar's collar. The dog trotted to the back fence and began barking at a noisy squirrel flicking its brown tail from atop the aluminum chicken-house roof. Abby latched the gate and strolled to the patio. If she got started soon, she'd have plenty of time to get everything done in town and return home before dark.

Before dark. The thought gave rise to a flash of

anxiety as Abby recalled pulling night duty with the Las Flores Police Department back in the day. Before Kat became her partner, she had worked many such shifts without backup and knew only too well how receiving a call from dispatch could power up her stress. Everyone from Chief Bob Allen down to the newest rookie comprehended that police work was arguably one of the most stressful jobs anyone could do, often fraught with crises involving unknown dangers and ambiguous situations. The unknowns would get your thoughts spinning and your mind playing tricks. You'd imagine the worst, and sometimes the worst happened.

It was that kind of stress that accounted for high rates of suicide, divorce, and alcoholism among cops. But Abby was no longer a cop. She worked a farmette. Farmers were up with the first light and down with the chickens. But since Jake's murder, the onset of twilight had brought Abby more than the welcoming thought of dinner and bed. Twilight triggered uneasiness. The darkness, which arrived earlier each evening as the calendar ticked down to the winter solstice, imparted in her a trepidation she could neither define nor name. It entered her flesh and bones as surely and stealthily as an illness that threatened to harm her health. With a sudden shiver at the patio slider, Abby realized she needed to get a grip on what was happening to her. More importantly, she had to find out how to get rid of the symptoms, which weren't going away by themselves. Her regular doc had a nurse-practitioner covering for him while he was away on sabbatical. It was high time to seek help from a professional.

After tossing the junk mail into the kitchen waste-basket and then sliding the twenty into her mason jar of change on the countertop, Abby stashed the egg carton on top of the fridge. She headed to the washer and dryer area. From the shelf over the appliances, she removed a small cardboard box packed with honey jars—all filled, sealed, and labeled. Next, she printed out an invoice for them, as well as a copy of the new flyer promoting her products. With those tasks completed, Abby entered her bedroom closet to find a change of clothes.

She pulled a fully lined wool dress from a hanger. The garment struck just above the knee, but Abby reasoned she could wear some warm tights to block the November chill. And a pair of flats would look nice with the dress, which also had a matching angora sweater in a shade of turquoise that set off the reddish gold of her hair. She reasoned that Paola, if awake, might also appreciate the splash of turquoise color amid the plainness of ICU blue scrubs and the white lab coats.

Twenty minutes later, at Twice Around Mark-downs, Abby pulled the angora sweater tighter around her bosom against the chill at the back of the store, where the bric-a-brac was kept. Kat loved stuff from bygone eras, especially Victorian collectibles, so Abby had decided to look through the castoffs in the display cases and on the tables. Her gaze swept over three well-worn trading cards and a book on how to crochet tea cozies, jam pot covers, and doilies. She passed on picking up a sepia-

toned daguerreotype image that looked like one
of those postmortem portraits that the Victorians
loved, and instead, she reached for a vintage ivory
or bone British Raj panel bracelet. Forming the
bracelet were individual links depicting elephants,
peacocks, and other images associated with the
vast Indian subcontinent. The bracelet latched
like a miniature belt buckle.

"May I help you find something?" the male sales-
clerk called out in a booming voice.

Startled, Abby dropped the bracelet and spun
around.

"Sorry. Did I scare you?" the man asked as he
tottered toward her. His voice sounded too loud
for normal conversation.

"Well," Abby replied, "I nearly jumped out of my
skin."

The man laughed and pointed to his hearing
aids. "I've got two of them, and neither works very
well. Wife tells me I talk too loud, but I hear too
soft."

Abby flashed an understanding smile. She
picked up the bracelet and positioned it back on
its display tree. Taking a few steps toward an old
clock, she told the man, "I'm just looking."

"I'll leave you to it, then," he said and wandered
away.

The round shape of a candy box caught Abby's
attention. She picked up the blue cardboard box
covered in a gilt Arabesque pattern and held it to
the light to examine it for damage. Fading seemed
to be the only issue, especially on its top surface,
which read LILLIPUTIAN CONFECTIONS. The image

was of a teenage girl standing beneath a banner. Judging by her blond curls fashioned into ringlets and the period dress she wore, the depiction of the young female had been inspired by the Victorian era, even if the box wasn't actually from that period.

The candy box sparked for Abby a new idea for Kat's birthday. She would clean the box and fill it with the foil-covered chocolate truffles that Paola had given her the day before the shooting. Paola had explained that properly stored in a cool, dark place—not the fridge—the truffles would keep for two weeks. Abby also remembered that she had antique silver candy tongs she'd found at an estate sale and never used. She'd give Kat that item, too.

"Sir," Abby called out. "How much for this box?"

The man didn't respond. Surmising that he hadn't heard her, Abby picked up the box and carried it to the cash register at the front of the store.

"You want that old thing?" he asked, holding it aloft and blowing off a layer of dust.

"Depends. How much?"

"No more than a dollar, though I'll wager my missus would put a higher value on it. Between us, I think my wife should have trashed it long ago."

Abby winked at him. "No need to bag it," she said, pulling a dollar from her purse and pushing it across the counter. The man opened the register and put the single bill inside, then nodded to her as she left.

Delighting in her find, Abby carried the box back to her Jeep. Kat, she was sure, would love it. The item needed cleaning, of course. But after that, Abby would line it with paper and fill it with truffles. A ribbon that anchored the tongs on the knotted bow would give the present a festive finish. With Kat's present crossed off her to-do list, Abby set the Jeep on a course for Maisey's pie shop.

CRAWFORD FEED AND FARM SUPPLIES, emblazoned on the side of Lucas Crawford's 1958 restored truck, grabbed Abby's attention. The vehicle was parked directly in front of the pie shop. Wheeling her Jeep in behind it, Abby felt her pulse skitter. After parking, she stared at the front door of the shop. The thought of seeing Las Flores's most eligible bachelor strolling out triggered a flood of emotions, like that of a teenage girl awaiting the moment when Boy Wonder would do a slo-mo walk toward her. Already, she felt hot.

Her thoughts tripped back to that late spring day many moons ago when he'd come calling with a box of empty jars in his red pickup. She had been working with the bees and had become trapped inside her beekeeper's suit. The day had been sweltering. When the zipper caught on fabric at the back of her veiled bonnet, Abby couldn't escape. She had asked him to help her free the slide from the fabric so she could unzip the hat and take off the blazing hot suit. Now the memory of smelling his aftershave and sensing his eyes on her as his fingers fiddled with that zipper triggered a quiver of excitement. Her secret admiration of Lucas had taken hold that day. It had never left her.

Despite the pitter-patter of her heart, Abby took a deep breath, hoisted the box of honey-filled jars and invoice into her arms, grabbed her purse, and climbed out of the Jeep. The bell on the door jingled, announcing her arrival. An apron-clad Maisey looked up from refilling a patron's cup with coffee. Flashing a warm smile that lit up her face, Maisey waved to Abby.

"You must have been reading my thoughts," Maisey said when Abby got to the counter.

"Yeah? What were you thinking?" Abby asked, setting down the box of honey.

Maisey lowered her voice to a conspiratorial softness. "I made those pies you were so crazy about last Thanksgiving. You know, the ones with whiskey . . . well, technically, bourbon. You know, bourbon is whiskey, but not all types of whiskey are bourbon."

Abby nodded, half listening, as her gaze swept across the room to the table by the window where Lucas had sprawled his muscular frame into a booth. The afternoon sunlight danced through the trees outside the window. The brilliant light splayed across his curly brown hair, highlighting its silver threads. Dressed casually in jeans and a woolen shirt that matched his eyes, the color of sunlit creek water, Lucas seemed captivated by his companion in conversation. Her long hair was the color of amber honey, with lighter tresses around her youthful face. Beyond her obvious attractiveness, she radiated a quiet vitality. Around the shoulders of her baby blue pantsuit, she'd wrapped a pretty paisley shawl. She hadn't touched her pie but held a mug of steaming coffee cupped between her hands.

"I've got two bourbon pumpkins left, and one has your name on it. So what do you say, Abby?"

"Huh? Okay."

"Did you hear even a word I said?" Maisey asked. She chuckled. "Or were your thoughts occupied elsewhere, perhaps with the folks in the booth by the window?"

Abby's cheeks grew warm. "Not at all. I was just thinking how much I love your custard pies, and especially the ones with rum, bourbon, or Kahlúa in them." She turned her full attention on Maisey and the business at hand. "Here are the extra jars of honey you wanted and the invoice. But maybe we should call it even if you're gifting me a pie."

"Now, who said I was gifting it? I said it had your name on it," Maisey teased. She let go a hearty laugh. "Of course it's a gift, sweet girl. And my giving it to you isn't motivated by the thought of getting free honey in return. You know I don't work like that. So just give me a minute to box up your pie, and we'll settle up on the honey. Coffee? It's on the house."

Abby nodded and eased onto a stool. She shot a furtive glance at the angled mirror above the counter, hoping to catch a glimpse of Lucas. Who was that stunning woman in blue he was with? Unfortunately, he and his companion sat out of reach of the mirror's reflection. So Abby sipped the coffee that Maisey had poured and bided her time, listening to Willard grouse on his cell phone about his suppliers' late shipments to his hardware store. "All," he said, "thanks to a truckers' strike back east."

Abby listened with disinterest. She longed to check out Lucas and the woman who shared his booth, but imposed an iron will of self-restraint. Had the best-looking guy in the county, who ministered to all the animal owners through his feed store, found someone to minister to him? Acutely aware that her heart paced at a breakneck speed, Abby realized that either she would have to let the man make a move toward her and respond in kind or she'd have to shut down her feelings for Lucas. For the latter, it might already be too late.

Maisey tied the pie box in a flourish of red string. Handing it to Abby, she said, "I'll write you a check and be right back." Abby contented herself with sipping her coffee and trying without success to turn a deaf ear on Willard's contentious conversation.

"You wouldn't leave without saying hello to a neighbor, now would you, Abby?"

The voice behind her sounded male, husky, and sexy. Abby knew who it was. She looked up into the mirror at Lucas. He stood an arm's length behind her. She was determined not to let him see any sign of the havoc she was holding inside.

"Hello, Lucas," she stammered. The pitter-patter of her heart quickened to a dizzying speed. His beautiful friend might have held his interest before, but now Abby caught him boldly assessing her. She held his attention now. Next to her, Willard eased off his stool, with his cell phone still plastered against his ear. He hurried away. Abby slowly twirled around on her seat, catching a glimpse of Willard pulling open the pie shop door to traffic. As she rose to greet Lucas, a car engine backfired. The loud explosion reverberated through Abby like a gunshot. Her heart scudded against her chest. Legs wobbled. Knees went weak. She reached out instinctively to steady herself on something . . . anything. Lucas caught her arms and held her firmly.

Eyes wide, Abby leaned back, sat down again on the stool. Lucas, not breaking contact with her body, sank down onto Willard's vacated seat. Abby forced a smile, more aware of her jangled nerves and the fight-or-flight battle raging inside her than of Lucas's hands still holding on to her. "What a klutz I can be, losing my balance like that. Thanks for the catch."

"Sheesh, that was loud," said Maisey, who turned and retreated to the kitchen through double swinging doors.

Lucas's companion spoke to him softly. "Be a dear, and get your friend here a glass of water."

Lucas released his grip on Abby, pushed off from the stool, and headed to the far end of the counter and the water station.

"It's okay," the woman told Abby. "A loud noise can't hurt you." She placed a tender hand on Abby's arm. "Breathe slowly. It will calm your thoughts and racing heart."

If Abby felt flustered by her intense reaction to the car's backfiring, she was caught off guard even more by the unexpected attention from the lovely stranger with Lucas. She tried to stand.

"No, just sit," said the woman. Her tone was re-assuring, even nurturing. "Focus on the breath. Slow. And even."

Abby hazarded a glance at her. The woman's light brown eyes met Abby's without judgment. "I feel rather foolish. It's nothing," said Abby.

"Well, you might want to believe that, but it isn't true. I'm a doctor. It's just a guess, but I think you've suffered some recent trauma. What's your name?"

"Abby. Abigail Mackenzie."

"Nice to meet you. I'm Lucas's sister, Olivia Crawford." She sank onto the stool next to Abby. "Right now your heart is pounding like a racehorse's and your anxiety level has just shot through the roof. You don't know whether to hurry out the door or do battle with something you can't see, hear, touch, or taste. But your body reacts to it all the same. Am I right?"

Had it been that obvious? While Abby appreci-ated Olivia's calm manner, she worried that Lucas would return at any second. *Not the time and place to discuss this. Particularly with a stranger, and even more so when the stranger is Lucas Crawford's sister.* Abby decided to excuse herself and leave. But her legs felt wobbly. The last thing she wanted to do was to create more of a spectacle.

Olivia fished in her handbag and produced a business card. Leaning in, she handed it to Abby and whispered, "Lucas told me that you had been attacked on your farmette after your town's celebrity pastry chef was murdered. And recently, when the winery heir and his wife were shot, you found them. Given your exposure to such traumatic events, it's not surprising you reacted the way you did, Abby. May I call you Abby?"

"Yes." Abby wasn't sure of what to make of this woman, who knew way too much about her already.

"Your symptoms are not unique. Bottom line, you don't have to deal with this alone. There are some excellent treatments."

Abby straightened. So maybe Edna Mae had been right about PTSD. Edna was a retired nurse. She'd probably seen this kind of thing before. Abby's thoughts raced on. She took no comfort in having Olivia—a total stranger—diagnose her on the spot, even if she was a doctor. Abby was not her patient, so there could be no expectation of confidentiality. She didn't much like the idea of Lucas and his sister discussing her mental health, not that they would. But then again, why wouldn't they? And there was no stopping gossip once it started spreading in a small town. The truth quickly became distorted and spread faster than foul brood in an infected hive.

Lucas came back and handed Abby a glass of water. She took a sip and wondered what he must have thought about her over-the-top reaction. Feeling a blush warming her cheeks, Abby glanced at Olivia's card.

"So your degree . . . is it in psychiatry or psychology?" asked Abby, trying to sound normal, like nothing had happened.

"Clinical psychology . . . I'm a therapist in private practice, and I have a doctorate. Lucas suggested after my partners and I split that I move down the peninsula, closer to the heart of Silicon Valley. I've heard there are plenty of stressed-out folks working in high tech who could use my services." Olivia chuckled.

"Makes perfect sense."

Olivia smiled. "You've got a nice town here, Abby. And the locals know their way to the only pie shop in town, so finding my practice around the corner shouldn't be too difficult."

"Absolutely," said Abby. She grinned sheepishly. "It's nice to meet you, Dr. Crawford."

"Oh, please, call me Olivia."

Abby's heartbeat was slowing to normal, but she felt a bit too shaky to stand. She puzzled over what seemed like a strange synchronicity that she should run into Lucas in the first place. And then . . . to find out that his sister was a therapist. And that the woman was moving her practice to Las Flores. It was just too weird. For a millisecond, Abby wondered if Maisey had something to do with arranging this serendipitous encounter.

She glanced at Maisey, who laid a check on the pie box and then busied herself with picking up dirty counter dishes and placing them in a rubber dishpan. *Nah.* Maisey could not have spun this manifestation of the surreal into being. Not without knowledge of my plans for the day. And Maisey would never divulge someone's emotional fragility. So how could the forces of nature have just lined up like this on the very day when she had decided to seek help?

Abby took another sip of water. She swallowed and set the glass on the counter.

"I hope you'll call me sometime." Olivia abandoned the stool and made a move for the door.

"Thank you for the card," Abby said, rising. "I'm on my way to the hospital to see a friend. I'd be happy to let the staff know about you. When will your practice open for business?"

"Monday morning." Olivia pulled her pashmina shawl tighter over her shoulders. "Some of my previous patients are following me here to my new location. But for new patients, I'm offering a free consult and reducing the cost of the first full visit to half price. I've got some slots open next week." Her smile seemed genuine.

Abby absorbed the information. "I hope the location will work as well for you. We have a wonderful, tight-knit community here," Abby said, trying to sound enthusiastic but noncommittal. She looked at Lucas. It was hard to fathom what he might be thinking. The intensity of his gaze sucked the breath right out of her. "Wouldn't you say, Lucas?"

He took a lot of time to say, "Yep."

Olivia turned back toward Abby and came to within an arm's reach. "I hope we'll meet again, Abby. From what Lucas says, you're quite an amazing woman."

Feeling her cheeks flush warm, Abby turned her attention to Olivia. "Can't imagine why."

"Just that whole commitment thing you have about the backyard food movement," said Olivia. "Keeping bees and chickens and a garden and orchard. It has to be a ton of work."

Abby tilted her head to the side. "Well, it's my passion, for sure. If you'd like to see the farmette sometime, perhaps Lucas could bring you by."

"Once the dust settles from my move, I just might do that."

"You still have my number, Lucas?" Abby figured he'd have kept it, even though he'd never used it. Texting and chitty-chatting on the phone weren't his way. When he wanted to reach out to her, Lucas Crawford always found a way to do it in person. And Abby liked that about him.

He tapped the breast pocket of his wool shirt. "In my cell."

Olivia started for the door. Lucas put on his cowboy hat and pushed it down over his curly locks. He leaned in close enough for Abby to smell the scent of lemon soap commingled with aftershave. "For two people who live so close to each other, Abby, we could be a lot more neighborly. Let's do something about that . . . soon," he said in his soft baritone.

Befuddled, Abby struggled to think of an appropriate quip, which didn't come. To agree enthusiastically might seem too eager. But neither did she want to appear too cautious. In the end, it didn't matter. Lucas touched two fingers to the brim of his hat, and before Abby could say anything flirty or otherwise, he followed Olivia out of the pie shop.

"I heard that." Maisey grinned like the cat that had just discovered the canary's hiding place. "You should take him up on that, because," said Maisey, "that man has a thing for you."

"Good Lord, if I didn't know you, Maisey, I'd swear that you've been sipping from the bourbon you're pouring into those pies." Abby winked at her and then tucked Maisey's check and Olivia's card in her purse. Picking up the pie box by its tied strings, she said, "Thanks for this, Maisey. Gotta run."

"Sharing pie is a good way to get to know a neighbor, Abby. Especially one so good looking."

"Yeah, yeah. I'm picking up what you're putting down." With a lighthearted laugh, Abby said, "See you soon." With the bourbon pumpkin pie in hand and hope in her heart, Abby strolled out of the pie shop. It was just possible, her luck might be changing.

Bourbon Pumpkin Pie

Ingredients:
Pecan topping:
½ cup all-purpose flour
1 packed cup dark brown sugar
1½ sticks (6 ounces) unsalted butter, at room temperature
½ cup pecan halves

Pie filling and crust:
1¼ cups pumpkin puree (fresh or canned)
½ cup milk
¼ cup bourbon (Wild Turkey or your favorite brand)
3 large eggs, separated

1½ tablespoons cornstarch
½ teaspoon ground cinnamon
¼ teaspoon freshly grated nutmeg
¼ teaspoon ground cloves
¼ teaspoon salt
1 pie crust (store-bought or premade), baked

Directions:

Preheat the oven to 350°.

Prepare the pecan topping. Pour the flour in a medium bowl and add ¼ cup of the brown sugar and 4 tablespoons of the butter (½ stick). Combine with your fingers until the mixture is crumbly. Add the pecans and mix well. Set aside the topping.

Prepare the pie filling. Place the remaining stick of butter and the remaining ¾ cup of brown sugar in a large mixing bowl, and using an electric mixer, beat them together at medium speed until fluffy, about 1 minute.

To the butter–brown sugar mixture, add the pumpkin, milk, bourbon, egg yolks, cornstarch, cinnamon, nutmeg, cloves, and salt. Beat until well combined and set aside.

In a medium mixing bowl beat the egg whites until stiff with an electric mixer. Gently fold the beaten egg whites into the reserved pumpkin mixture until all traces of white disappear.

Pour the pumpkin–egg white mixture into the prebaked pie crust and sprinkle the reserved pecan topping over the pie.

Bake the pie on the middle rack of the

oven for 1 hour, or until golden brown. Remove the pie from the oven and check the doneness by inserting a knife one inch from the crust edge. If the knife comes out clean, the pie is done.

Allow the pie to cool before serving.

Serves 4

Chapter 10

Sowing a seed is the hope—not the
guarantee—of fruit to come.

—*Henny Penny Farmette Almanac*

On Saturday Abby circled the Root Cellar parking lot for ten minutes, hoping someone
would back out a vehicle so she could pull in. Frustrated that she'd be late for Kat's birthday dinner,
she reluctantly parked behind the Pantry Hut, a
restaurant supply shop. Ordinarily, she would
never choose to park in a lot where she'd have to
walk up a dark alley.

Bundled against the cold in a calf-length flared
coat over wool slacks, a silk shirt, and scarf and carrying her purse and Kat's gift bag, Abby set off
down the alley sandwiched between the Pantry
Hut and the Root Cellar. When she had walked
halfway into the alley, a car pulled in perpendicu-
lar to the entrance and stopped, its engine idling.
The automobile blocked Abby's exit. She stepped
into a shadow. Hid. Waited. Watched. It was an old
habit: Take evasive action for protection when

faced with an ambiguous situation. Assess for danger.

Was she overreacting? Where was the threat? Abby tried to shake the sense of vulnerability eroding her confidence. *I'm okay.* She remained hidden, observing. *Why aren't you moving, dude? What are you waiting for? The next taxi to Timbuktu?* From the store, a woman wearing a hoodie that concealed all but a forelock of platinum hair approached the passenger side of the car.

The vehicle door opened from inside. Dome light came on. Abby could not see the woman's face. But she could tell that the driver was a man wearing a multicolored, slouchy beanie over a ponytail. With the gift bag and purse in a vice-like grip, Abby watched the car roll forward a few inches and brake. The red lens cover was missing on one of the taillights. Alarm bells went off. Without success, she tried to throttle the energy coursing through her. She pressed her body against the wall and tried to still her shaking hands. Abby stared at the taillight. The memory of the murder resurfaced. That night, a car had rolled by her hiding place, and the killer or someone else in the car had waved a flashlight, searching for her. Was it the same sedan? Same driver?

Rooted to the wall, in the shadows, she watched the car merge into traffic. Her stomach churned. A bilious taste seeped into the back of her throat. She doubled over with dry heaves.

"Are you okay?" A man wearing mechanic's overalls and a single hoop earring, which glinted in the moonlight, pulled his arm free of his companion—a pregnant woman bundled up against the chill. He hastened toward Abby as the woman waddled behind. "Ma'am, you all right?" he asked.

Abby repeatedly swallowed until the wave of nausea subsided. "Yeah. Dry heaves."

"Pregnant, right? With our last one, wife puked nonstop for three months. You want us to walk somewhere with you?"

Abby steadied herself. *There isn't always going to be a Good Samaritan in the alley to help you out. You've got to face this fear.* Abby cleared her throat. "No, no thanks." She slowly emerged from the shadows and walked toward the man. Maybe she was trying too hard to make a linkage between the cars. *Taillight covers are broken all the time. A coincidence? Maybe.* But then again, deep down, she didn't believe in coincidences.

"Where you headed?" the man asked. His tone reflected genuine concern.

"Root Cellar," said Abby. She lifted the gift bag. "Birthday celebration."

"Oh, cool," said the man. "In that case, the Root Cellar is located on the left after you exit the alley."

"Uh-huh." Abby forced a smile that she didn't feel and set off again. She'd grown weary of being over-vigilant every waking hour, distrustful of everything and everyone around her. Her whole life, she'd been strong in the face of adversity, but this challenge of dealing with nightmares and intrusive imagining was unrelenting and insidious in the way it robbed her energy and made her question her sanity.

By the time she'd reached the heavy wooden door of the Root Cellar, she'd decided to have only one celebratory glass of wine and to make it an early evening. Afterward, she'd lock up her farmhouse, soak in a bath, and drink some warm honeyed milk to beckon sleep. And when the weekend was over, she would call Olivia and secure the earliest appointment available. It would be a calculated move meant to seal Olivia's lips in a doctor-patient relationship. Abby would get help with her panic attacks and ongoing anxiety while at the same time ensuring no one else in town, especially Lucas, would ever know. Without the county's critical incident stress management team to help her, like when she'd worked on the force, Abby reckoned this would be her best option.

Entering the warmth of the tavern-style bar and eatery, with its Tuscan paintings, mica-lighted booths, and walls glazed in old-world shades of umber, red, and gold, Abby hid her anxiety behind a party face. She threaded her way through the crowd to the tufted leather booth on the second level where Kat stood waving. Dressed in a fitted black dress with sheer sleeves and a bateau neckline, Kat had chosen a simple pair of black pearl drop earrings, which looked sublime against her fair skin, blue eyes, and nearly white blond hair, moussed in 1920s-style finger waves.

"Well, don't you look fabulous," Abby said, handing Kat the gift bag. "Hope you like it."

"Oh, you shouldn't have," Kat said after bussing Abby's cheeks. "But I'm glad you did."

"I had fun finding it," Abby said. And it was the truth. She loved poking around in antique shops, consignment outlets, and thrift stores. Such outings were even more fun when Kat was with her.

After removing her scarf and coat and relegating them to the booth, Abby pushed her reddish-gold mane over the shoulders of her sea-green silk shirt. She slid into the booth, then scooted to the middle so she wouldn't have to shout to be heard over the clatter and chatter. From the mid-booth vantage point, she also had a clear view into the heart of the tavern. It was another old cop trick picked up from her days on the force—always sit with your back to the wall and in a spot where you can see what's coming.

"So . . . you started without me." Abby grinned and pointed to the empty wineglass on the table.

"Exactly why I like this place," said Kat with the smile of a Cheshire cat. "When I told the headwaiter that it was my birthday, he brought me a complimentary glass of wine and said something in Spanish. *Felice,* I think." Kat eagerly reached into the bag, took out the candy box, and loosened the ribbon from around the antique tongs.

"*Feliz cumpleaños,*" Abby said. "Means happy birthday."

"Yeah, that was it." Kat admired the scrollwork on Abby's gift of tongs.

"Where is he?"

"Well, unfortunately, when I got here, he had just finished his shift and was on his way out. And here I was, hoping we'd have the whole evening to flirt. Bad timing."

"I guess. There'll be other times," Abby said with optimism, although not entirely sure that Kat and the headwaiter would last long enough for there to be another time. Keeping track of Kat's boyfriends wasn't easy. There were a lot of them, and they were a diverse lot, to boot. If Kat were a seed saver, she'd have the most interesting collection around.

"Wait until you see him," Kat said. "The girls in Dispatch weren't wrong about him." She gestured with her hands, as if she'd just touched a hot burner. "What a hunk."

"You are so off the hook, Kat. Have you even had a date yet?"

"No. But, boy, I can tell we click. He's already given me his phone number." Kat batted her eyelids like a coquette. "I don't think it's going to take him long to make a move. And if he doesn't, I will."

Watching Kat set aside the silver tongs to study the box, Abby had to marvel at Kat's self-confidence when it involved men.

"This is so like you, Abby," Kat said, looking pleased. "Working seven days a week and you can still find time to search out something special. It's perfect. You need to apply the same diligence to finding a good man."

Abby appreciated Kat's enthusiasm but didn't want to go there. "Look inside the box."

Kat eased off the lid and took out a foil-covered truffle. "What do we have here?" She peeled back the foil from the confection to expose a triple-layer cube of white, milk, and dark chocolate. "Zowie, Abby. Do you know me or what?"

"So, these were made by Paola. Eight in all. Each is different," Abby explained. "There's an apricot-coconut, one with raspberry filling, and a sea-salt caramel, but my favorite is the limoncello– white chocolate truffle."

"Wow."

"You've got to pay attention to what happens on your tongue when you eat one of these treats. Paola once told me that each truffle must tell its unique story in a single sensational bite."

"So I shouldn't park myself in front of the tube, watch *Antiques Roadshow,* and mindlessly gorge on them?"

"I didn't mean that. Just, you'll enjoy them more if you savor each morsel."

"Got it." Kat rewrapped the triple-layer chocolate and returned it to the box. She peeled back the foil on a chocolate truffle dusted in gold luster and licked her fingers. "Wow . . . chilies with the chocolate."

"I think Paola calls that one Aztec Royale."

"Well, I suppose I'll have to expand my horizons from those plain milk chocolate bars in the family-size bags."

"Atta girl. Aim for a more sophisticated palate." Abby chuckled.

"I'm all for that, but just so you know, I got plenty of that 'try this' and 'try that' from my last boyfriend."

"The chef with the tats of vegetables over his forearms? You ended it, right?"

"Well, not exactly. I thought I'd dumped him. But then he called to see if I wanted to go away for a weekend. You know, to one of those fancy bed-and-breakfasts near a winery. Tastings. Mud baths. Massages. The whole shebang. How could I say no to that?"

"If anyone deserves the whole shebang, it's you, Kat." Abby glanced at her watch. Twenty minutes seemed like a long time to have been seated and not served. Not even a menu. She checked out the bar area—not a single stool open and already the crowd stood shoulder to shoulder, waiting for tables. Abby resigned herself to what might be a long evening, instead of that early night she'd planned.

"So, Kat," said Abby, figuring that this was as good a time as any to broach the subject of the case. "When we last spoke, you said Lieutenant Sinclair was on his way to interview Paola about the murder. Learn anything?" Abby pushed back against her seat and crossed her legs.

"Not really. Docs say it's a little too soon to be grilling Paola."

"What about the bullet? It had to pass through both sides of Jake's skull, which would have slowed it down before it passed out and hit her. I'm assuming that she slipped down and forward in a defensive position or that it might not have hit her at all."

"That's what the bullet trajectory suggests."

"Maybe she saw that the killer had a weapon and ducked. Did you find the casing? Know the caliber or anything else about the bullet?" Abby realized that the rapid-fire sequence of her questions made her sound terribly eager for information. Kat was her best friend, but Abby knew it would be prudent not to let Kat know she was secretly working the case.

"None of us are ballistics experts, even if we do have the casing and the lead from the bullet." Kat scanned the room, then threw a hand up to flag down a waiter. "We know the ammo was nine millimeter."

Abby's thoughts raced. "Well, street thugs like to spray and pray with their semiautos, and nine is cheap ammo. The military uses it, too. And Brianna Cooper kept a Sig Sauer model P229 in the middle drawer of her desk at the winery. With it were boxes of nine-millimeter ammo."

Surprise claimed Kat's face. Her eyes narrowed. "And I suppose her desk drawer just happened to be standing wide open, with the gun and ammo in plain sight?"

Abby arched a brow. "Kind of. So, didn't Brianna tell you all about the gun? Because I know if you have the casing and lead from the bullet, it's possible to match them to a suspect gun. I mean, if you had a suspect gun."

Kat looked suspiciously at Abby. "Which we don't. But you can bet we'll be having a chitty-chat with Ms. Cooper. I'd love to have a look at that gun of hers." Kat put the truffle box back into the gift bag and dropped in the tongs. "I'll just put this under my coat so I don't forget it when we leave."

Abby reckoned it was time to shift the conversation. "Did you know Lucas Crawford has a sister?"

"News to me," said Kat. "Where's she been hiding?"

"Living and working up the peninsula, I guess. I recently saw Lucas in the pie shop, and she was with him. Olivia is her name. Seems nice."

A waitress approached and diverted Abby's attention.

"About time!" Kat whispered.

The waitress, dressed in a black shirt, tie, trousers, and a crisp white ankle-length apron, set a basket of warm bread and pats of butter on the table and handed them menus. "We're swamped tonight," she said. "What can I get you ladies to drink?"

"Two white zins," Kat said. "And I have a couple of questions about the specials—eggplant parmigiana and the osso buco with polenta."

As Kat quizzed the waitress about those and other menu options, Abby allowed her gaze to sweep the room. When the waitress had left, she told Kat, "Don't look now, but the mayor and his wife are dining over in the corner, and Chief Bob Allen is there, too, sitting with his back to the wall."

Kat strained to see him. "Well, that's a surprise. The mayor has the chief on speed dial. They were at each other's throats yesterday. The mayor says the chamber of commerce members are on his back and have convened an emergency meeting to see how they can attract more people to our downtown during the holidays. Local businesses should be seeing an uptick in shoppers, but it's been just the opposite. Solving the case would help, of course, but, like the chief says, we don't need city hall on our backs, telling us to get on with it." Kat pursed her lips and then continued. "Really . . . like we're somehow not taking the murder seriously. And like the mayor could rustle up some more resources if we just told him that's what we needed, when we all know he can't deal with the budget shortfall this year."

Abby leaned in and said, "Sorry, Kat. It sounds like you are under a ton of stress." She decided against talking about her own issues.

"Yeah, well, everyone needs to take a deep breath

and a step back." Kat plucked a slice of bread from the basket on the table and buttered it. "Lieutenant Sinclair is a micromanaging controller, and Chief Bob Allen is constantly checking our work. We're in a pressure cooker, for sure, but all for the greater good, I guess." She pushed the bread basket toward Abby.

Abby waved the basket away. "Well, I'm an outsider now, but it seems that focusing on Emilio is a waste of time and resources. He's—"

"Not a suspect anymore. Passed a poly yesterday. We've moved on."

Abby hid her delight by shaking out her napkin and laying it across her lap. No point in harping about Emilio now. Maybe she'd have some bread, after all.

"It's good for Emilio but not swell for us," said Kat. "Somebody killed Jake. And so far we've got zip."

Abby understood the difficult challenges facing the cops during the initial phase of an investigation. "With all the people in Jake's orbit, there must be quite a pool of possible suspects, especially women with whom he's had affairs, resentful boyfriends, and ticked-off spouses."

Kat swallowed a mouthful of warm bread and seemed ready to say something when the waitress reappeared and set two glasses of wine on the table.

"Ready to order?" she asked.

Kat ordered first. "I'll have the cheese fondue and more of this bread." She handed the menu back to the waitress.

"I'll have the spinach salad with goat cheese,"

said Abby, "and the salmon with the honey-miso glaze." She glanced at Kat. "Let's you and me split the salad," she told her.

"You got it." The waitress tucked the menus under her arm and scurried away.

"So . . . I've been checking Jake's cell phone log for calls and texts," Kat said before taking a sip of the chilled rose-colored wine. "During his last twenty-four hours, he took several calls from Brianna Cooper and also the sous-chef. Lina Sutton sent a text, too, saying pretty much what she said on the steps of the church."

"Accusing Jake of killing her sister?"

"Yep."

Abby lifted her glass and touched it to Kat's. Taking a sip, she savored the chilled wine and wondered why Brianna would call Jake repeatedly in the hours before he was to renew his wedding vows with Paola. After returning the glass to the table, she touched the cloth napkin to her mouth. "Why do you think Jake's female employees were calling him right before he was murdered?" asked Abby. She made a mental note to jot down the linkage on her incident poster on the living room table. She would also be adding Lina Sutton's name to the board.

"Don't know yet."

"Well, what bothers me is the strange posturing of the sous-chef. When I asked her if she knew where Emilio was, she jerked a thumb toward the back parking lot. So why did she tell Lieutenant Sinclair that she didn't remember pointing me anywhere and that she thought I might have returned to the party?"

"Dunno. But she has a rock-solid alibi—waiters and the dishwasher were in that kitchen when the murder happened."

"What's Lina Sutton's story?" Abby asked.

"Student nurse. She works in the hospital's emergency room. On the night her sister was brought in, she was working a shift."

"Oh, that had to be horrible for her," Abby said. "Such a tragedy. No wonder she's so angry with Jake. Could be a motive for murder." She sipped the chilled wine from her glass, set it down, and dabbed her mouth with her napkin.

"Yeah," Kat said, looking pensive. "But she's got Father Joseph as an alibi. She went back to talk with him after leaving the church in a huff." Kat tucked a tendril of hair behind her right ear and continued. "Jake was right. Lina's sister had gotten drunk after their breakup and should have called a cab. Luckily, no one else was in the path of her car when it veered from the road and hit the tree."

Abby posed another question. "So the sister died in the ER?"

Kat nodded. "We interviewed the physician in charge that night. He told us that they did everything they could to save her." Kat lapsed into silence.

Abby refolded her napkin and thought about how difficult it must have been for Lina to have witnessed any part of a frenetic scene in which the hospital staff worked to save a life—a scene Abby had seen on more than one occasion. "What did the winery's CCTV show?" she asked.

"Not much. The fog that night was thick. We hoped to find the killer on camera, but we didn't."

"What about a getaway car?"

"If that's what it is. It's a fuzzy image at best." Kat took a sip of wine, pushed her glass aside, and leaned in. Looking intently at Abby, she asked, "Do you know something about that car? Is there something else you want to share . . . 'cause if you do, I'm all ears."

"Okay, this is going to sound crazy. I gave my statement that night, but . . . as it turns out, it might not be entirely complete."

"And why would that be? Why would you leave out anything?"

"Faulty memory?"

"What? Don't be silly. Right after the murder, as I recall, your statement was the first taken down. You can't get impressions fresher than that."

"I know, but I felt flustered. Everything had happened fast. I think it's possible I might have seen more than I thought I did that night."

Kat's expression darkened. She leaned back and reached for her glass. "I'm listening."

"Well, let's start with that older-model, light-colored sedan that rolled past me that night."

"We know that from your statement."

"Yes, but the car was missing the red lens cover over one of its taillights. Passenger side. That detail was not in my statement, was it?"

Kat straightened. "No. Is that something you saw? Or you think you saw?"

"I'm pretty sure I saw it."

"Pretty sure? You either saw it or you didn't, Abby." Kat clearly was pushing her to take a position on that detail. "So which is it?"

Kat had slipped into her cop persona. Abby felt flustered. Warmth surged into her cheeks. She swept aside her doubt. "I saw it."

Kat stared at the folds in the napkin that she'd not yet put on her lap and seemed to be reflecting on the significance of Abby's new information. "Well, that particular detail is backed up by the CCTV. Because of the fog, we couldn't see much, but we could sure make out the missing taillight lens. So anything else?"

Abby shrugged. Though validated by Kat's revelation, she wasn't ready to go out on a limb with thoughts, hunches, and ideas she couldn't validate or prove, not that she didn't have plenty of them. False info and bad leads equaled a lot of wasted time for investigators working a murder case against the clock, which was always ticking. And . . . this one was already a hot mess.

"If you remember any new details, let me know ASAP." Kat handed her a coconut-covered white-chocolate truffle. "For your dessert."

"Sure." Abby's thoughts wrapped around the runner she believed she saw in the dark parking lot at the time of Jake's murder. That idea yielded another. Might the woman wearing the hoodie and getting into that car outside the Pantry Hut have been the sous-chef? Whether or not it had been Dori Langston, Abby couldn't be certain. But searching for stemware and jelly jars might be the perfect ruse to ask someone if they perhaps remembered Dori shopping there.

Coconut-Covered Limoncello White Chocolate Truffles

Ingredients:
½ cup heavy whipping cream
20 ounces white chocolate (chopped into small pieces)
2 tablespoons Limoncello Italian liqueur
½ tablespoon finely grated lemon zest
Parchment paper, for lining a cookie sheet
½ cup shredded dried coconut

Directions:
Slowly heat the whipping cream in a small pan over low heat until it is just boiling. Remove from the heat and set aside.

Melt half of the white chocolate pieces in the top of a double boiler. Pour the reserved cream over the melted chocolate and stir until the mixture becomes uniform. Add the Limoncello and the lemon zest and stir to combine well. Cool the truffle mixture on the counter for 1 hour, and then refrigerate it overnight.

Line a cookie sheet with parchment paper. With gloved hands and a melon scoop, form the chilled truffle mixture into 1-inch balls. Place each truffle ball on the lined cookie sheet and stick a toothpick into each.

Place the remaining white chocolate pieces in a double boiler and gently heat over low heat. Stir the chocolate continuously to distribute the heat evenly and melt the pieces. When the chocolate has melted, dip each truffle ball into it to coat. Set each dipped truffle back on the parchment paper–lined cookie sheet.

Sprinkle the coconut over the dipped truffles while the outer coating of chocolate is still warm. Let the truffles cool before enjoying.

Makes 48 truffles

Chapter 11

On a quiet, clear morning, the gobble
of a wild turkey can be heard a mile
away.

—*Henny Penny Farmette Almanac*

On the Monday before Thanksgiving, Abby strolled into the Pantry Hut, half expecting elbow-deep shoppers in the store. Instead, she found a party of two—herself and the clerk.

"Whatcha looking for?" called out the twenty-something woman from where she stood on a ladder positioned in front of shelves of paper products. "It's almost Thanksgiving. Need a turkey roaster? Basting brush? Or kitchenware?"

"Well, Charlotte," said Abby, taking note of the name tag on the young woman's bib apron, "I'm looking for stemware and screw-top glass jars." Abby watched as the clerk lined up boxes of napkins and then arranged them on the top-tier shelf.

Charlotte wore a headband with a fabric flower,

dark yoga pants with a cell phone pocket on the hip, and a yellow shirt, which was partially covered by a green apron with ties so long, they wrapped around the girl's waist twice. "We got plenty of both," Charlotte boasted. "I'll show you." After straightening the last box of paper napkins she'd pushed into the row, she dropped the empty cardboard box on the floor and climbed down.

Abby's gaze swept a dozen or more aisles lined with shelves filled with everything from dishware to deep fryers.

"Our jars are over there." Charlotte pointed toward the wall on the other side of the room. "Stemware is this way."

"It's my first time here," Abby said, hoping to engage the young woman as she followed her down a long aisle of wineglasses and goblets. She picked up a two-and-one-half-inch stemmed glass with a midsize bowl and studied it. "I've seen this style before."

"Our best seller. It's practically unbreakable. Lots of wineries use it for tastings."

"Yeah? Like the Country Schoolhouse Winery?" Abby set the glass back on the shelf.

"Yes." The young woman plucked an expensive piece of crystal stemware and handed it to Abby. "But this is the one they purchased for engraving for that recent party."

"You mean the one where . . ." Abby noticed a frown claiming the clerk's expression.

"That guy was killed? Uh-huh."

"Awful business." Abby handed back the stemware and asked, "So, how did you hear about Jake Winston's murder?"

"My housemate."

Abby asked, "How'd she know about it?"

"She worked there that night."

"Yeah? Doing what?"

"Supervising the kitchen."

Abby ventured a wild guess. "Are we talking about Dori Langston?" She watched the young woman's expression, wondering if the two were close.

"Yeah. She's a great cook."

Abby pushed on. "So . . . does she shop here?" It was a stroke of luck that she was able to get to that question so quickly.

The clerk led her down another aisle. "Yeah. Matter of fact, just last night she came in around six. Do you know her?"

"Know of her. I hear Chef Emilio Varela's kitchen puts out some fantastic pairings of wine and food. So Dori must be what? About ten years older than you?"

"Uh-huh."

"So how does she like working for a chef from Argentina?"

"She hopes he'll leave so she can have his job. So I guess that means she doesn't like him that much. Or cops."

"Oh, really? What she got against law enforcement?"

"Questions. They interrogated her half the night, as if she had something to do with it."

"Did she?" It was a provocative question, Abby knew, but it might lead somewhere.

Charlotte drilled her with a strange look.

Abby backpedaled. "I just meant maybe she saw something or someone, perhaps even the killer."

"No, she didn't." The young woman selected a box and removed a similar glass. Holding it up, she asked, "How about this one?"

"Don't care for the bowl. It's too big for such a fragile stem."

Charlotte returned the glass to the box and looked around for another option.

Abby asked, "So how'd Dori take Jake Winston's death? After all, he was the big boss, wasn't he?"

"Not as upset as I would be if my boss got killed. But she told me the next day that she is going to get top chef job now."

"Oh, really?" If Jake, Abby reasoned, had refused to terminate Emilio, it would give Dori a motive for murder. But Jake's death didn't automatically mean Emilio would leave, so where had Dori gotten the idea that things would be otherwise? Abby picked up another glass, grimaced, and put it back. "How would that be possible?"

"She was always saying affirmations that the chef would move on. Now it looks like he'll be cooking inside the slammer."

"Say what?"

"Well, you hear gossip. The cops are pretty sure that the chef is Jake Winston's killer."

Well, that's wrong, but whatever. "Did a cop tell you that?"

"Nope. Heard it from a customer."

"I'm curious, Charlotte. Where'd Dori get her culinary training?"

"You'd have to ask her." The store clerk seemed tired of the conversation and Abby's inability to select stemware.

"I sort of like these," said Abby. "Suppose I should get them before they're all gone."

"You don't have to worry about that. I mean, look around. We aren't exactly swamped with customers."

"Well, that could change now that the holidays are here."

"Boss says we're slow because of the murder. We're depending on locals instead of all the tourists for our holiday business this year. A family takes care of its own. And we're all family in this town, right? I mean, you get to know everyone, don't you?"

The young woman clearly was trying to seal the sale. Abby seized upon the opening. "Well, true . . . mostly. But we can't know everything, can we? I mean, take your roommate Dori, for example. She's not from around here, is she?"

"True." The clerk picked up the box of glasses Abby had chosen and turned to walk toward the front register. "But you got to give it to Dori. She's always figuring out a way to change things in her life."

"Like what?" Abby saw the chance to probe and took it.

"Well, she was a wild child, parents pushed her out, but she learned to cook and used that to land jobs. Worked the east part of the valley until she got that winery gig."

Abby knew about some lovely areas, but the eastern side of the valley had some rough neighborhoods where rival gangs made life miserable.

"Did she join a gang?"

Charlotte's expression darkened. She frowned. "God, I hope not."

"Just curious," Abby said, then quickly shifted to another question. "So, how did she end up moving in with you down here?"

"Five of us share an old Victorian over on Wisteria Lane. Only five houses on the street, and ours is the largest. We have room for six. She called the number in our newspaper ad. Then, when we discovered she cooks at the winery, well, that was a bonus."

"I'll bet. When did she move in with you?" asked Abby, handing her credit card to the young woman.

"August first," said the clerk. Ringing up the purchase, she added, "But I think she's moving out, because she told me she had met a rich guy and they were getting a place together. Wouldn't mind a rich boyfriend myself."

"Well, my dear, money can buy a lot of things," said Abby, "but happiness isn't one of them. That comes from inside." She leaned over to check the price she'd been charged and inhaled a sharp breath. As she returned her credit card to her wallet, she was already having buyer's remorse. It wasn't like she was preparing a big sit-down dinner for her friends on Thanksgiving—it was going to be a low-key affair with Kat. She chalked the expense of those crystal glasses to the cost of digging for information. But she was darned sure she'd be returning them in a day or two.

Abby straightened her spine and looked squarely at Charlotte. "I take it you never met that boyfriend of Dori's?" Just as quickly as she'd asked the question, Abby wished she had not. *Better slow the roll. You sound fixated on Dori.* "You know," Abby said, forcing a little laugh, "because he might have a rich younger brother."

The clerk giggled. "You think I didn't ask?"

"Did she ever mention his name? I know many of the local families."

"Like I told the cop lady who came in here, Dori didn't say much. Her boyfriend was an only child. Wealthy, I think. But recently the relationship had cooled." Charlotte's look could have frozen the tail feathers off a turkey. "Are you a cop, too?"

"Heavens, no." Abby asked, "Do I look like a cop?"

"I dunno. I didn't think the woman with the Roaring Twenties hair was a cop, either, but she flashed a badge and asked a lot of the same questions."

Abby suppressed a smile. So Kat had already questioned the clerk.

With an inquisitive expression, Charlotte asked, "Did Dori have something to do with that murder?"

"I wouldn't know," Abby said. "But murder makes you wonder what the heck is going on up there, doesn't it?"

"It's all anyone in this town ever talks about when they come in here," Charlotte said.

"People are on edge. They want answers. When the answers don't come, they seek comfort in sharing information, I guess."

"Dori wants answers, too. Always asking me what I hear from the locals. You'd think she'd just ask the people she works with up at the winery. Everybody talks, but no one seems to know anything."

Abby surmised that Jake had seduced Dori, like he had so many others. Remembering what Edna Mae had said about Jake coming in with his interior decorator in the short skirt who knew nothing about quilts, Abby figured that Dori would set up the love nest and Jake would foot the bill. But if Jake's intentions toward her had cooled, maybe the money flow had slowed to a trickle or ended. Wouldn't that give Dori a motive for murder? Maybe.

"Oh, jeez, I forgot a case of your four-ounce jars," said Abby, picking up her purchase. "Next time then. I've got what I came for."

Midweek Abby walked into Dr. Olivia Crawford's waiting room at half past two for her appointment. Hanging her denim sweater jacket on the coatrack, Abby felt her phone vibrate in her jeans pocket. After sliding into an armchair by a small table with a lamp and a green-leaf orchid on it, Abby took out her phone and peeked at Kat's text. It contained an apology. She couldn't make their Thanksgiving dinner at the farmette because she had to work the murder case with the guys.

Abby texted back. **No problem. Solve the case. We'll meet up at the Black Witch and order something with Wild Turkey in it.**

"So glad to see you, Abby."

Abby looked up to see Olivia closing the door behind the patient who'd just left.

"Come this way, please."

Abby turned her cell on vibrate and dropped it into her daypack. She followed Olivia into the inner chamber. The clean scent of lemon and cedar permeated the room. A massive French fruitwood bookcase with glass windows revealing rows of neatly arranged books dominated one wall of the room. A narrow rectory table had been positioned in front of the bookcase. It held a crystal vase of silk peonies and roses. Alongside lay a coffee-table book about Edwardian tea service pieces and another about ancient Scottish clans.

Appreciating the aesthetic of the room, Abby quickly grasped that she and Olivia shared similar tastes. This gorgeous room was the kind she could only dream of creating in her farmhouse. After dropping her daypack onto the ivory and gray accent rug that covered the wall-to-wall Berber carpet, Abby took a seat on the sofa.

"You know, Abby, I've been thinking about you," said Olivia as she pulled open the rectory table drawer and took out a clipboard with forms attached. "Tell me how you've been doing since the pie shop episode." The psychologist sank into a high-back armchair. Her tone imparted genuine concern.

Abby grunted softly. "To say I'm still under siege would be putting it mildly. But when you said some treatments could help, it gave me hope."

"I have some ideas about ways you might manage your symptoms, Abby, but we're getting ahead of ourselves. First, there are some forms I'd like you to read and sign, authorizing me to treat you.

Then I'd like very much to hear what you desire to get out of the therapy sessions and for us to explore together not only your symptoms but also what led up to them. Why don't you start on the forms? I'll just get something I would like to read to you before we go too much further. Would that be okay?"

Abby relaxed into the curves of the couch and read through the consent form and a questionnaire about her general health. With the pencil attached to the clipboard, she wrote her signature in the blanks provided, and then she handed the clipboard back. Olivia turned to a section in a book she'd retrieved from her bookcase and read aloud two definitions—one for panic attacks and the other for post-traumatic stress disorder. Abby felt her brow furrow. *Sounds like what I've got.*

Listening to the gentle modulations of Olivia's voice explaining the similarities and differences between the two and how a shocking or traumatic event served as the trigger in both, Abby felt reassured that she'd made the right decision in consulting with Lucas's sister. In Olivia, she sensed integrity, honesty, and compassion. Here was someone who didn't talk down to her and who clearly understood that for Abby, labeling the problem, outlining solutions, and building trust between them was paramount.

Abby decided to address her most pressing concern. "I repeatedly have disturbing memories of the night of the murder. I'm constantly reminding myself to let the police investigators do their jobs. But then my police training kicks in. I obsess about connecting the dots between the homicide and what I don't and do remember. The physical symptoms are awful."

"Like what, Abby?"

"I feel startled and jumpy. My heart races. I'm apprehensive and worry a lot."

Olivia leaned slightly toward her in an actively listening pose and nodded her head from time to time to indicate she understood. "You know, Abby, during a traumatic event, fear generates split-second changes in the body and brain. These are normal, natural responses for protecting or removing the body from danger."

"Are they panic attacks, or do I have PTSD?"

"So, let's take some time to talk about that." Olivia outlined the four criteria necessary for a diagnosis of PTSD in an adult. She emphasized that a patient had to have experienced all the symptoms for at least one month.

Abby had been symptomatic for only three weeks and now found cause to feel optimistic. "The fact that it hasn't been a month yet and that we're treating this early . . . Are the chances good I could move past this?"

Olivia's features relaxed. "I think so."

"There's something else," said Abby. "There are details from the night of the murder that have me perplexed. I second-guess myself as to whether or not I really saw what I think I saw. Can you help me with that, too?"

Olivia tilted her head slightly. "Possibly." She placed the book and the clipboard on the rectory table and returned to her seat in the wingback chair. "We have tools. Medication and modalities, such as talk therapy, EMDR, hypnosis. Have you ever been hypnotized, Abby?"

"No," Abby replied. "I'm not sure it would work with me. You have to give over your power. I couldn't. Or wouldn't."

"I see. And what about EMDR?"

"I don't know what that is."

"Eye movement desensitization and reprocessing," explained Olivia. "It's a nontraditional but controversial reconstructive modality for treating trauma. I've found it to be an effective therapy for cases like yours." She pushed a tangle of amber-honey hair away from her face and took her time explaining further.

"In theory, Abby, the modality uses your rapid eye movements to tamp down the emotionally charged power of your memories of the traumatic event. The effect is to desensitize you to the memory. You will always remember the traumatic event but with therapy come to view it as though it was an article in an old newspaper clipping."

"Meaning no physical responses like what I now have?"

"Exactly."

"Will it work fast?"

"Depends on you. The therapy will allow you to create a new mental relationship between the memories you associate with the trauma and a healthier way of looking at it. But, Abby, we'll proceed at whatever speed you feel most comfortable with."

Feeling nervous energy bound up in her hands and legs, Abby uncrossed her legs and folded her hands in her lap.

"We can start the EMDR today if you like. The way it will work is this. You'll hold the memory of the trauma in your mind, taking note of the details of what you saw and heard, as well as your emotions and bodily sensations. You don't have to tell me or anyone else what happened. As I instruct you, your eyes will follow my moving fingers, which I will hold in front of your face. Like when you read a book, your own rhythmic, rapid eye movement will enable your mind to remember the event and your thoughts to process whatever wasn't processed during the trauma. A moment or two later, I'll guide you to think about something pleasant. And then I'll ask you to rate your level of distress. Our aim will be to reduce those stress levels."

Not relishing the thought of having to relive the dark emotional potency of that night all over again, Abby felt her heart beginning to tick faster. *I'm here to deal with this and to end this misery. It has to be done. If not now, when?*

Olivia waited for a sign from Abby that she had considered all the options and was ready to begin. "Take your time."

Abby moistened her lips against her dry mouth. Medication, hypnosis, talk therapy, or the controversial EMDR? She didn't want to be doped up on pills. Hypnosis was definitely a no. Talk therapy . . . she'd had plenty of that in the past, when she had served on the force and following protocol meant seeing the police shrink for particularly gruesome scenes. The new modality EMDR sounded like New Age quackery—eyes moving back and forth like when reading a book. Seriously? But if it worked, did it matter?

She stared at Olivia's rose cashmere sweater and matching pants with a ribbed cuff at the ankle—a feminine look that would have been enthusiastically embraced by Kat and Paola. Unsure of how she'd expected a professional doctor of psychology to dress, Abby felt that Olivia's sweater suit on such a chilly day and her ballerina flats, well worn but in good repair, suggested she was a pragmatist. She wore no jewelry or symbols of some driving ideology or religious belief. *All good. So, make up your mind, already. You can always leave if it gets too weird.*

In what sounded more like a suffocated whisper than a full-throttled declaration, Abby heard herself say, "Let's try the EMDR." If she had to think about wandering around in the dark and discovering the bodies again, at least she'd have Olivia with her. And they'd be right here in a safe, secure environment. It was time to get beyond the craziness that was claiming her life.

"Would you like a glass of water before we start?" Olivia asked. "Patients are often nervous during the first session. A little water helps with the dry mouth."

Remembering the bottled water she always carried in her daypack, Abby said, "No thanks. Let's just get this over with."

"Good. I suggest you drink plenty of water and sleep as long as you need to after we've finished our session today." Olivia smiled reassuringly. "The body can get so tense and hold so much stress that when it releases it, a person can feel like a wrung-out washcloth. And let's face it. You've held tremendous stress in your body for weeks. Letting it go will feel liberating. Now, tell me, do you have anyone who could drive you home or stay with you tonight?"

"No. I'll be fine."

"Shall I ask a neighbor or perhaps Lucas to look in on you?"

"No, no. Please don't," Abby said, a little too emphatically. She added, "I don't want him to know about this. You can't tell him." She drilled Olivia with a stare.

"Of course not. It would violate doctor-patient confidentiality. You needn't worry about that, Abby." Olivia leaned far forward, as if to emphasize her next word. "Ever."

Reassured, Abby settled back into the soft cushions of the couch.

"Ready?" Olivia asked, still leaning in.

"As ready as I'll ever be," said Abby.

"Rate your level of anxiety, Abby. On a scale of zero to ten, with ten being a high level of distress and zero being no distress, how would you rate the way you feel now?"

"I guess maybe ten."

"Where in your body do you feel the most distress?" Olivia asked.

"I'm trembling inside. My heart is racing. I feel shaky."

Olivia gestured toward a blanket throw on the couch. "Use that if you feel cold. Now, I want you to relax by taking a few deep breaths." Olivia flashed a reassuring smile. "As you can see, I'm holding up my forefinger about twelve inches from your nose. I want you to see it clearly—not too close or too far. So, is this a good spot?"

Abby nodded. Already, this seemed a little weird, but then again, what did it matter if Olivia's technique worked?

Olivia traced an invisible horizontal line in the air from the center position in front of Abby's nose to the left side. Then she moved her finger back to center and followed the line the same distance in the other direction. "Keep your eyes on my finger," she said.

Abby focused and followed as instructed—back and forth, back and forth. She soon realized that with each invisible line tracing, Olivia's finger was dropping a smidgen lower.

"Close your eyes."

Abby didn't need the command. Her lids were all the way down.

"You are safe. Nothing is going to happen that you don't want to happen." Olivia fell silent, perhaps to allow time for Abby to feel reassured. "Now, when you are ready, I want you to go back to the night of the trauma."

Olivia's soothing, soft tone did little to assuage Abby's anxiety. With her head resting on the sofa pillow, Abby sank a little deeper into the cushions and tried to breathe more slowly.

"Now, I want you to focus on the trauma. We'll do this in short bursts of fifteen or thirty seconds. What do you feel? Abby, what do you smell? Where is the light? Or are you in total darkness? What do you see as you look around? Notice the details." Olivia's voice sounded as soft as a dove's cooing.

In her mind's eye, Abby stood alone in the dark parking lot. The fog wafted past her in heavy, wet sheets. She heard the shot. Flinched. Then, as if in

slow motion, the memories flooded in. A figure
ran uphill. A car engine turned over. Headlights
beamed on her. The car sped away. The imagery
shifted to Jake . . . and then Paola. The event in all
its minutiae played out in her mind. Abby shifted
slightly on the couch and slowly opened her eyes
to look at Olivia. The therapist was staring intently
at her.

"How's the anxiety now, Abby, on a scale of one
to ten, with ten as the highest and one as the low-
est?"

"Seven, maybe," Abby said.

Olivia smiled. "That's a good start, Abby. There
are several phases to this modality, and in between
treatments, you'll need some coping mechanisms
that you can use to calm yourself. We'll talk about
those next. Of course, we'll keep working to lower
your anxiety and reduce your symptoms. Sound
good?"

Abby felt more relaxed than she'd felt in weeks.
"Absolutely wonderful."

Wild Turkey Trivia

If Benjamin Franklin had gotten his way,
the wild turkey, not the bald eagle, would
be America's national bird. The wild
turkey, with its dramatic iridescent feathers, is a popular game bird and is hunted
throughout North America. This bird finds
suitable habitat in forests, swamps, and
grasslands. Wild turkeys eat seeds, snails,

insects, nuts, berries, and even small snakes. Like the peacock impressing the peahen, the tom turkey will fan out his tail and strut about to attract the female turkey's attention. He's the one that gobbles; female turkeys cluck. The latter lays pale tan eggs with dark speckles that are twice the size of a chicken's eggs and have yolks of a golden-orange color.

Chapter 12

Healing the maladies of our gardens
heals us in the process.

—*Henny Penny Farmette Almanac*

After the therapy session with Olivia, Abby returned to her farmette and struggled against fatigue to do a few chores. The last one was applying a dormant spray to control the overwintering peach leaf curl that made her peach trees sick in the spring. Later, after a warm shower and a small meal, she dressed in pajamas and bed socks and crawled under a down comforter. Her head rested on a lavender-scented pillow. Her feet snuggled up against Sugar's warm body.

After the EMDR, perhaps erroneously, Abby had anticipated some kind of a shift in her psyche. For a while, she lay quietly, listening to the doves coo their plaintive lament and the chimes beyond the window intone prayerful harmonies. Then, from the shadowy margins of her consciousness, her thoughts began to slip into a penumbral darkness. Like untethered leaves, her thoughts drifted downward, deeper, beyond the realm of dreams, into a peaceful abyss.

Upon awakening, Abby discovered that the anxiety she'd felt since the night of the murder had lessened its hold. Not only did she feel rested, but also her thoughts seemed alert, bright, and reflective. She had not gotten up in the middle of the night to check over her house or awakened after imagining a gunshot, one that forced her to check the driveway for a light-colored sedan. Now, sipping her morning coffee with a renewed sense of well-being, she gazed uphill at the silver gambrel roof on Lucas Crawford's barn. Like that roof, with its two equal slopes on either side, their friendship had evolved a similarly balanced curvature. Both she and Lucas seemed to be waiting for some kind of signal that the other was open to discovering how to bridge the distance between them.

The words Lucas had spoken to her at Maisey's pie shop made it pretty clear he wanted to be more than just a good neighbor. And behind the image of the fearless, independent woman that she showed the world, Abby secretly longed for that special someone with whom to share her life. Even the remotest possibility that it could be Lucas Crawford sent her spirits soaring.

A woodpecker whacking at the dead eave of the front porch and the rocker's runners rapping the patio floor where she sat at the back of her house lulled her into a flight of fancy. With her fingers curled around her morning mug of coffee, she relished the sun warming the marrow of her bones. She hunkered deeper into the sheep's wool jacket over her pajamas and robe and proffered silent thanks for the EMDR and Olivia Crawford, who knew how to help her find peace again, and for Lucas, who was quietly awakening in her something mysterious and beautiful.

Her stomach growled, a reminder that she hadn't eaten. Setting her half-empty coffee mug on the patio table, she pushed her feet, still covered in thick socks, into a pair of garden clogs. After easing up out of the rocker, she strolled toward the orchard to pluck a ripe persimmon.

The sound of metal rattling stopped her in her tracks. She pivoted in the direction of the sound and saw someone throwing down the chains that secured the gate to the fenced-in property behind hers. Only the landowners entered from the road on the far side. She strained to make out the identity of the visitor and then grimaced when she realized who it was. Henry Brady was wrestling with the unwieldy gate. Struggling, he nevertheless managed to pull it open over the old gravel driveway.

Arghh. Should have known you'd be back. Abby made a beeline to her patio and entered the kitchen. A folding door separated the kitchen from the washer and dryer area. Intent on helping that man get on his way as soon as possible, she began pulling clothes from the laundry basket. Soon attired in jeans, a cotton turtleneck, and a thick sweater, Abby noted that the hands of the wall clock read ten o'clock as she left the kitchen. After pulling the slider closed behind her to keep Sugar inside, Abby crossed the yard, still damp with morning dew, and headed for the chicken house, the metal fence, and a possible confrontation.

She watched Henry drive his Ford F-150 into the driveway, overgrown with dried stalks of star thistle and wild oats from all the horse manure spread around the property last year to keep the weeds down. Behind the truck, he towed a seventeen-foot RV with peeling paint and windows that looked like they'd been soaped and left to dry. Instead of parking on the concrete slab hidden from view, he parked beneath the eucalyptus trees near where the old water tank once stood. Dust clouds rose from the double wheels of the RV. Abby marched halfway across the weedy acre in Henry's direction, covering her nose with her arm against the dust.

She halted in mid-stride when she realized Henry had brought friends. Following the RV into the desiccated drifts of weeds were two guys in a Chevy Silverado and another man in a gray beater with the truck hood and a door primed but not painted. She hadn't noticed the country music playing from the beater truck, but now the driver turned the volume to a deafening level. The music's bass boomed. Abby could feel it in her gut. She decided in the interest of self-preservation, it would be wiser to offer a friendly greeting to Henry and find out what was going on before she got up in his face about what looked to be the start of a party.

Seeing her approach, Henry called out, "Morning, Abigail. Nice to see you again."

"Uh-huh." Abby tapped her fingers against her ears, hoping Henry would realize they could not converse with the music at that volume.

Henry waved his arm and yelled at the guy in the beater truck. "Yo, bro, cut that damn radio.

Can't hear myself think." Addressing Abby again, he said, "He doesn't mean to be rude, but then again, he doesn't concern himself much with what other folks want."

Abby arched a brow but said nothing. She plunged her hands into her sweater pockets and waited for Henry to explain why he and his pals had come, although parking the RV, she surmised, was the likely reason.

"Hope we're not bothering you," Henry said when the radio volume had dropped. "We're here to load up our gear and guns."

That Henry's pals had climbed out of their trucks but kept their distance had not escaped Abby's notice. "Folks who live out here like it quiet, Henry—"

"Yeah. Sorry about that. Prying my recreational vehicle from the wife's clutches proved worse than I'd ever imagined. But now the Prowler's cleaned up and ready for the road," he said, his tone reflecting a sense of pride.

Giving Henry a look of surprise, Abby said, "You named your RV?" She stared at the two tanks of gas tied with bungee cords, and the duct tape holding pieces of trim in place.

"Yep. Good one, huh?" He drilled her with a look of self-importance.

Oh, jeez, like I could care. On the other hand, I don't much like the idea of you coming and going and bringing your buddies back here. Abby forced a smile. The time had come to face reality. The tranquility she'd enjoyed from that empty wooded acre likely had come to an end.

She hadn't thought much about the possibility that the heirs might allow friends to use the place. It wasn't any of her business who came or went back there, and she chastised herself for feeling so territorial. It wasn't that she didn't appreciate the drama Henry must be going through with his divorce. The loss of a mate was tough, especially during the holidays. She got that. But she doubted these guys cared a fig about stewardship of the land, the protection of animals, or the level of noise they made.

"So . . . hunting trip, huh? Be gone long?" Abby dug the toe of her garden clog into the plant detritus.

It'll be a short trip," said Henry. "We're leaving before dawn tomorrow. Be back before you know it." He pulled out a pack of cigarettes and offered her one. She waved it away. He lit one for himself.

Turning her face away from the smoke he blew in a thick cloud, Abby uttered a silent curse that these four fellas had messed up an otherwise fine morning, and there was nothing she could do about it.

Henry took a long drag off his cigarette. "Holidays are no big deal. Wife has cut me out of her life, and fine by me." He blew a couple of smoke rings. "I'd rather spend Thanksgiving with my buddies in any case. But these guys are married, and there'll be hell to pay if they aren't back for their kids." He blew smoke through the side of his mouth and grinned.

"Uh-huh." Abby looked over at Henry's friends, who stood together in a pack. They smoked their cigarettes near the beater pickup. Then she saw they had popped open tabs on cans of beer. *Seriously? At ten in the morning? Get real.*

"Please don't use those beer cans for target practice back here," Abby said in the sweetest tone she could summon.

Henry looked surprised, as though he hadn't thought of that. "Oh, heck, no."

"I'd better go, let you all get to your packing." After turning back toward her farmette, Abby strode through the weeds to her side of the chain-link fence. Rather than allow disappointment to overtake her and further ruin what was left of the morning, she would do her chores and check the mail. Last day for it, since tomorrow was Thanksgiving.

After pouring crumbles into the chickens' hanging feeder and filling their water canister from the water hose, she inspected the hives, which she'd covered with blankets now that the nights had turned colder. Then it was back to the patio. There she grabbed her coffee mug from the table, opened the slider, and stepped into the kitchen. Sugar managed to squeeze between her feet as she walked to the sink with the mug.

"Good grief, sweetie. I know you're hungry," said Abby, "but I won't get that bowl filled any faster if you knock me to the floor." Sugar slapped her tail against Abby's legs as she poured kibble into the dog bowl.

With the dog fed, Abby walked out to Farm Hill Road and opened the mailbox. Amid the bills, she found a postcard from ethnobotanist Jack Sullivan. After turning it over, she read the message.

I'm having a pint of plain and thinking of you,
as it's coming on Thanksgiving there in a wee bit.
Now, don't you be losing faith in our friendship,
Abby. I know I've not written until now. But Bor-
neo is keeping me busy. If you'd be so kind as to
write me back, I'll take it as a sign to keep oiling the
hinges of our friendship so we can hang together.
Happy Thanksgiving. Jack.

Abby grinned as she reread his note. She could
almost hear him saying the words in that feigned
Irish brogue of his. The memory of her previous
case was a bittersweet one. Jack had sought her
help after his sister Fiona's death. He'd told her
once, "Get your wild on, Abby." She chuckled at
that memory and wondered if there was anything
about Fiona's murder that could somehow help
her understand and sort out Jake Winston's death.
Fiona had been a free spirit, living an unconven-
tional life on her own terms. Jake Winston also was
guilty of that. *Live by your choices. You might die by*
them, too.

Abby entered the house and propped Jack's
card on her antique Queen Anne chest. In the
kitchen, she pulled out the cookie sheets, wondering how long it would take for a package of cookies to reach the island of Borneo. If she mailed
them on Friday, wouldn't he get them by the end
of the year? Regardless of how long it might take,
Abby decided to send him some. She upped the
count of cookies needed to five dozen—for Kat,
Paola, the Varela family, and Jack Sullivan.

After washing and drying her hands and tying
on an apron, Abby removed a large mixing bowl

from the cabinet. Then she took out the bag of cookie cutters she kept in an old bread box. Reaching into the fridge for the butter and eggs, she heard her cell phone sound with Kat's ringtone. After removing the phone from her sweater pocket, she slid a finger over it to answer the call.

"Ten guns that crazy woman has in her condo. Can you believe it, Abby? Ten. And thousands of rounds of ammo. So I asked her, 'Why the arsenal?' " Kat's tone sounded frustrated.

"Whoa, little missy. Back up the train for a minute," Abby said. "Who are we talking about here? And BTW, isn't it customary to say hello first?"

"Yes, so hello. I'm talking about Brianna Cooper, that graphic designer at the Country Schoolhouse Winery."

"Okay, what did she say when you asked her about her guns and ammo?"

"Said she's a serious collector. Goes to the range every month and fires off two or three hundred rounds. According to her, she needs lots of ammo for plinking, competition shooting, and hunting."

"So she collects and shoots. Unless one or more of those guns are illegal, she has the right."

"True, but she withheld information about having those guns. She lied about her alibi. She lied about the nature of her relationship with Jake. It's frigging aggravating to have people who, instead of wanting to get a murderer off the streets, stonewall us with lies."

"I hear you." Abby took a package of butter and the carton of eggs from the fridge and set them on the counter.

"But you won't breathe a word of this to anyone, will you, Abby?"

"Oh, stop. We're in the same boat on that score. You know I won't. So what's got Brianna Cooper under your microscope?"

"Well, it has a little something to do with an eight-by-ten package of compromising pictures of her and Jake. Then we found some regular trans-actions from his bank account into hers that don't match her payroll checks. She's turned over the pictures. We know she was blackmailing him. She denies it, of course, and swears she didn't kill him."

Abby breathed in a sharp breath and let it go. "If he was paying up, why would she kill him and stop the money flow?"

"Who knows? She says he paid her to pose for pictures . . . wanted to improve his photography skills. Is that lame or what?"

"Well, for sure, Jake was one weird character. And the people around him, except for the Varela family, were equally strange." Abby put her cell on speaker. She removed a measuring cup from a drawer of baking utensils and took the bag of flour out of the pantry. Placing it on the kitchen counter, she opened the bag and measured out five cups of flour into the mixing bowl. "So I take it you're still looking for a suspect gun?"

"All but one of Brianna Cooper's guns are ac-counted for. She says she loaned it to a cousin for target practice. He lives in Idaho," said Kat. "She could be lying about that, too." Kat's tone sounded frustrated. "Tedious, girlfriend. Really tedious tracking these details."

"I hear you. When I get bogged down, I do something physical, like hacking away on a brush pile or treating myself to a tea and pastry break." Abby reached for the container of baking powder and took out the measuring spoons.

"I'd like to bust something right now," Kat said.

"Seriously? Then why not do some of your kick-boxing after work today? Exercise clears the mind and diminishes stress."

"Can't. Lieutenant Sinclair has me tracking down Brianna Cooper's cousin. We've got to eliminate him and locate that gun. Could be a late night."

"So, you're no longer scrutinizing Dori Langston?" Abby took a five-pound bag of sugar from the cupboard.

"Not again with the sous-chef, Abby."

"Kat, I can't shake the feeling that somehow she's connected."

"So you've told me. And I will ask for the umpteenth time. Explain to me how she could be in two places at once."

"You know I can't, but—" Abby was about to reveal that she saw Dori Langston hooking up with a guy in a suspicious vehicle after leaving the Pantry Hut. And then she wanted to tell Kat about her encounter with Lucas Crawford's sister and the EMDR stuff, but Kat cut her off.

"Oh, hold on, Abby. I've got an incoming from dispatch. I'm going to mute you. Be right back."

Abby heard a female voice start briefing Kat through her radio. Then silence. A moment passed and then another. Kat clicked back into their conversation.

"Abby, we've got a floater in the reservoir up by the Country Schoolhouse Winery."

In disbelief, Abby stared at the granulated sugar. "Male or female?"

"Jane Doe. And not dressed for a walk around the reservoir in November."

Abby's thoughts swirled. "Identifying marks?"

Kat said, "Butterfly on her neck. Tall woman. Light hair."

Abby's fingers tensed around the bag of sugar. "Dori? You know, I've seen a butterfly tattoo. Yes, now I remember. When you and I were filing out of the church after the wedding vow exchange between Jake and Paola. It was on the neck of a tall woman with platinum hair."

"Yeah?" Kat said. "Fits with it being Dori Langston, doesn't it?"

Abby inhaled sharply. She knew the cops would need a positive ID and cause of death and would be calling in Millie Jamison, the coroner. "Has anyone reported Dori missing?"

"No."

"Jeez, if it is Dori, that means two of the Country Schoolhouse Winery workers are now homicide victims. Are you thinking what I'm thinking?" asked Abby.

"The deaths are linked—oh, you bet. I'd like to get into it with you, Abby, but seriously, I've got to run."

With her mind preoccupied with this troubling new situation, Abby was hardly in the mood to make cookies. Still, she would stand down, stay away from the crime scene, and let Kat get back to her when she could. In the meantime, Abby reasoned that baking would give her hands something to do while she mentally reviewed all the facts and tried to figure out if she'd misinterpreted some piece of information and how this new complication might fit into the case. She walked back to her incident poster, picked up a felt pen, and wrote *victim* next to Dori Langston's name under *suspects*. She drew in the simple shape of a butterfly next to the name.

Around twelve o'clock, as the baked sugar cookies were cooling, Abby spotted Henry Brady making a beeline through the weeds toward her chicken run. Abby wiped her hands on her apron and walked out to meet him before he stepped a foot onto her farmette.

"So . . . I'm about to split," he said. "My friends left already. Look, is there any chance I could leave my extra RV key with you?"

"No chance," said Abby, turning her head slightly so she wouldn't have to smell the scent of booze and chain-smoked cigarettes. She wondered if he'd left the butts on the ground. "I don't want that responsibility." Abby wasn't against helping out a friend, but she hardly knew this guy. "Try a magnetic key box," she said. "Just stick it to the undercarriage." She glanced past him, expecting to see a pile of beer cans, too, but didn't spot any.

"Don't take this the wrong way," Henry shot back in a tone tinged with sarcasm, "but only an idiot would do that. Why not hang a sign, too, for any burglar intent on swiping my vehicle?"

"We haven't had any burglaries out here," Abby said. "And besides, your RV is locked behind a chain-link fence, hardly in a high-target area."

He seemed vexed. "Wife always called me an airhead because I have trouble keeping track of things. Lost more keys than I can count. Couldn't you just hang it up somewhere and forget about it until I come around to get it?"

Abby wasn't sure why she felt so put upon. It wasn't a big request, like asking her to donate a kidney or something. The simple truth was she didn't want to be the keeper of the key to Henry Brady's RV. But apparently, neither did his buddies, because if it was so important that a trusted other party hold on to his extra key, then surely he'd already asked them.

His jaw had set into a firm line beneath his unshaven cheek jaw. "I'd be grateful if you'd just hang on to it until the hunting trip is over." He dropped his smoldering cigarette butt into the dirt and crushed it with his boot.

Abby tensed. "So when is that again?"

"Back after Thanksgiving weekend. I'll get it from you before I take off again."

"On another hunting trip?" Abby asked, buoyed by optimism that he'd soon be gone again.

"After this trip, I'm moving up to Bellingham, Washington, up by the Canadian border. I'll need the RV to haul my stuffed trophies. That's all I'm getting out of the divorce settlement with the drama queen."

She'd been hard on Henry and felt remorseful. "Oh, all right. Give me the key. But I'm taking it on the condition that you don't show up at my door in the middle of the night, asking for it back." She wanted to add the words *drunk or high* to that sentence but decided against it. "I'll hang it on the hook next to my oven mitt."

"Thanks," said Henry. After giving her the key, he turned and walked back to his truck. Abby watched him take out his cell phone and call someone. They chatted a few minutes. After that, he slid the cell into his pocket, locked the gate with the chains, and drove away. Her gaze swept back to the Prowler parked in the open. *What happened to stashing it where I wouldn't have to see it? Figures.* Abby bent down and picked up Henry's cigarette to deposit in her trash.

Pushing Henry from her thoughts, Abby walked back to her kitchen. Despite the positive changes she felt from the EMDR, a low-level anxiety plagued her. Knowing she would be seeing Olivia in a few days for the next in her series of weekly treatments, Abby tried to ignore it. She would do some deep breathing and meditation to calm down later, as Olivia had counseled her to do. For now, she would mentally tick through the questions for Chef Emilio Varela tomorrow. Time he shed some light on his now-dead sous-chef and his missing gun.

Easy Sugar Cookies

Ingredients:
Cookies:
2 cups granulated sugar
1½ cups butter
4 large eggs
1 teaspoon vanilla extract
5 cups all-purpose flour
2 teaspoons baking powder
1 teaspoon salt

Royal Icing:
1-pound box (3½ to 4 cups) confectioners' sugar
3 large egg whites
lemon juice squeezed from one large de-seeded
    lemon
Food coloring (optional)

Directions:
Prepare the cookie dough. Combine the sugar and butter in a large mixing bowl and cream until smooth with an electric mixer. Add the eggs and vanilla to the mixture and beat until well blended. Stir the flour, baking powder, and salt into the sugar-egg mixture.

Cover the bowl with plastic wrap and chill the dough for 1 hour, or roll the dough into balls, cover tightly with plastic wrap, and refrigerate overnight.

Bake the cookies. Preheat the oven to 400°. Roll out the chilled dough on a floured surface until the dough is ¼- to ½-inch thick. Cut

it into the desired shape using a cookie cut-
ter.

Place the cookies 1 inch apart on an un-
greased baking sheet, and bake for 6 to 8 minutes, or until golden brown and no longer
springy to the touch. Transfer the cookies to a
metal rack and allow them to cool completely.

Meanwhile, prepare the royal icing. Combine the confectioners' sugar and egg whites
in the small bowl of an electric mixer. Using
the paddle attachment, beat the sugar-egg
mixture on the mixer's low setting until moist.
Add the lemon juice and beat on medium for
4 minutes. The icing should appear light and
fluffy. Tint the icing with food coloring, if desired.

Decorate the cooled cookies with the icing.
Or if you wish to decorate them later, the
icing can be stored, covered with a layer of
wet paper towels and then plastic wrap, for
up to 24 hours.

Makes 5 dozen cookies

Chapter 13

Few things in life stink more than fresh
manure, a rotten egg, or a rush to
judgment.

—*Henny Penny Farmette Almanac*

The earsplitting cackle of chickens brought
Abby to an abrupt awakening at six thirty. It
was still semi-dark out. Rubbing sleep from her
eyes, she rolled out of bed and pulled back the
sheer curtain at the window to see the cause of the
commotion. A small gray fox standing on its hind
legs clawed at the double layer of poultry wire over
one of the chicken-house window frames. And it
wasn't the first time she'd seen that fox or the only
time it had tried to break in.

After throwing her pink fleece robe on over her
cotton pajamas and plunging her feet into the garden clogs she'd left by the slider, Abby ventured
into the breaking dawn. Sugar followed right on
her heels. Concerned about the dog's welfare,
Abby grabbed Sugar's collar and coaxed her pooch

back to the safety of the farmhouse. "Extra hugs and a treat when I get back, sweetie." But Sugar was not interested in promises of later rewards. She pawed the slider and protested by barking.

An Arctic chill assaulted Abby. She shivered against the bone-chilling cold that penetrated her nightclothes. Cinching her robe tighter, she peered toward the chicken run. The fox could have been passing through her property if it lay between its hunting areas, but it seemed more likely that the animal had remembered her chickens from a previous visit.

Trapping and transporting the fox to another territory meant it would have to defend itself in a new location while disoriented. Abby dismissed that idea as a bad option. "Oh, boy, what am I going to do with you?" she uttered under her breath. "I sure hope you haven't dug a den or found another predator's hole and taken up residence nearby." Abby could think of only one remedy for getting rid of the unwanted fox—saturate the mouth of the hole that the fox was using as a den—if she could find it—with urine-soaked kitty litter. Where was she going to get that? She could use noise maybe. There might be fallout from angry neighbors, but if it meant the fox would leave, it was a risk she'd willingly take.

After taking the metal garden trowel on the patio table and grabbing the lid from the galvanized garbage can, Abby levied several hard whacks of the trowel against the lid. The animal took notice but didn't retreat. Instead, it lunged around, searching for another way in, and then resumed clawing. Abby banged. The fox clawed. Frustrated,

Abby set out over the wet grass, hammering the lid as she marched forward.

The fox rushed the fence and scrambled over the wire and down the other side. Watching the streak of gray lope away, Abby remembered her grandmother Rose's admonition to keep still and think fast when a cunning fox was around. Of course, her Scots-Irish grandmother's advice was often laced with a little Celtic folklore that involved tall tales about foxes as shape-shifters. Still, her grandmother Rose was right about one thing— one must keep her wits about her when a predator fox was on the prowl. Watching the animal take refuge under Henry Brady's RV, Abby's hope surged that the ugly vehicle would be leaving, too, but she worried that Henry unwittingly might drive over the poor creature. Well, there was nothing she could do about that now.

After checking the poultry wire over the chicken-house windows to assure herself that her small flock would remain safe, Abby turned back to the warmth of her farmhouse. She would permit the fox a Thanksgiving Day reprieve and search for its den some other time.

After attaching the lid to the garbage can, Abby laid the trowel on top, yawned, and took one last whiff of the pungent pine and wood-smoked air before heading inside. She grabbed a biscuit for Sugar and allowed the pooch to find her treat in her bathrobe pocket.

"See there, big girl, I keep my promises. Now, go and enjoy your biscuit while I check the TV for the weather. I don't want a freeze to take out my citrus trees." After stifling another yawn, she dropped a slice of bread into the toaster, made coffee, and then went to the living room and hit the ON button of the TV remote.

"Police confirm it's a local winery worker who's been found dead at the regional park reservoir," the anchor said.

If she felt sleepy before, Abby was now wide awake and tuned in. The reporter promised to return after the commercial break with the weather and traffic. Abby hustled from her living room/dining room back to the kitchen. There she poured her coffee and slathered butter and jam on the toast. A moment later on the couch, with a cup of coffee in hand and a plate of toast on her lap, Abby intently watched the images on TV. Two men lifted the stretcher bearing the victim's body into the rear of the coroner's van. The camera panned back to the on-scene reporter and Chief Bob Allen, who were standing by the dock where Abby and Emilio had recently sat together, discussing his conflict with Scott Thompson. Abby munched her toast and listened to what her old boss, Chief Bob Allen, had to say.

"We have recovered a body. It's female. Gunshot to the head. We're withholding the name of the deceased until we can notify the family. There's a press conference at four. That's all." The chief stepped away from the microphone.

Hoping for more details, Abby was disappointed that the reporter lobbed the conversation back to the meteorologist. She heard "frost tonight" before she hit the OFF button on the remote. As she sat still as a stone, her thoughts swirled. *Another winery worker shot in the head. Wow.*

Abby raised her coffee cup to her lips and sipped one mouthful after another as she tried to make sense of the bizarre development. She rose and carried the cup and plate into the kitchen, where she deposited them in the sink. Beyond the greenhouse window above the sink, she stared at a family of crows sitting atop the pine tree. For most wineries, the work was seasonal, swelling during harvest season and slowing after. So how many winery workers had the winery employed this time of year? Had they all been working a shift on the night of Jake's murder? If not, who hadn't been there? she wondered. Abby looked over at her incident poster. The only winery personnel names on it were of those working the event the night of the murder. Abby realized she needed more information. After grabbing her phone from its charger on the kitchen counter, she texted Kat. **Can we talk?**

Kat texted back. **Not now.**

Abby chewed her lip. Should she ring Otto? Or maybe just drop by the police station? He was working this case, too, albeit it was likely from a different angle. A plate of homemade cookies might get him to share info. At the very least, she would try. But to Emilio's place first. She had to know more about the sous-chef and whether or not Emilio knew where the woman was. Surely he could shed some light on that subject.

An hour later, Abby pulled in front of Luna Varela's Spanish-style bungalow with the Jeep's front seat loaded with the gift boxes and a wrapped paper plate full of cookies for the cops. The Jeep's dashboard clock read ten o'clock. Abby took a quick look at a message she'd got from Kat. **Leaving the crime scene. Dori Langston was shot in the back of the head and dumped.**

Execution style? Abby knew if the body was dumped at the site, the crime happened somewhere else. With a professional hit, the killer would shoot but would not move the body. Point of fact, Jake was shot and left in the car. But Dori was shot and moved. So moving a body would take some thought, time, effort, and possibly advanced planning. *Why do that? Not to get caught, for sure.* But perhaps the killer feared the cops finding a personal connection between them.

Abby's thoughts continued streaming around unanswered questions: Two killers or only one? Were the killings by a professional or an amateur? If Jake had been the killer's first victim, was the killer learning as he continued his crime spree? And if the two murders were for revenge, what was the killer's anger, resentment, or grudge all about? *Which begs the question of how many workers were employed by the winery and where they all were during Jake's death and Dori's murder. Who would know this? Don Winston would have access to the employee roster for that day. Of course, the police would already have asked for it.*

Jarred from her thoughts by a hand waving in her peripheral vision, Abby yielded to the distraction. Luna Varela was standing at her front door, signaling Abby to join her in the house. Abby reached for the cookies and a bouquet of late-blooming red roses. She got out of her Jeep.

Hustling up the walkway, she called out, "Happy Thanksgiving, Luna."

"Same to you. I saw you drive up. Come in."

She hurried up to the dark-eyed young woman and handed her the flowers and the box of cookies. "A little something for you."

"How sweet, Abby. Thank you."

Abby suspected that if anyone knew where Emilio was on this chilly holiday morning, it would be his sister. "What's the chance Emilio is here? I drove by his place, and he didn't answer my knock."

"He's not here. Is it important that you find him?" Luna gestured for Abby to lead the way inside the house. The scent of coffee permeated the Varelas' living room. From the kitchen, the loud outburst of a child's giggling told Abby that the toddler was up and having breakfast, perhaps with her parents.

"I'd like to talk to your brother again. And, yes, it is kind of important."

Luna's expression darkened. "Should I be worried?"

"There's been another murder," said Abby, breaking the news as gently as possible.

Luna's free hand flew to her mouth. "Who?"

"The winery's sous-chef, Dori Langston."

Luna collapsed onto the couch, still clutching the flowers and the box. Her eyes widened in fear. "You can't believe Emilio knows anything about that."

"Well, I'm not convinced he does or doesn't. I just want to talk with him before the police do another knock and talk, which I'm sure they will."

The stricken look on Luna's face made Abby wish she'd kept the information to herself.

"This is terrible. Why is this happening to our family?" a stricken Luna asked.

Abby tried to soften the blow. "I'm so sorry, Luna. Here I've gone and upset you, when that was never my intention. I'll find Emilio. No worries." Like it or not, she'd created drama, and now she needed to extricate herself. "I should go. Will I see you at the hospital later, visiting Paola?"

Luna looked bewildered. "Yes, I suppose." It seemed clear that she was still thinking about Emilio.

"Great. I want to see our girl, too. Hope to catch you there." Abby turned to leave, but Luna grabbed her arm.

"Should I call a lawyer? I mean . . . for Emilio?"

Abby hesitated and swallowed hard. "I'm afraid that's Emilio's decision. Talk with him." She left as quickly as she'd entered the house.

After dashing back to her Jeep, she pulled out onto the street and headed straight for the Las Flores Police Department. Eight minutes later, she strolled into the lobby with the plate of cookies. Waving to the ladies in Dispatch, she walked over to the speaker in the glass window. On the other side of the window, Nettie was tidying up some paperwork while a uniformed county sheriff's deputy looked on, apparently waiting for her to locate some document he needed.

"Good morning," Abby called cheerfully, holding up the plastic-wrapped plate of cookies.

Nettie, who handled records keeping and patrol

when she wasn't doing the CSI work for the department, looked up. Her eyes brightened. "Well, hi there, Abby. I didn't know you were coming by."

"Working the holiday sucks. Been there, done that, so I brought your gang some cookies."

"Super." Nettie plucked the document from a pile she had been searching through and handed it to the deputy. They both headed for the security door that separated the visitors' lobby from the rest of the facility.

As the sheriff's deputy walked past her to exit the building, Abby met Nettie at the doorway and handed her the plate. "Any chance I could speak to Otto?"

"He's prepping for an interview."

"What about Kat?"

"Expected back any minute."

Abby swallowed hard against her next idea, as unpalatable as it was. "Lieutenant Sinclair, maybe I could speak to him for a minute?"

"Took an early lunch and went for his run along the creek to clear his head. And the chief is with the mayor right now."

"Maybe I could help?" Nettie asked, eyeing the cookies.

Just then Kat's voice sounded from behind Nettie in the corridor. "Which interview room, Nettie?"

"One," Nettie called back.

Leaning in and glancing past Nettie's shoulder, Abby peered in the direction from which she'd heard Kat's voice. She saw Kat escort Emilio to an interview room after entering from the station's rear, where a jailer kept watch over two twenty-four-hour holding cells and a booking room.

"I'd better go," said Nettie, as if afraid of being caught dawdling instead of doing her job.

Abby nodded. "I'll pick up my plate tomorrow."

"With any kind of luck, we'll have a confession by then."

As the security door clicked shut behind her, a shiver shot down Abby's spine. *God, I hope not Emilio's.*

Jobs Honeybees Do

In the complex community of a honeybee hive, there are tens of thousands of bees. Some bee-keepers assert that a healthy hive can have forty thousand-plus bees. The vast majority are infertile female bees, referred to as *workers.* There are also males, called drones. Some of the worker bee tasks are as follows:

- Foragers and scouts: gather nectar, pollen, and water

- Nursemaids: feed the queen and the larvae

- Builders and cleaners: create the wax and build cells and keep the hive clean

- Guards: seal the hive openings from intruders

- Bouncers and undertakers: evict the males from the hive in the late autumn, when they are no longer necessary; clean away bee corpses from the entry of the hive

Chapter 14

Honeybees are calm when the scent of
their queen indicates she is strong and
healthy; agitation comes when the
queen becomes old, diseased, or
injured and her scent wanes.

—*Henny Penny Farmette Almanac*

In the antiseptic-scented room, Abby gazed upon her friend Paola, lying asleep in the freshly made hospital bed. Where the small flap had been removed from her skull to create a brain/bone window, her head had been wrapped with a fresh dressing. The doctors, Abby learned, had frozen the skull bone and would reattach it with screws approximately six weeks after their patient had been discharged home. But that discharge, according to the family, wouldn't come for another week. For now, Paola's long black hair had been cut and plaited into two short braids that barely touched her shoulders. For Abby, Paola still exuded a beautiful vulnerability as she rested against white cotton pillows.

After placing her gifts of a magazine and the box of cookies on the bedside table, next to the plastic water pitcher, Abby eased down into the worn leather armchair next to Paola's bed. The quiet whir of a bathroom fan, turned on and forgotten, created white noise that invoked a monotonous yet peaceful ambience. Within minutes of her arrival, however, Abby heard the voice of the hospital operator cut through the paging system as she asked for an X-ray tech to report to the ER.

Paola's eyes fluttered open. She stared blankly at Abby. Seconds ticked away and then her lips formed a faint smile of recognition.

Gently grasping the hand that had apparently once supported an IV needle but had become infiltrated and now appeared swollen and bruised, Abby asked, "So . . . how are you, sweetie? *Cómo estás?*"

Paola touched her tongue to her dry lower lip and pointed to lemon glycerin swabs in sealed packets on her bedside table. Abby stood up and plucked one from a plastic cup that held three. She ripped open the packaging and stroked the swab across Paola's cracked, dry lips. After pressing her lips together, Paola said in a hoarse voice, "I'm alive."

Abby slipped the swab back into the cup. "And so you are. Happy to hear it." Abby had tried to sound cheerful. But as she sat back down in the chair and gazed at Paola, she soon realized a gloom had settled over her friend.

Paola's features contorted slightly, reflecting concern. "The night you found me . . . did you check on Jake, too?"

"Of course I did." Abby struggled with what to say next. Had Paola been lying there all these weeks, thinking otherwise? "He was already gone, sweetie. I'm pretty sure it would have been quick."

Paola's dark lashes swept over her cheeks. A tear rolled down her cheek and disappeared into a braid. Abby pulled a tissue from the box on the bedside table and dabbed it at Paola's eyes. What could she possibly say to ease the pain? Abby remained silent to allow Paola time to take in the information.

Paola sniffled. When she again spoke, it seemed clear she wanted to talk about something other than the murder. "Tell me about your farmette. Are you busy?"

"Busier than a worker bee," said Abby, effortlessly launching into the story about finding the fox at the chicken house. When she'd finished, Paola smiled and gazed at her, as though there were a million things to say, but she had no command of the words to say them with. The two again sat in an emotionally potent silence.

After several minutes, Paola said in a small, resolute voice, "I miss him."

Abby bent her head, studied Paola's hand as it reached to wipe away tears. "I'm so sorry, sweetie. I can hardly believe he's gone." She added, "But the good Lord saw fit to keep you around."

"Why? Life is poison to me now." She shot a challenging look at Abby. "I don't want to live. Not with this pain in my heart."

Abby cringed. Running through her mind were all the platitudes that people offered in moments like these. She thought about how dark and alone and anxious she'd been over the weeks since the murder. The nightmares. Lack of sleep. It surely had been horrific for Paola.

"I can't know the suffering you're going through," Abby said, her voice barely rising above a whisper as pain squeezed her own heart. "But to have the gift of life is a privilege. The healing of your body will take time. And of your spirit, well, that will depend on you and your Maker." Abby reached out and stroked Paola's arm. She focused her gaze on the purple bruise and the swelling of the hand where an IV must have infiltrated. It was her way to avoid looking into Paola's grief-stricken eyes. "Prayer can be a poultice, if you believe in such things . . . and I think you do."

Paola's lips quivered. After a long moment, she said, "That night . . . our party . . . Jake parked. We talked. It was good. Better than seven years before."

Abby turned toward a sudden clatter in the hallway. The chatter and shuffling of feet soon subsided. She looked back at Paola. The large dark eyes still shimmered with tears, but Paola seemed more composed.

"He changed. Months ago, it started. He feared no consequence for anything."

A frown creased Abby's forehead as she grasped for meaning. "Why was that?"

Paola shrugged slightly. "The last time he went to Buenos Aires, he caught a brain fever. When he came back, he was forgetful. Demanding. Physically needy."

"Maybe he regretted time spent away from you?" Abby asked.

Paola twisted slightly, adjusting her position in the bed. "No."

"Well, then, what?" Abby leaned in. "I don't understand."

Paola's expression darkened. "It's weird, the way he was. Always wanted attention. And from different women. He didn't used to be like that." Her lips tightened. "He would be angry if I told you. It's too strange. He would hate me to tell anyone."

"A secret, then?" Abby asked.

Paola turned her face toward the window. Birds and bees and butterflies flitted in the fifth-floor rooftop garden beyond her window.

After a moment Paola changed the subject. "I saw the shooter."

"Yeah?" She would wait and see what more Paola might say.

With a small nod, Paola added, "A man. Looked like a bum."

"You recognize him?"

"No."

"Did Jake know him?"

"I think so." She reflected in silence and then said, "The man knocked. Jake lowered the car window." The lids of her eyes fluttered, as if her mind was trying to push out other images, perhaps the sound of the shot and the scene of her husband dying.

A stab of guilt drove Abby from further probing.

A female voice interrupted them. "Ready for lunch?" A woman dressed in a white nurse's uniform with a blue name tag strode in, carrying a plastic lunch tray with a plate under cover, a carton of milk, and a piece of pie. Abby rose and removed the cookie box and magazine she'd placed on the bedside table and laid them on the window-sill.

"Salisbury steak today," said the nurse as she slid the tray of food onto the table. "And you have visitors to keep you company while you eat." The nurse called out, "She's awake. Come in."

Abby glanced toward the door. Luna, her husband, and their daughter entered the room, bearing smiles and gifts. Luna carried Spanish-language books. Her husband brought yellow mums in cellophane tied with a big ribbon. Abby rose from the chair to make room. "How does she look to you, Luna?" asked Abby, stepping out of the way so Luna could kiss her sister.

"Looking stronger every day," said Luna, stroking her sister's arm. "Your doctor tells us to get ready. They're going to send you home maybe next week."

Abby scooted to the foot of the bed. "Such wonderful news. I think on that note, I'd better go." She blew a kiss to Paola. "Great to see you, sweetie. Eat your lunch. You're going to need your strength."

Luna followed Abby to the door. "Abby, could I have a moment?" she said, stepping into the hallway behind Abby. "What about Emilio? He hasn't returned any of our calls. We're worried."

Abby maintained a poker face. She didn't want to telegraph concern in any way. "I'll call you just as soon as I hear from him," she told Luna. She wasn't exactly lying. While she'd glimpsed Emilio in the police station corridor, they hadn't talked.

Luna said, "Whatever you can do, we thank you for it."

Abby took a step, stopped, and pivoted. Lowering her voice to a whisper, she said, "Months ago, Paola told me that Jake seemed changed after his last trip to South America. Did she talk with you about that?"

"Yes, he'd gotten sick."

"With what?"

"A brain fever . . . I think encepha-something. I can't recall the name."

Abby reflected a moment, wondering if some kind of sickness might not have underpinned Jake's abnormal behaviors. She gave Luna a quick hug and strolled toward the elevator, her thoughts preoccupied with the run of bad fortune Paola had experienced over the past few months. The display light on the wall above the visitors' elevator indicated it was stuck on the first floor. Abby waited and searched for the stairwell. Pivoting, she stared down the corridor in the opposite direction, past the nurses' station. Perhaps she should take the service elevator down there or the stairwell next to it.

As she contemplated that option, Abby spotted a man wearing a beanie crocheted in rainbow colors. He shrank back into a doorway and stared in her direction. Alerting on her gazing back at him, the man walked quickly from the room and hurried to the stairwell. In a moment of intuitive recognition, a shiver shot down her spine. *Jeez. You've been following me.* Abby's heart scudded against her chest wall. The elevator came and went.

She willed herself to the window to scan the parking lot. At the lot's edge a coffee kiosk and a fall produce stand had been set up. The number of people coming and going during the lunch hour seemed enormous. In due course, however, Abby spotted the rainbow hat. She tracked the man as he began weaving among the parked cars. She watched him slow his gait to peer in the vehicles, as though casing them for valuables, but as he rounded the coffee kiosk, she could no longer see him.

Abby walked back to Paola's room. She stood in the doorway, waiting for Luna to look up. Since she did not know what the man's purpose or intention was for being at the hospital, it made no sense that he'd be on this floor, Paola's floor. Abby tried without success to calm her galloping heartbeat. *Breathe, Abby. Slow and easy calms the heart.*

Seeing her, Luna hurried over. "What's wrong?" she whispered. "You look like you've seen a ghost."

"Call it a premonition or whatever you like, because I know this sounds silly, but I don't think Paola should be left alone."

"Why? Is she in danger? What is it? Abby, tell me."

"I don't want to alarm you. I just saw someone suspicious. A scuzzball in a beanie. I can't see any reason why he'd be on this wing of the surgical ward."

"A visitor, you mean?" Luna asked.

"I don't think so. But to that point, have any workers from the winery come to visit Paola?"

"Jake's parents came once. Paola was friends with Scott Thompson, but he hasn't been by, nor has anyone else from the winery, unless you count Emilio."

"I feel strongly about this, Luna. Schedule family member visits in shifts, if you have to."

"Why? There are many doctors and nurses and other staff here."

"And they won't guard and protect Paola like you will."

Luna's eyes swept the corridor. "Okay," she said and headed back into the room.

Minutes later, Abby reminded herself to include the guy with the beanie on her incident poster and to try to find out who he was. She guided her Jeep from the hospital parking lot and navigated the course to town. She headed down Chestnut, turned on Lilac, and then onto Wisteria Lane, where Charlotte had said she shared a Victorian with Dori Langston and others. Parking next to a sycamore tree with white bark and yellow leaves three houses from the end of Wisteria Lane, Abby reckoned the only sure way to know which house Dori had lived in was to knock and ask for Charlotte and/or Dori at each one. From the console, she took a pen and a spiral-bound notepad and jotted down the addresses of the Victorians on the street for later reference. Still holding the writing materials, she looked up to see two people in the rearview mirror.

The couple walked their dog on the same side of the street as the Jeep was parked. As if a divine hand were orchestrating a piece of good luck just for Abby, the two tramped right past her. Abby realized the woman was Charlotte. With her was a man in his late twenties, wearing cargo pants, a thermal pullover, and a tattered sweatshirt. But as Abby studied him, she began to think he looked a lot like the dishwasher with the stringy, long ponytail in the kitchen the night she'd encountered Dori Langston slicing persimmons. The couple led the dog up to a distinctive white Victorian with turrets and a wraparound porch. Abby circled the house number on her notepad and then placed the pad and pen back on the console.

She watched Charlotte hand off the dog leash to her companion and unlock the door. The dog bounded inside. With the door closed, Charlotte and the man talked. The conversation grew heated. Abby rolled down her Jeep window to listen, but too late. Charlotte stormed inside the house, then slammed the door behind her. The man turned, trotted down the steps of the Victorian, and walked back in the direction from whence they'd come.

Well, well, Miss Charlotte, you knew the sous-chef but said nothing about knowing the dish-washer. Why was that? Abby thought.

After adjusting the view of the mirror, Abby watched Charlotte's companion. He pulled his cell phone from his pants pocket and made a call. Perhaps he wanted to summon Charlotte back outside. Or maybe he'd called someone else. Abby twisted in the driver's seat and observed him until he reached the end of the lane, put away his phone, and pulled out a pack of cigarettes. He lit up. Paced and smoked. After about ten minutes of chain-smoking, a motorcyclist arrived to give him a lift. After he climbed on behind the driver, the two sped away.

Tempted to follow, Abby decided instead to question Charlotte. She grabbed the remaining box of cookies, meant for Kat, thinking that Charlotte might view Abby's sudden visit less intrusive if Abby came bearing a holiday offering. With her gift in hand, Abby rang the doorbell.

"What are you doing here?" Charlotte asked, peeking out the crack of the partially opened door. "Is there something wrong with the stemware?" Charlotte pushed her dog by the collar back behind her, stepped outside, then closed the door.

"Oh, no. Not at all." Abby cleared her throat. "Think of it as paying it forward. You know, you do something nice for someone. Then they do something nice for someone else. I'm taking homemade cookies around to all my friends. Just now, I saw you and remembered how patient you were with me at the Pantry Hut. I was so indecisive over those glasses. So these sugar cookies are for you."

"Yeah?" Charlotte studied the decorated box that Abby held aloft. "Thanks."

"And I'm so sorry to learn about Dori's death," Abby said, jumping right into the subject of murder. "I saw it earlier on the TV news. You must be devastated."

Eyeing Abby with suspicion, Charlotte shrugged. "I guess we didn't really know her *that* well. Sure will miss her cooking."

"At least now you have cookies," said Abby.

Charlotte eyed her with curiosity. "What about your guests?"

"What about them?" Abby asked, not sure where she was going with the question.

"Isn't that why you needed the stemware?"

"Oh, yes," said Abby, racking her brain for an excuse that wouldn't appear too lame. "But you know how iffy guests can be when they're driving in from out of town. Late and later." She sniffed and looked out over the lawn. The dog whined on the other side of the door. Abby pushed on. "Hard to believe, isn't it? You and I were just talking about Dori at the Pantry Hut. Now she's gone. Have the Las Flores police been around yet?"

"One officer," Charlotte said. Her voice assumed a hint of hostility. "He questioned us for an hour or more before allowing us to take my dog for a walk."

"I saw you with the dog and a young man."

"My boyfriend. Trevor Massey. He works at the winery, too. Shares a shift from time to time with his cousin Gary Lynch."

Abby, thinking these were two more names for her incident board, said, "Oh, and what's his job at the winery?"

"Buses tubs of glassware, washes dishes, recycles, collects the trash . . . whatever needs doing."

"And did they ride to work together?"

"Of course. She lives here, and he practically does, too. And they work at the same place."

"I don't see his car here."

"That's because he rides a bike. His cousin has his car today."

"Cousin?"

"Yeah, cousin. Why all the questions?" Charlotte's brows knitted into a scowl.

"I'm just trying to understand the people who were her friends or were in her orbit. Yesterday was Wednesday. She would have been working, right?"

"No, they were both off."

"She was found floating in the regional park

reservoir, and I'm trying to understand how she got there." Abby had already surmised that if Dori had died someplace other than the reservoir, her body would have to be transported there for dumping. That likely meant she'd been in a car or a truck, not on a motorcycle.

"How should I know? Last night I worked until closing. When I got home, she was leaving to have a drink with a friend." The frantic scratching of canine nails against the inside of the front door diverted Charlotte's attention away from Abby. The dog's whining had progressed to full-on barking. Charlotte's face contorted with stress. "Sorry, but I've got to deal with my dog."

"How can I reach Trevor?" Abby knew she was pushing hard, but there was a lot at stake.

"Why are you asking me all these questions? You said you weren't a cop. What then? Private investigator?"

With no clear way to evade the question, Abby met Charlotte's direct gaze. She took out her phone and said, "You've figured it out. Help me contact Trevor. I'll never bother you again." Abby proffered her phone. "Please."

Charlotte's lip curled. Clearly, she was fed up. But she took the phone Abby handed her and punched in some numbers. Glowering, she thrust the phone back into Abby's hands and disappeared inside the house.

The door slamming in her face did little to dampen Abby's enthusiasm. She dialed Trevor and got a message machine. *No answer, no good.* Back inside her Jeep, Abby added Trevor's number to her contact list and called him one more time.

"Yeah," answered a male voice, clearly annoyed.

"Trevor Massey?"

"So what if it is?"

"I supply honey to the chefs, Emilio and Dori, up at the winery where you work."

"So?"

"So, I'm calling about Dori. I've got a couple of questions."

"Nope. I answered the cop's questions. I don't have to answer any more of them, especially from a beekeeper."

Abby protested, but the line went dead. It had been a long shot, but worth a try. *If you won't talk to me, maybe your new boss, Don Winston, will.*

Tips for Feeding Bees When Food Sources Are Limited

Beekeepers understand that their honeybees derive nourishment from honey and pollen. Honey provides calories the bees need for energy, while pollen provides minerals and protein. The following tips involve the proper feeding of honeybees during winter or other periods when pollen sources and access to honey are limited.

- Do not take honey from the hive if doing so means you'll then have to feed the bees come winter.

- Ensure the bees have access to their sealed combs of honey. Alternatively, feed them sugar syrup (made with white cane sugar, not brown, because of bee digestion issues).

- Make certain honey destined as food for the bees comes from a source free of disease.

- Use as little heat as possible for food destined to be consumed by bees, since heating honey produces a compound shown to cause honeybee gut ulceration.

- Avoid feeding high fructose corn syrup to the bees, since much commercially grown corn involves the use of pesticides and often GMOs.

Chapter 15

Pomegranates are an ancient symbol of
fertility; jelly made from the juice of the
ruby-red seeds makes a lovely filling for
layers of a trendy
wedding cake.

—*Henny Penny Farmette Almanac*

Abby lay low for a while, lest word got around
that she was badgering witnesses, gathering
names, checking out old-model sedans, and demanding phone numbers. But laying low didn't
mean she wasn't dealing with her anxiety. She'd
been steadily working on the incident poster, adding new info as it became known. The poster with
lines and notations in different colored inks had
taken on the look of a road map rather than an organized chart. And even with the case always
within view, she still could make no sense of Jake's
murder. As a distraction more than anything else,
she resorted to reworking Edna Mae's quilt. Then,
unexpectedly, a neighbor called. The old curmud-
geon, who had served in the military and lived

down Farm Hill Road from her, called around four o'clock in the afternoon to ask if she'd be willing to bring him two dozen organic eggs and a one-pound jar of lavender honey. His wife, he said, "had the hankering to do some baking."

Abby and Sugar hadn't yet gone out for their walk, and taking a delivery to a shut-in was a good reason to get out. With the items tucked into a basket, along with some pickles and corn relish she'd canned over the summer, Abby and Sugar set off down Farm Hill Road. Within a half hour, they came to the short lane lined with tall redwood and pine trees where the neighbor lived. A half century ago, he'd bought that old adobe house, probably never realizing that a small tract of houses with lawns and families with pets would sprout up around him. But it had. No sooner had Abby and Sugar arrived than the man met them in the yard with money in hand. Eighty-five years old and nearly deaf, he gave her a jar of pomegranate jelly with the money and sent her on her way. Abby surmised that being polite and neighborly wasn't his way. She and Sugar turned around and made it back to the Henny Penny Farmette just as dusk painted the deepening blue of the sky with large swaths of apricot and lavender-gray.

Abby reasoned that if the pomegranate jelly tasted good, she might try her hand at making some next September, when the fruit on her trees ripened. It would be a messy business extracting the juice from the seeds held inside the leathery peel. Potentially, the jelly making from those seeds could turn the kitchen into a disaster area. And although they hadn't yet produced a lot of fruit, she had planted six pomegranate trees on the outer edge of her small orchard. If she could sell pomegranate jelly to the upscale deli-market that already had purchased her homemade apricot and wild plum jams, the mess making the jelly could be worth it.

Abby was still thinking about adding pomegranate jelly to her repertoire of organic fruit jams and jellies the next day, as she drove to another EMDR session with Olivia.

"How's the anxiety level?" asked Olivia after Abby had recapped the last week and they had gone through another therapy session.

"Four or thereabouts," said Abby. "The heart palpitations aren't coming like they used to. Almost never now. And when I do get worked up, the meditation and deep breathing calm me. And . . . I've been doing some reprocessing of my own."

"How so?" asked Olivia.

"I created an incident poster for Jake Winston's murder, and I've been working it like a puzzle in my living room."

"And when you're working on the case that way, how does it make you feel, Abby? What does it bring up for you?" Olivia asked.

"I feel like I'm doing something to confront the darkness . . . all the unknowns. That's where my demons hide. The more I know, the more I can plug in facts and new information, the less tense I feel."

Olivia smiled. "In its own way, that's a breakthrough, Abby. I doubt you'll need many more sessions with me, but let us at least book one for next week."

Abby nodded. "Sure. I don't know if it's the EMDR or my tackling the case that is helping me. Or both. But something is working. The memories still surface, but not like before, with all the shaking and heart racing and fight-or-flight response. Now, those images are just ordinary, like reading a report."

"Good. See you next time," Olivia said.

Around noon on November 24, Abby called the Country Schoolhouse Winery's main number. No one answered. Knowing it would be a long shot that anyone might be around and working after Don Winston began laying people off, she nevertheless drove to the site. Life for Don Winston had to be pretty bleak. How would he restore the winery's reputation now that two murders had tainted the business like a barrel of bad grapes? How would he plow forward without the innovative ideas involving food and wine that had been Emilio's strength or without the forward-thinking business vision that had been Jake's gift?

Abby strolled straight to the entrance door of the Country Schoolhouse Winery. It was Thanksgiving. Kat was still working the case and now had a new crime to solve. Abby reckoned they would not be able to get together for a glass of wine this evening, so she might as well visit the winery, have a glass, and ask more questions. Alas, the place appeared to be shuttered and locked. Charlotte had told her that neither Dori nor Trevor had worked recently, because Don had temporarily closed the tasting room and kitchen—a fact confirmed by the sign on the door. But Hannah had told her they would be working with a skeleton staff while Emilio and Scott were temporarily laid off. Still, as far as Abby could tell, she alone walked on the premises. When her cell sounded with Kat's ringtone, Abby had been peering through one of two stationary windows at the front of the winery.

"Whatcha doing?" Kat asked.

"Poking around. I'm up at the Country Schoolhouse Winery. Hoping to find Don Winston."

"Why?"

"I have some questions."

"Your presence there wouldn't involve our two open murder cases, right? Because meddling in our active, on-going investigation would not be welcome."

"I know what the official position is, Kat. No need to remind me. But would you answer a couple of hypothetical questions?"

"Like what?"

Abby seized the opportunity. Her questions might point Kat to another vein of inquiry, while Kat's answers might reveal new details. "What if Jake's murder was a hit, arranged and paid for by Dori? And what if she gave the killer the gun for the hit, as well as providing the shooter with an alibi during the time of the shooting?"

"That's just off the hook, Abby. Is that a half-baked theory you are floating, or do you seriously believe that's what happened?" Kat asked.

"Well, I don't believe Emilio killed anyone, even if he had military training with weapons. He would never risk a shot going wild and hitting his sister. He loves her."

"Abby, he might not have intended to hurt her. But you can't always guess exactly how a bullet is going to behave. And you can't truly know a dark heart."

"Emilio has a good heart," Abby said. "And he's never been anything other than an upstanding member of our community."

"Whatever. I don't see the relevance of your alternative theory. We've got a suspect gun now. We know it is Emilio's weapon."

Abby cringed. "So you've tracked it from Dori's body to our local gun shop owner. And I'll bet he had copies of the documents Emilio filled out when he purchased the gun."

Kat replied, "You got it. We've got our own copy now of the firearms transaction record."

"Yeah, yeah, I know. You've got the ATF Form forty-four seventy-three." From the bridge of her nose, Abby brushed a spiderweb thread she'd walked into while attempting to peer into another window. "So think about this. What if Dori was the thief who stole Emilio's gun?"

"Oh, why would she? Check her Facebook page. Amid pictures of her culinary creations are words of praise for Jake and also Emilio." Kat cleared her throat. "So now I have a hypothetical for you, Abby. Say we can match Emilio's gun to the casing found at the scene, and we also have the lead the docs pried from Paola's skull. Wouldn't you agree that we can match the casing and bullet to the gun that fired them?"

"Yes," Abby said.

"Of course, finding Emilio's fingerprints on the gun would be golden, but we don't know about that yet. Still, with what we do know, I'll wager that Emilio's gun never went missing. He had to have lied about that." Kat's tone sounded confident.

"And yet he took and passed a poly." Abby turned away from the window and walked along a path, where she checked out the irregular shape of the cell phone tower atop the church on the horizon. "What about that cap in the parking lot? Recover Emilio's hair from it?"

Kat didn't respond.

"So I guess that's a no," said Abby.

"Be that as it may," Kat conceded, "Emilio Varela must have something to hide. He's hired a hotshot lawyer and is no longer cooperating."

Abby stared at the tip-top of the distant communications tower. "Have you checked Dori's cell phone? She and her killer's paths crossed at some point. What if it was for drinks?" She added, "Maybe sometime after seven o'clock p.m. They could have set it up during a phone call. Check her phone."

"We don't have it. It wasn't on the body."

"Well, maybe the killer has it. Regardless, cell phone records will work, too," Abby said.

"How do you know she had a date for drinks?" Kat's querulous tone concerned Abby.

"Don't get upset with me."

"But Abby, this is the type of meddling that concerns the chief and Sinclair."

"I'm not meddling. I've been asked by friends to help them understand the dire circumstances their brother is in right now. But don't I always pass along what I learn to you and Otto?"

"Suppose I can't quibble with that. . . . So what do you have?"

"She was last seen by one of her housemates between six thirty and seven o'clock, going out to
have drinks with someone. Kat, you and I both
know that we've got one bar in town, the Black
Witch, and that bar has CCTV. I'd love to know if
anyone saw Dori leaving the bar and, if so, who was
with her."

The phone went quiet. Abby surmised Kat was
digesting the information. "So I'll get on that, girlfriend, right after lunch. And that brings me to
why I called," said Kat. "Otto made reservations at
Zazi's to treat his wife, but she's stuck in Utah on
ambulance company business. Whaddya say you
and I join him there for a bite together?"

Abby glanced at her wristwatch. "It's nearly one
thirty."

"And the reservation is for two o'clock," Kat
said. "How soon can you get back here?"

"Twenty minutes," said Abby.

"On the prix fixe menu today, along with pumpkin pie," said Kat, "they've got an assortment of
desserts, including a rustic ginger-pear galette. So
you know what I'm having."

Abby chuckled. "Just like you to pick out your
dessert before the meal. See you there in a few."

Twenty minutes later, Abby navigated her Jeep
up Main Street. The only parking near Zazi's
opened right before her at the police station
across the street from the bistro. No sooner had
she grabbed her purse and exited the Jeep than
she ran into Chief Bob Allen, who walked toward
her, seemingly in a hurry.

"Hey there, Chief. Working the holiday?" Abby asked. She stepped aside to avoid them colliding.

"Nope," he said. "I'm dropping off some paperwork." He stepped past her.

"If you've got a minute, Chief?"

Bob Allen turned back. "Yes."

"You know Paola Varela?"

"Of course."

"This may sound like a weird request, but is there any chance a guard could be posted on her for the next few days, until the hospital discharges her?"

Chief Bob Allen's mouth tightened; his facial expression reflected what he perhaps construed as the impertinence of her suggestion. "Now, why would we do that? She isn't a prisoner in custody. And with the killer or killers still at large, I'm not allocating cops to babysit. I need two to a cruiser for their safety."

"But I think Paola is in danger."

"*You* think she's in danger?"

"Two winery workers are dead, and she's recovering from injuries inflicted by a bullet that killed her husband."

"Tell me something I don't know, Mackenzie."

"When I visited her at the hospital. I saw someone—a man—in the corridor on her floor. I'm positive it's the same person who gave Dori Langston a ride the night I met Kat for her birthday dinner. It was outside the Pantry Hut. And when that guy saw me at the hospital,he took off running like a rooster with his tail feathers on fire."

"This guy have a name?" asked the chief. His

body language told Abby he wanted to keep moving and was annoyed that she'd stopped him.

"I don't know him or his name."

"So basically, you think the person you saw at the hospital might want to harm Paola Varela. But you have no real evidence she's in danger at the hands of this man. You're just basing it on a hunch. Furthermore, you don't know who he is or whether or not the two have a history. Do I have all that right?"

"Yes, but—"

The chief's lips thinned beneath the sparse mustache he'd grown. "Request denied." He started for the station door.

"But—"

With his back to her, Chief Bob Allen raised his hand to gesture that it was the end of the conversation. Abby turned to face the opposite direction. *Whatever.* She crossed the street with the light and walked into Zazi's, where Kat, phone plastered to her ear, gazed out the plateglass window, absorbed in her call. After sliding into a chair and hanging her purse straps over the chair back, Abby watched the traffic pass on Main Street and tried to tune out Kat's date-making arrangements for drinks with the Root Cellar's headwaiter.

Otto soon joined them at their table for four, just as the waitress took away the extra chair and returned for their drinks order—iced teas for Kat and Otto, a glass of house red for Abby, to wash down the bad taste in her mouth from her encounter with the chief. Well, at least she'd tried to get Paola police protection.

As the waitress delivered the drinks, Abby noticed a light-colored sedan roll past on the street outside the window.

"Excuse me. I'll be right back." Abby pushed off her chair and, with her cell phone in hand, hurried outside. Tapping the camera app on her phone, she attempted to capture the vehicle's license plate. If the car's movement made it difficult for Abby, the other cars obstructing the view made it nearly impossible.

Back inside, she sat down again and scrolled through the sequence of shots.

"What gives?" Otto asked.

"A bunch of blurred images," Abby replied, disheartened. "I know that car. I saw it near the Pantry Hut. The driver was waiting to pick up Dori Langston. And I'm not a hundred percent sure, but it looks a lot like the car that drove out of the winery parking lot after Jake's murder. And that car that just drove by has the broken taillight lens."

"Yeah?" Otto got up to look out the window.

Kat, now off the phone, chimed in, "Girlfriend, I'm worried about you. Running after a car driven by a skinhead?"

Frustrated, Abby tucked her cell phone back into her purse. She reached for the white cloth napkin and gave it a sharp shake before placing it on her lap.

"I've heard street gossip, Abby," said Otto, sitting back down. "When you're nosing around, word gets out on the street. When I told you to watch your step, I meant it."

"Yeah, yeah." Abby gestured with her hand, as though flicking off the comment. "So I ask questions of people. Like everyone else, I'd like to understand how two in our community ended up dead. I've got a theory, but I can't prove it."

"Yeah. Are you going to share it or make us ask you questions?" Kat twisted in her chair.

"Give me a sec," said Abby. She picked up her phone and looked for Trevor's number. Locating it, she said, "You all might want to save this phone number."

Otto's pen failed as he tried writing the number on a tea napkin. Kat took out her phone and stored the number in it for later reference.

"So, this number," said Abby, "belongs to Trevor Massey. He's the boyfriend of the Pantry Hut clerk named Charlotte. And I've got something else for you."

The waitress brought a tray of appetizers that included baked Brie with rosemary crostini and sweet potato bites with toasted mini marshmallows.

Abby went on. "Find out if this dude had access to the sedan with the broken lens cover over the passenger-side taillight. Maybe the car belongs to a relative or friend. He and Dori both worked at the winery, and he sometimes gave her rides to work. I think he's involved in some way."

"I hate to disappoint you, Abby, especially when you are on a roll," Otto said, "but Massey has a solid alibi for the time of the murder. He's not a skinhead, and the only vehicle he's got registered in his name is his motorcycle."

"I know he's not a skinhead, but maybe he knows the killer. I don't know. Dori provided him with his alibi. I'll wager that he was hers. Am I right?"

Kat and Otto exchanged a look that told Abby she'd guessed correctly.

"Why would Dori lie for Trevor if she believed he had something to do with the murder?" asked Kat.

"Why else? To cover up her involvement." Abby knotted the napkin in her lap and then untied it. It gave her hands something to do to release the energy she felt tensing her muscles.

Otto waved over the waitress for another glass of tea. "Oh, so Dori Langston, who is now dead, was somehow involved in Jake's murder. Pray tell me how."

Abby took a sip from her water glass and locked eyes with Otto. "I think she killed Jake. She didn't pull the trigger, since she was in the winery kitchen. But I think she got someone to do it for her in return for the promise of drugs, favors, money, or something else."

Otto looked at her. Apparently, he remained skeptical. He ran a pudgy hand across the lower half of his face.

"You say Dori had an alibi, but Emilio had one, too," said Abby. "Months ago, when his gun went missing, Dori had been crashing at his place. Let's say she took it. She could have given it to Trevor Massey or someone else to kill Jake. Then, instead of giving the gun back to her, he or the killer could have hung on to it. The how and why details, I haven't worked out."

Abby inhaled a sharp breath and let it go. "But it seems so obvious to me that if a killer got the gun to kill Jake and kept it, he could have used it to shut Dori up about his role. And don't you find it just too convenient that Emilio's lost gun was right there near her body? Emilio goes on the hook for two murders, while the real killer goes free. Neat."

"Neat would be if the killer had left the victim's purse at the scene and it bore the killer's fingerprints, fiber, and blood," Otto said, clasping his hands around the back of his head, as if thinking about what evidence they did have to work with.

The three sat in silence until their food came. Abby reckoned she'd done everything she could at this point to paint an alternate picture of what might have happened. Otto and Kat would have to find the holes and plug them. And God forbid that she should be wrong about Emilio. Fiddling with her napkin, she decided to ask her friends why the police chief was in such a dour mood.

"I asked him a question, and he acted as if he had a burr up his butt," said Abby. "Is it just me or what?"

"He's not happy about something that happened early this morning," said Kat, looking at Otto, as if for permission to go on.

"I'm all ears," said Abby.

"Let's just say he's not happy today with Lieutenant Sinclair," Kat said. She rolled her eyes and let Otto pick up the thread.

"Well, we shouldn't make too big of a deal out of it. It's not like it hasn't happened to cops in other city police departments." Otto reached for his iced tea and took a swig.

"Oh, for God's sake," Abby said, leaning forward. In a whisper, she said, "Tell me already."

Lowering her voice, Kat said, "He went for a run

to clear his head. I told him not to park under the bridge along Las Flores Creek, where the running trail begins. The park rangers check that area only once each day. Lots of cars have been broken into down there." She drew a pattern with her finger on her napkin, as if leaving it up to Abby to figure out what might have happened.

"So someone broke into his car," said Abby. "What was taken?"

Kat yielded answering the question to Otto, but he was ogling the food the waitress had brought on a large tray to the next table. Kat leaned in and whispered to Abby, "His service revolver."

Abby's eyes widened. She made a soft whistling sound. "Oh, boy."

Otto's attention returned to their conversation. "At least the press hasn't gotten wind of it."

"Yet," said Kat, leaning back in her chair. "You'll keep silent about this, won't you, Abby?"

"Of course." Abby's thoughts drifted back to the hospital parking lot and the guy wearing the slouchy beanie. She'd watched him peer into cars, but he hadn't jimmied open any doors or smashed windows. He hadn't committed a crime that she'd witnessed. But, boy, he was weird. And Abby wished she knew why he was at the hospital, on Paola's floor, and whether or not he had any connection to the winery other than knowing Dori. On her incident poster, Abby had written him in as "Weirdo."

Desserts arrived. Kat plunged a fork into the rustic ginger-pear galette placed before her. The look on her face suggested it tasted as good as it looked. Her eyes swept over Otto's pumpkin pie and onto Abby's French apple tart with almonds and apple brandy. In a seemingly mellower mood than before their late lunch, Kat said, "Won't it be lovely when we get the two murders solved, the downtown freeway exit closed so the holiday horse and buggy can travel up and down Main Street, and have all the decorations and holiday lights up in the downtown?"

"The fire department doing that again this year?" asked Abby.

"Uh-huh," Kat said. She dabbed her mouth with her napkin.

"Yeah, well, I'd like to find Sinclair's weapon," said Otto, pushing another forkful of pie into his mouth. After chewing and swallowing, he added, "Love to beat the crap out of whoever took it."

"How did the thief get it? Was the lieutenant's car damaged?" asked Abby.

Kat said, "Not really. I think the perp had some experience using unlocking tools."

Otto finished his pie and pushed back from the table. "Yeah, well, about that dream you have for the perfect winter holiday, Kat. Personally, I think it's not a good idea to have a jingle-bells horse and buggy trotting up and down Main at the same time as cars full of folks gawking at holiday lights."

Kat and Abby locked eyes. Otto abruptly had shifted the conversation again..

"If you ask me, it's a recipe for disaster," said Otto.

Kat reapplied her lipstick and then looked squarely at him. "You really don't have a romantic streak in your body, do you? I'll bet your wife wouldn't mind a buggy ride under the stars in a horse-drawn carriage. Try to picture the two of you sitting real close. With a glass of hot mulled wine and a blanket to warm you, things could heat up real fast." Kat looked at Abby and winked.

Otto grinned. "And can you picture what will happen if traffic spooks the old nag? I'm talking about the horse here."

"Of course you are," Abby said, muffling a chuckle behind her napkin.

"Oh, please," said Kat. "I'm sure the buggy driver knows the drill."

Otto grinned and fiddled with his duty belt, pushing it lower over the belly he'd just filled.

Abby put down her fork, brushed the crumbs from beside her plate into her napkin, and laid the napkin on the table. She relaxed, listening to the easy banter between Kat and Otto. Her two friends and former fellow officers at times could be adversarial, but they had a genuine affection and were fiercely loyal to each other.

"There's going to be a big celebration in the park for the holiday tree lighting next weekend," said Kat. "Why don't you invite that handsome rancher who lives up the hill from your farmette? We could meet next to the tree in the downtown park."

"And then what?" Abby asked.

"Hang out," Kat said.

"Somehow I don't see Lucas Crawford just hanging out," said Abby.

"For once, Abby, I wish you'd lighten up. You don't have to fall in love with the guy. Or force a relationship. Just have a little fun. Or have you forgotten how?"

Otto arched his brows.

Kat wouldn't let it go. "Ask him when the opportunity presents itself."

"Assuming it will," Abby said. The idea did rather tantalize her.

Rustic Ginger-Pear Galette

Parchment paper, for lining a baking sheet or tart pan
All-purpose flour, for flouring a cutting board
Pastry dough, enough for 1 large pie crust (made from scratch or store-bought)
¼ cup granulated sugar, plus ⅛ cup for sprinkling on the pie crust
1 tablespoon cornstarch
1 pinch kosher salt
4 large ripe pears
¼ cup finely chopped candied ginger
2 tablespoons unsalted butter
1 large egg
4 tablespoons apricot jam

Directions:

Preheat the oven to 400°. Line a baking sheet or tart pan with parchment paper.

Sprinkle flour over a cutting board and then roll the pastry dough into a 14-inch round. Place the round on the lined baking sheet or tart pan and refrigerate for at least 30 minutes.

Combine the ¼ cup sugar, cornstarch, and salt in a medium bowl. Cut the pears in half. Use a melon baller to remove the pithy centers and then slice each half into ¼- to ½-inch-thick slices to lay them out in a fan shape. Coat the pears with the cornstarch mixture and place them on a large plate.

Remove the pie crust from the refrigerator. Position the pear slices on the pie crust, starting from the center of the dough and working outward, leaving a minimum of four inches of dough to fold back over the fruit. Sprinkle the candied ginger over the pears. Place dots of the butter all around the galette. Press the dough around the edges over the fruit to hold it in place.

Beat the egg with a whisk in a small bowl. Use a pastry brush to apply the egg wash to the edges of the dough. Sprinkle the egg-covered dough with the remaining ⅛ cup sugar. Bake for 1 hour, or until the crust is golden brown. Remove the galette from the oven to a wire rack.

Spoon the apricot jam into a small saucepan and heat thoroughly. Brush the warm jam over the pears and serve the galette.

Serves 4–6

Chapter 16

Citrus trees need protection from frost,
so cover them with sheets of burlap or
blankets on frosty nights.

—*Henny Penny Farmette Almanac*

Driving home after her late lunch with Kat and
Otto, Abby listened to the four o'clock press
conference on the Jeep's radio. Chief Bob Allen
and the mayor presented the facts about Jake's
and Dori's murders and reminded the community
to remain vigilant until law enforcement caught
the killer or killers. A reporter raised a question
about witnesses that echoed Abby's concern for
her and Paola's safety.

On the evening news, the local media dug into
Dori's past. The product of a broken home, the re-
bellious teenager had initially found work in food
service but had forged gang ties and had more
than a few brushes with law enforcement. Shady
characters from Dori's past painted her as a mas-
terful manipulator. But Abby reckoned that Dori
had smarts and cooking talent, too. Abby could al-

most hear Father Joseph emphasizing during a homily that no person was all good or bad.

On her incident poster, Abby studied the lines she'd drawn from Jake to all the people who had had a relationship with him. His name was in a circle to indicate he was deceased. Now Abby drew a circle around Dori Langston's name. Returning the cap to the felt-tip pen, she studied the lines that connected everyone. Several people had motives. Others had the means. But the column labeled "opportunity" remained problematic. Abby wondered if it would do any good to drive to the hospital emergency room and interview that student nurse Lina Sutton. Perhaps she would remember some small detail she hadn't shared with the police. She uncapped her pen and jotted the intention on the poster.

Edna Mae called at sunset with gossip, as if it were a breaking news story. Paola was going to be discharged over the weekend, and her parents were leaving for Argentina in the morning—at least that was what an old friend at the hospital had told her. Was it true or not? Abby told her yes and explained that Luna had told her as much in a late afternoon phone call.

"I wish I could chat more with you, Edna Mae," said Abby, "but I've got to cover my citrus trees with blankets. It's supposed to freeze tonight. And I've got to do it before dark. You understand, don't you?"

"Oh, sure, Abby," said Edna Mae. "And let's talk about how the quilt is going the next time we chat."

"Of course," Abby said. "Next time." She didn't want to explain to anyone, least of all Edna Mae, why she was working on an incident poster instead of finishing that darn quilt.

She also didn't want to get into her concerns about Paola returning to the home she'd shared with Jake. The part-time housekeeper had agreed to work three days a week to help out. Also, Eva and Luna would be taking turns checking on their sister. The family had arranged with a local medical staffing company to have a per diem nurse at night, when the family members returned to their own homes. Abby promised to help Paola get settled and to drop by often to check on things.

On the following Monday, Abby made good on her promise. She helped Eva and Luna move Paola home. Paola was improving incredibly fast, considering what she'd been through. Abby felt her concerns assuaged when she observed Paola in the kitchen of her house, spreading some of Abby's wild plum jam onto pieces of toast she'd made after deciding she was hungry. It was a delight to watch. Luna and her toddler stayed with Paola the first night. Eva and her husband and child stayed the second night. Then the nurse took over night duty.

On the third day after Paola's discharge, Abby stood at the chain-link fence at the rear of her farmette, in pitch-black darkness. She watched circles of bright Maglites bobbing around. Henry and his buddies were guiding the RV onto the concrete slab behind the oleander bushes, out of the sight line of Abby's farmhouse. When her cell phone rang, Abby pulled the phone out of her jacket pocket and answered, "Mackenzie here."

"Thanks be to God, Abby. I have reached you." Paola's voice quavered. "Please help me."

"What's wrong? Have you hurt your head?" Abby knew that Paola's doctors would not reattach the small piece of bone taken from Paola's skull for another six weeks. She pivoted and sprinted back to her kitchen.

"No, my head is fine," said Paola. "It's the phone. It keeps ringing."

"Probably just a wrong number," said Abby.

"Not my phone. Jake's."

Abby's brow furrowed. "Wait . . . the cops took his phone."

"No. Jake had another. In his coat. Can you come now?"

A chill ran down Abby's spine. She stepped through the slider, then pulled it closed with her free hand. "Of course I'll come now. What does the caller say when you answer?"

"Nothing. Just breathes."

"And how many times has he or she called?"

"Three."

Abby could hear a faint melody. "What's that?"

"Jake's cell. Ringing again."

"Don't answer it." A knot formed in Abby's stomach. She frowned. Who didn't know that Jake was dead? Was someone making a silly prank call, or was this something more nefarious?

Paola cried out in a high pitch, "Ayeee. Abby, the patio light. It has turned on."

Abby's thoughts raced back to several months ago, when Jake had installed motion-detector lights on the outside patio wall. His house and others on their street bordered green space with bushes and trees and abundant wildlife. The green space separated the backyards from a creek bed that swelled with water during the rainy season. On the far side of the stream, uphill, was another tract of houses.

"Where are you? Can he see you?"

"In the kitchen." She gasped. "*El diablo*!" Paola began to cry. "He's there. I can't see him now, but I feel his eyes on me."

"Flip the light switch." Abby tried to sound calm. "Listen to me, Paola. Get out of the kitchen." She could hear Paola sniffling. "Is the house-keeper there?"

"No. She just left."

"What about your sisters? The nurse? Is anyone in the house with you?"

"*Sí.* The nurse is on her cell to the doctor about my medication. Eva left before Luna. Ten minutes ago."

"The doors and windows are locked, right?"

"Yes, I think."

"Good. You and the nurse need to get into a bathroom. Lock the door. Keep the lights off. I'll call the cops on my way. Leaving now."

"Hurry, please, Abby."

"I'll call you back."

"*Sí. Gracias.*" Paola's call clicked off.

From her bedroom dresser, Abby snatched her purse and car keys. Her sudden movements trig-

gered Sugar's frenzied barking. Not wanting to
waste a minute but needing to soothe her dog,
Abby called out gently, "Come on. You're going
with me." On the way out of the kitchen, she
grabbed Sugar's leash from the top of the fridge.

Navigating from the driveway onto Farm Hill
Road, Abby hit the contact for police dispatch.
When it rang, she tapped the cell phone speaker
icon.

"What's your emergency?" asked the dispatcher
who picked up.

"Abigail Mackenzie here. I'm calling in a ten-
seventy. The location is at three-nine-nine Thornhill Way. The home owner was recently discharged
from the hospital and is in the house with her
nurse. They are alone. There's a prowler at the
rear of the residence."

"Copy that. A squad car is in the vicinity."

"I'm on my way and will meet your officers
there."

"Roger that."

Speeding to the end of Farm Hill Road and
then turning off on a shortcut known to the locals,
Abby hit the contact for Paola and listened for the
ring. It seemed entirely possible that Paola's
prowler might be of the four-legged variety. But
after all that had happened, checking it out seemed
prudent.

Paola's shaky voice answered. "Abby?"

"The police are coming now," Abby said.

She could hear Paola exhale relief.

"Could you see the prowler? Could you tell if it
was a man or a woman?"

"Not possible," said Paola.

Abby heard the faint wail of a siren through the phone. "Okay, you're going to have to meet the responding officer in another minute or so. I am almost there, too. Make sure it's a cop before you open the door. Understand?"

"Yes."

Abby could hear the siren wail louder and then abruptly shut off. Paola had ended the call. Abby pressed down on the gas pedal. With Sugar in the passenger seat, she focused on taking every shortcut she could remember, until at last she pulled up and parked behind the cruiser with its light bar still flashing.

Abby decided to keep Sugar in the vehicle. She walked swiftly toward Paola's front door. A blinding flashlight beam struck her in the eyes.

"Stop right there."

Abby stopped mid-step at the surprise and her heart thumped in response. "I'm Abigail Mackenzie, the one who made the call to dispatch," said Abby. "The home owner inside has asked me to provide assistance."

"Show me your ID."

Abby reached into her purse and pulled out her driver's license.

The cop examined it and then handed it back. "Ex-cop, right? Go on in. My partner's inside with her and her nurse."

Abby hurried to the door. She tried not to register surprise at seeing Officer Bernie de la Cruz when the door opened. So the chief had him picking up calls now that Kat and Otto were working

the murders. Abby met his gaze, noticed the twin-
kle of recognition in his eyes. Women in the LFPD
knew well Bernie's reputation as an incorrigible
skirt chaser. His favorite line exposed the truth of
how he viewed any romantic relationship—*I'm here
for a good time, not a long time.* His personal life
aside, he was a good cop who worked the evidence
room, logging items in and releasing them when
cases had been adjudicated.

Before Abby could speak, Paola called to her.

"*La policía . . . muy rápido.*" Paola let go of the
nurse's hand to hug Abby. "*Gracias, mi amiga,* for
coming." She adjusted the blue print scarf around
her head, which hid the missing section of bone
the size of tea party gingersnap. Scarves would be
part of her daily attire now. Paola led Bernie, the
nurse, and Abby into the kitchen. There she stood
next to the sink and pointed out the window at the
illuminated backyard. Whatever had triggered the
sensor when Paola and Abby were on the phone
would remain a mystery. But now, Abby reckoned,
the officer who'd stopped her out front had probably gone around to the back to check the rear of
the house and the yard. His movement likely had
tripped the sensor light.

An hour later, Bernie and his partner—a twentysomething cadet who carried no gun—had done
a thorough search of the property and found
nothing. Before they left, they checked Jake's
phone, jotting down the number that had been recently calling. They wrote out Paola's and the
nurse's statements for the incident report. And
they instructed Paola to keep her doors locked

and to dial 911 if there was further suspicious activity.

Abby put her hand on Paola's arm. "Listen, why don't you consider discharging the nurse for tonight and coming to stay with me and Sugar for a few days?" She struck a lighthearted tone. "The couch bed is almost as comfortable as mine. And in the morning, I'll prepare us a big breakfast, farmette style—fresh-squeezed orange juice, rosemary potatoes, sausages, chunks of French breakfast cheese, toast, and homemade wild plum jam. Whaddya say?"

The cops regarded Paola for a reaction that didn't immediately come. "Abby's right," said Officer de la Cruz. "It might be good for you to stay somewhere else tonight. I doubt whoever had been out there will be back, but you never know. Sounds like you'll be in good hands over at Abby's place. Personally, I'd never pass up that breakfast she's offering." He stole a glance at Abby, which she disregarded. No way did she want Bernie to think she might have the slightest interest in starting something with him or inviting him to breakfast. Her focus was now completely on Paola and moving past the dark events of this evening.

Paola smiled. "Abby is my sister and my angel."

Abby escorted the officers to the door. "Thanks for taking a look around," she said. "We'll be leaving soon, too."

The kitchen clock wall above Abby's sink read nine o'clock straight up when Abby had finished locking the doors for the night. She and Paola had changed into pajamas and robes. Preparing the sofa bed with clean sheets and pillowcases took more time than usual because Sugar considered it a game. On Abby's upswing, Sugar would see the billowy sheet and launch herself at it. This new game went on for several throws, until Abby redirected Sugar to a legitimate toy—a chewed-up rag doll that had a pocket for tucking in a treat.

"I love it here," Paola said.

"You and me both," Abby said. Although she and Paola were in the cozy living room, Abby could hear the wind chime beyond the master bedroom window clanging. Abby said, "That wind is bonechilling cold and strong as my grandmother Rose's favorite hot toddy."

"Toddy?"

"It's a little drink my grandmother would whip up on cold nights. Generally, it would include her favorite Scottish whiskey, some water, herbs, and honey," said Abby. "But I'm going to make us something less potent to help us sleep." Abby walked to the kitchen to take out a pan and a jug of milk and set about warming the milk. She wondered how to explain to Paola not to be alarmed that the twiggy branches of the twenty-foot elm would scrape across the roof with the wind gusts. Then, there would be the pitter-patter of raccoon paws across the rooftop as the animals made their way to the Brown Turkey fig tree on the northwest side of her place. And the pine tree, too, would drop cones with a thud whenever the wind blew hard.

Abby poured the warm milk into a teacup and added honey. She walked back to Paola and handed her the cup. "Try this." After returning to the kitchen, she poured a cup for herself and again rounded the kitchen counter to sit at the antique dining table. Addressing Paola, she said, "The stone house in back has a bad roof. Pieces of corrugated tin break off sometimes in a wind gust. It makes a fierce racket."

Paola smiled but said nothing, apparently content to sip the beverage.

Abby sipped her milk and wondered how to explain mid-century roofing material that would snap off and blow away. What words could she substitute in Spanish for *polycarbonate* and *corrugated aluminum*? She decided not even to try to explain all the sounds that might wake Paola.

Paola looked up from her teacup and nodded. "We'll be fine." She lowered her gaze and finished her warm milk in silence. After she set aside the teacup and yawned, she asked, "Extra pillow, *por favor*?"

"Of course," said Abby. "Two aren't enough?"

"I want to wrap one. I brought Jake's pajamas." Her dark eyes grew shiny, and her expression became melancholy. "Maybe I see him tonight."

"In your dreams, you mean?" Perhaps Jake's pajama shirt still carried the scent of his soap and his body. That, too, would soon be gone. Abby looked at her tenderly. Unable to fathom the depth of Paola's suffering, Abby could easily understand this small act of love.

"In dreams, yes," Paola said, lifting the sheet to crawl into the bed. "You think it is strange?"

"No, I get it," said Abby. She set aside her teacup and rose to fetch the pillow. Sugar bounded up from resting on her haunches under the table to follow Abby. "Oh, I almost forgot," Abby said. "Ordinarily, Sugar sleeps at the foot of my bed. I don't know how she'll behave, since I rarely have guests. Feel free to call me to come get her."

Paola smiled. "Not necessary."

From the closet in her bedroom, Abby took the extra pillow from the shelf. She found a freshly washed pillowcase and wrestled it on. That Paola would beckon Jake to visit her in her dreams seemed touching. What if it worked? Abby wondered whom she would summon. Her thoughts conjured images of Ian Weir, Jean-Louis Bonheur, and Jack Sullivan. No, if she could invite anyone into her dreams, it would be that enigmatic Lucas Crawford. She placed the pillow on a chair and pulled out a comforter from a zipped storage bag. After taking the two items to the living room, Abby handed the extra pillow to Paola and spread the comforter over the bed. While Paola wrapped Jake's gray-and-blue-striped flannel bedclothes around the pillow, Abby did a final check of the door and window locks.

"Sleep well, my friend," said Abby, her hand on the light switch. "Tomorrow's a new day."

Paola had already turned away from her to embrace the pajama-clad pillow.

Abby murmured, "My grandmother Rose would say, 'In this world, when we doubt too much and dream too little, we miss the sweet mysteries of life.' And doesn't love always begin with a mystery?" Abby flipped off the light. "Sweet dreams, Paola."

How to Make a Garden Wind Chime from a Pot Lid

What country garden would be without a wind chime hanging from a branch of a tree or a garden shed? It's easy to make a chime using old pieces of silverware and hanging them from a pot lid that has a handle or knob.

The tools you'll need are a felt-tip pen, scissors, and a drill with a bit (to make small holes in the pot lid and the silverware pieces). The materials needed include a nine-inch round pot lid with a handle, a spool of fishing line, ten small washers, and old forks, knives, and spoons (ten total). Find these at tag sales, thrift stores, and consignment shops. Beads will add color and interest.

Use the pen to mark places on the pot lid and the silverware handles for holes and drill them. Cut the fishing line into ten pieces, each measuring twelve inches, and tie a washer on each piece of line. Thread the pieces of the line through the top of the lid so that the washer holds each line in place. Add beads to each piece of fishing line, on the underside of the pot lid. Tie a piece of silverware at the end of each line. Hang the chime using fishing line or a piece of cord or wire threaded through the pot lid handle.

Chapter 17

Smoke is a by-product of combustion—
so where there's smoke, you can
bet there is or was a fire.

—*Henny Penny Farmette Almanac*

Abby huddled under the bedcovers, trying to make sense of the dream she'd just had. In the dreamscape, she'd been standing in dense, damp fog. Her left hand rested upon a fence post. A raven descended and perched on her hand. Her dreaming mind sensed a familiarity about the bird. Its presence, though ephemeral, transmitted an indefinable heaviness of energy that penetrated her being. In some ways, it felt akin to the weight of grief or unexpressed love when a person bottled those feelings inside. The bird stayed only long enough for her to sense that burden. Without warning, it lifted off the post and took flight. But the dark and heavy encumbrance that the dream presence had brought stayed with her.

Cocooned in blankets and a comforter, Abby listened to the howling wind and a tarp that must have ripped away from its moorings and now whooped, slapped, and flapped. She'd stretched it over an old frame to create a makeshift potting shed on the southeast side of her house, near the herb garden that she and her late friend Fiona Mary had designed and planted. Beyond the windows, these noises added another chorus to nature's cacophony. As Abby thought about it, she had likely incorporated the flapping sound into her dream as the bird flew away. But why had her sleeping mind conjured the symbol of the archetype trickster in the first place?

Her grandmother Rose believed the raven to be a messenger. And that black bird, with its shaggy throat feathers and bowie-knife beak, portended bad tidings, failure, and loss. Remembering the terrible misfortune that had befallen poor Paola, now sleeping in the other room, Abby surmised the dream might have simply been her subconscious throwing up an image to represent the darkness associated with death.

Sugar stirred. Wide awake, her ears shot up. "What is it, sweetie?" Abby asked, rubbing the sleep from her eyes. She glanced at the clock. The hands indicated it was a little past midnight. Sugar bounded to the living room, barking her head off. Abby rolled from under the warm bedcovers. After tucking a small penlight on the bedside table into her bathrobe pocket, she trotted after Sugar to see who or what was calling at this late hour.

Paola awoke. "What's going on?"

"Shhh." Something caught Abby's attention through the art deco glass panes. Out beyond the porch, a red circle glowed. Someone was smoking a cigarette. Who was there, and why? Heart thumping, Abby recoiled against the wall. She leaned down and touched Sugar, but there was no comforting the dog. She continued barking.

A second or two later, Abby stooped and again peered through the glass. The cigarette burned brighter, as though someone had just taken a drag. Then it darkened. Abby's stomach knotted. Her back and neck muscles tensed. Adrenaline pumped through her. Perhaps the prowler had watched them leave Paola's house and had followed them to the farmette. Abby's skin went prickly hot. A sudden suffocation claimed her. A bigger question loomed—what was going to happen when the smoker finished that cigarette?

Abby watched. The cigarette torched a rag, and the rag blazed. The intruder tossed it onto a blanket she had spread over each of her blood orange trees. *What the . . . ? My God. He's going to burn down the place.*

If she'd been alone—just her and Sugar—she might have loaded her gun, slipped out through the kitchen, and crept around to the front to see who was standing in her driveway. Having Paola inside complicated things. Although her young friend had regained mobility and was healing fast, she was still in recovery mode. One thing Abby knew for certain. She would protect Paola and Sugar regardless of the risk to her own life. But there wasn't a moment to lose.

"Sorry," Abby whispered as she touched Paola's shoulder. "But we have to go. Put on your shoes and bathrobe. No lights. Wrap yourself in this comforter." Paola started to ease out of the bed. She reached back for the pajama-covered pillow.

"Leave the pillow. There's no time."

"Why? Where are we going?" Paola stood adjusting the scarf over the vulnerable part of her head.

"I think your phone-call stalker has followed us here. So now we've got to hide." Abby helped Paola put on her robe and tie it. "Here are your shoes. Slide in your feet. And then wait here."

Abby hustled back to the bedroom, where she yanked her cell phone from its charger. She tapped the side button to bring up the lighted dial and then tapped the number for county communications.

"Dispatch. What's your emergency?"

"Abigail Mackenzie here. It's a prowler. He's set a fire near the front porch."

"Mackenzie. You called before. Same address?" asked the dispatcher.

"No. Send fire and police out to the Henny Penny Farmette at the end of Farm Hill Road. There's a chicken on the mailbox."

"Are you inside the house?"

"Yes, but not for long."

"Emergency vehicles are on the way. Can you stay on the phone with me?"

"Sorry. Can't," said Abby, then hung up. She pushed her feet into her house slippers and tried to think of where to hide. Preferably, as far from the house as possible. Her thoughts latched onto Henry's RV. Thank God, he'd come back on schedule. This time, he'd parked the RV behind the oleander bushes, where it couldn't be seen. She snatched the blanket from her bed and wrapped it around Sugar.

After carrying her swaddled dog into the dark kitchen, Abby whispered to Paola, "Follow me."

Next to the oven mitt, on a hook, Abby located the RV key. Pushing the key deep into her robe pocket where she'd put the cell phone and pen-light, she one-handedly unlocked and opened the sliding glass door. Throwing the blanket off Sugar, Abby held the dog by her collar. The two women slipped onto the dark patio, with Sugar yipping her high-pitched alarm. After sliding the door closed, Abby reached for Paola's hand while at-tempting to restrain and quiet Sugar. Steering clear of the backyard's wet grass, Abby chose to lead Sugar and Paola along the flat terrain of the gravel path. They passed the garden swing and fol-lowed the path to the end of the chicken run.

"Where are we going?" Paola whispered.

"There's an RV hidden in the back. We can hide there."

At the end of the run, next to the metal gate of the chain-link fence, Abby peered into the black pitch, trying to make out the shapes of the olean-der bushes. The wind's whistle through tall pines and pin oaks sounded more like a roar. Gusts lifted and smacked the eucalyptus branches and their long strands of leaves against the ridges of trunk bark. A broken piece of aluminum roofing rattled as the wind lifted and dropped it.

"Gad, what's that smell?" Paola asked.

"Skunk spray and manure." Abby held her breath against the stench and hoped that no raccoons, bobcats, or other wild creatures might be roaming.

But then again, it was a frosty night, made colder by the wind. So maybe not. She smelled smoke now, too.

After unhooking the metal gate, Abby struggled with Sugar and also tried to help Paola through. Tripping over an exposed root, Paola stumbled and then leaned against the gnarled trunk of the pepper tree. Abby had forgotten about the root and stumbled, too, but quickly recovered. She tried to guide Paola away from the tree. Disoriented, Paola turned in the wrong direction and latched onto the chain-link fence for support. It rattled. Sugar continued her high-pitched yip. Abby froze. Surely, the intruder had to know the dog was out and behind the house. She hoped Sugar's barking would strike fear in the prowler. If he believed the dog would find and attack him, he might flee. She stole a glance back at the house.

Flames licked the sky. Showers of red sparks rained down. The muscles in Abby's chest tightened. Rising anxiety threatened to paralyze her. Refusing to let tears come, she cried out softly, "Oh, my God, no. Please, not my house!" Swallowing the lump in her throat, Abby forced herself to turn away. She whispered to Paola, "Keep calm and keep moving. Our lives depend on it."

Pop . . . pop . . . pop. The sound stopped them in their tracks. Then a loud explosion erupted. The two women huddled together. Grasping Paola's hand, Abby tried to sound reassuring. "Loud noises can't hurt us. Don't let go of my hand."

"I won't," Paola said. "But that fire. It's your house."

"God help us," Abby whispered.

Sugar's high-pitched yipping reached a frenzied pitch. Abby picked her way toward the oleander bushes. "Quiet," she commanded Sugar as she struggled with the dog.

They stepped behind the six-foot-tall oleanders. Abby's teeth chattered. The cold night wind penetrated the thin fabric of her pajamas and robe. "Hold on to my belt," she told Paola. "This way."

Afraid the intruder would detect them if she turned on the penlight, Abby lead Paola in baby steps across the landscape she knew by heart. Still, being familiar with the terrain didn't make the going any easier. She worried that Paola might trip again. Falling could cause dire consequences for someone with a piece of her skull out. Abby extended her hand in front of her and walked with outstretched fingers until they touched cold, damp metal. Running her hand up and down, she felt the rectangular box of the taillight where it jutted out from the rear of the RV. Slowly, Abby inched her way around and felt for the entrance door on the side. Reaching into her robe pocket for the penlight and key, she realized the items were in the other pocket.

"Can you hold Sugar real tight until I can get the key out?" asked Abby.

Paola whispered, "*Sí.*"

Placing Paola's hand around Sugar's collar, Abby said, "Do not let her wiggle free. She'll jump."

"I have her," said Paola.

Abby retrieved the key and penlight from her pocket. After placing the penlight between her teeth, Abby inserted the key in the padlock. The round doorknob also had a key lock, but Henry hadn't locked it. Abby opened the door and fought against the fumes of spilled beer and stale cigarette butts. She held the penlight on the interior until Paola and Sugar were safely inside.

Paola's teeth chattered. "It's freezing in here," she whispered, struggling to hang on to Sugar. As Sugar leaped from her arms, raced out the RV door into the dark, and barked loudly enough to be heard halfway down Farm Hill Road, Paola put her hand over her mouth and shrieked, "*Nooo.*"

Cursing under her breath, Abby thrust her cell phone and penlight into Paola's hands. "Call nine-one-one again. Lock this door behind me. Do not leave until I come back for you."

Paola was safe in the RV. She had the comforter for warmth and the cell phone to call for help. Using Sugar's bark to guide her, Abby raced off into the pitch-black night. With her heart galloping like a wild mustang, she ran, lifting her feet high to keep from stumbling as she raced over the weedy field, past the oleanders, back to the fence. The gusting wind lifted her robe, blew her hair into her face. Thinking that the fire in front of the house had been set to smoke them out, Abby surmised that the intruder could be lying in wait at the rear of the house. If he laid a hand on Sugar, what in God's name would she not do to save her dog?

Her body tense as a wound spring, Abby needed a weapon, but with no time to get her gun and load it with ammunition, she unhooked the heavy shovel hanging on the chicken house. Flipping on the backyard light would diminish the intruder's advantage. She hustled across the wet grass to the back door. Yanked it open, half expecting the assault to come from any direction. She flipped on the outside light. Spun around with the shovel raised. Her gaze swept from one side of the backyard to the other. No sign of any movement.

Sugar took off again like she'd been hit by buckshot. She dashed along the dark north side of the house. Abby followed. One hand held the metal shovel head against her chest, and the other grasped the shovel handle, as if she were holding a medieval jousting shield and lance. There he was. On the other side of the front porch. Twentysomething, maybe. A shaved head and dressed in a sweatshirt under a camo jacket, he sloshed fuel from a five-gallon gas can against the tarp of her makeshift potting tent. He'd already set the blankets over her citrus trees and her Jeep on fire. Tall flames leaped upward to ignite the elm tree. Its branches overhung the roof.

Sugar loped toward the man, barking and snarling, then rushed at the man's legs.

The skinhead set down the gas can on the gravel. The man removed a lighter from his pocket and flicked it at the dog. Sugar continued snarling, lunging, attacking, biting. The man kicked his way over to a pressure-treated length of board lying on the front porch. He threatened the dog with it. When he spotted Abby striding toward him, he called out, "Call your dog off, or I'll smash its head in."

"Sugar, come. *Now.*" Abby knew the dog wouldn't come. Sugar rarely obeyed any of her commands. Abby regretted that she hadn't found the time in her overscheduled life for dog training. Both she and Sugar needed it.

The man lunged at Sugar, who renewed her attack. The intruder kicked and swung at Sugar, hitting her back leg. She limped back with a yelp. "Drop the shovel." The man took a threatening step toward Abby. Sugar snarled and lunged again. "Call her off, or I'll douse her. One flick. She's gone."

Abby's heart throbbed. Her pulse pounded in her ears. "Come, Sugar." Abby might as well have been talking to the wind.

The man threw down the board and picked up the gas can. He pointed the nozzle at Sugar. The dog lunged at the military-style lace-up boots protecting his ankles. With a violent shake of the can, the man doused Sugar.

Abby screamed, "You bastard. *No!*" Up went the shovel into hard-assault position. After taking aim, Abby lunged with the full force of her body behind the thrust. She levied a hard assault to his head. He partially blunted the hit by using the gas can as a shield. The blow reverberated back through the handle into Abby's arm and shoulder. She winced.

Blood trickled from the man's wound as he let go of the can. After snatching the shovel from her, he heaved it onto the gravel. It skidded away. Then he snagged a handful of her hair and yanked her to him. Held her tight. Attempted to jerk the belt from her bathrobe loops. All the while, Sugar waged a battle of her own.

Fearing the man would strangle her, Abby relied on her instincts. One of the many judo moves she'd learned on the force was the big hip throw—*O goshi*. But she had to move fast. Abby seized the man's left sleeve with her right hand and snatched his jacket at the small of his back with her left. Right foot first, she hopped, skipped, and pivoted in a split-second maneuver. Her buttocks and back pressed against the front of his body, and with her back straight, she bent her knees and yanked hard. The man flew over her hip.

He held on with the grip of a mechanical vice. Abby hit the ground hard just as sparks crackled and sprayed from the Jeep. The cold gravel pieces punctured her back and buttocks through her robe. The man squirmed on top of her. Pinned her arm under her. A searing pain sliced through her right shoulder. He delivered a blow against her left cheek. With an agonizing scream, Abby writhed. Struggled to wrench free. Tried to reach the pile of river rock she'd stacked beneath the tree. She stretched her free arm over her head in the direction of the rock pile and felt around.

Her fingers latched onto a stone the size of her fist. Writhing upward enabled her to inch closer until she had the rock in hand. But her attacker jerked her bathrobe belt free. Abby sucked in a sharp breath and hammered the rock into the man's head. His body went slack upon her. Summoning what little energy she had left, Abby pushed him off. He rolled toward the Jeep, which was still smoldering, smoking, and blazing in places. Lying facedown, the man remained motionless even as Sugar continued the battle. The metallic scent of blood mixed with the acrid smell of smoke and the Jeep's burning wires and electronics permeated the air.

Nauseated by the stench, Abby cried out in pain and shivered on the cold gravel. Overhead, the burning elm crackled. Beside her the Jeep's blaze roared on. Bleeding and unable to move her injured shoulder or arm, Abby prayed the man would not regain consciousness for a while. *Dear God, please spur Paola to make that call if she hasn't already.* Sugar whined and barked and stood sentry next to Abby's attacker.

"Sorry. Come here, Sugar. Please. Come."

A vehicle pulled in, and headlights shone on Abby, lying under the tree in her front driveway. Tires screeched to a stop. The driver's door flew open. A man leaped out and sprinted to her. She heard a heart-wrenching baritone cry. "Abb-yyy. My God, what's going on here?"

Lucas? Oh, thank the Lord. Abby looked helplessly at him as he knelt and wiped her tangled hair away from her face. She could feel the blood oozing from the cut on her cheek and sharp pain in her hands, where broken windshield slivers had pierced the skin. The rocks beneath her dug into her back and scalp.

"My God, Abby. You're bleeding." Lucas reached to lift her.

Abby cried out in pain. "I can't . . . my shoulder."

"What's that man done to you? I'll kill that son of a—"

Wincing, Abby said, "I think I've already done it."

Lucas fired questions. "Who is that a-hole? Did he set the fire?" He took out his cell phone. "I'm calling the cops. And the fire department."

"Should be on the way. I've already called," Abby said through chattering teeth. Shivering, Abby didn't know if it was the shock of the assault or the freezing temperature. Regardless, Lucas's touch was warm and gentle. "Let me roll toward you, Lucas. Take my hand and tug on my good arm."

With Lucas's help, Abby was soon standing. Two sirens wailed on the approach to the farmette from Farm Hill Road. Abby's knees buckled as she tried to walk on her own. "Sure hope my attacker doesn't have a gun on him. Guess if he did, he would have used it by now."

"I'll check just as soon as I get you settled in my truck," said Lucas. He hoisted her into his arms and carried her to his vehicle, with Sugar barking all the way. Crying out in pain at the jostling of her shoulder, Abby stole a look at her house. Already, flames engulfed the elm tree's lower limbs where they scraped the southwest corner of her roof. Light from the blazing Jeep and the tree danced on broken shards of glass from the blown windshield.

"You heard the explosion?" Abby asked Lucas.

"Like a cannon. Feared the worst."

Abby's mouth felt as dry as henhouse straw. She tried to swallow. "That idiot poured gasoline on Sugar and threatened to set her on fire. I've got to get her water, Lucas."

"Sure. I'll get her some. But you come first," said Lucas. He helped her onto the truck's bench seat, turned up the heater fan to warm her, and was starting to close the door when Abby called out to Sugar.

"Come, girl."

Sugar leaped up into the truck with Abby.

Engine eight screamed into the far side of her driveway, which had two entrances. Following the fire engine was a police cruiser. Abby's trembling began to subside. But the thought of Paola freezing caused Abby to tense again. As soon as the scene was safe, she'd send Lucas to get Paola. Two law enforcement officers exited their cruiser. Abby realized they were Officer de la Cruz and his cadet. Their shift must not be over. Watching Bernie talk into his shoulder radio, Abby reckoned he was reporting to dispatch that he'd arrived on scene. Seeing the injured man on the ground, he would check him out and call for an ambulance. Or a coroner's van.

Abby watched the police duo help the firefighters do a four-man lift of her attacker to move him out of harm's way. The firefighters, working like ants on a honey bucket, began to spray water and pink retardant on the blaze. Lucas talked with Bernie, while the cadet checked the man on the ground, most likely for a weapon. The cadet, probably a new hire from the local academy, found something, because he motioned Bernie over, and the two put on nitrile gloves so as not to contaminate any evidence they might recover.

The fire medic trotted over with a doctor's-type bag and administered first aid to Abby's attacker. After checking for a pulse and examining the man's head, he broke an ampoule and waved it under the man's nose. Abby's attacker began to move his limbs. When at last he sat up with help from the fire medic, he was facing Lucas's truck. Abby breathed relief when the cops cuffed him. Locked in the police car, the man couldn't hurt anyone now. Lucas and the fire medic turned and trotted toward her. Abby noticed that Lucas had positioned himself so that she didn't have to see her attacker while the fire medic examined her.

"It hurts like nothing I've felt before. I can't move my shoulder," Abby said.

"Your left shoulder is lower than the right, and there's a lateral deltoid depression. My guess is you've got a subluxation of the left shoulder. Quite possibly, you could also have a fracture of the humerus."

"In English, please," said Lucas.

"I believe she's got a classic partial dislocation of the left shoulder. And for some first-time dislocations, there can also be an upper arm or shoulder girdle fracture. Need an X-ray for that."

"Can you reposition it?" Abby asked. "I can't take this pain. My muscles are drawing up tight in that area. Help me if you can. Please."

"Wouldn't you rather be transported? There's an ortho doc on call in the ER tonight."

"If you've had the training to reset the darn thing, let's not argue. And if you need me to sign a permission form for you to treat me, I promise I will."

"Okay, then," said the fire medic. He helped Abby out of the truck and stepped behind her to reposition her arm. "Count to three." The fire medic placed his hands strategically on her shoulder and arm.

Abby counted, "One, two, three." She felt a snap and instant liberation. "Ohhh, my God in heaven," Abby murmured. "Relief at last."

The fire medic treated her cheek and then asked to see her hands. Taking each of Abby's hands in turn, he examined them. "I don't see any embedded glass. It looks like the cuts are superficial. Still, I advise you to let the ambulance transport you to the hospital. You need to be thoroughly checked out."

"Yeah, I know. You have to say that. But I'm worried about my friend Paola Varela. She's in an RV at the back of my property. Hurry," said Abby.

The fire medic said, "Of course. And it's your choice to be transported or not, but you've been assaulted, and you really ought to get medically evaluated. I assume that you'll want to press charges."

"Oh, I'm pressing charges, all right, and for what it's worth, that guy is facing more than an assault charge."

"Good enough, then." The fire medic put away his medical bag and joined his team to get someone to go check on Paola.

"You're made of stronger stuff than any woman I know," said Lucas. He removed his coat and slipped it around her shoulders. Then he reached into his truck and turned the key to cut the engine, leaving the lights on for the firefighters, who had begun the mopping up. "Let's get you and Sugar inside your house. Fire will soon be out. This nightmare is over."

"Could you do something for me?"

"Do you have to ask?" Lucas encircled her with a

muscular arm. With the front door of the house still locked, they walked along the north side to the back patio. Sugar followed and raced into the house as soon as Lucas pulled open the slider.

"Put out some fresh water for Sugar. She's panting so hard. She's my hero . . . well, one of them."

"You got it." Lucas closed the slider and helped Abby walk to the living room sofa bed. While Sugar slurped from her bowl of water, Lucas got another, larger bowl down from the cabinet and filled it from the sink with fresh water. After setting it on the floor next to Sugar's water and food bowls, he looked over at Abby. "How about I make us a pot of java? I know where you keep the coffee, and your friends out there would likely appreciate a cup on this cold night."

Abby chuckled. "Good idea. Coffee for them, but none for me, thanks. I've had enough adrenaline pouring into me to last a lifetime. Assault and arson are two things you think will never happen to you," said Abby, leaning against the sofa cushions. "What a nightmare."

"That guy didn't just assault you, Abby. From the looks of it, he was trying to kill you," said Lucas. His expression darkened. He left the kitchen to go to her bedroom. Within seconds, Lucas reemerged with the comforter from her bed. He laid it over Abby, pulled it up to her neck. "What am I going to do with you?" He kissed her lightly on the head. Then, after walking back to the kitchen, he went to the cupboard located nearest the sink and took down the coffee canister.

The patio slider opened, and a firefighter walked Paola into the kitchen.

"We're going to be okay now, Paola," Abby called out from the sofa bed. "Come sit with me." She patted the edge of the sofa bed. "What a night. My Jeep's destroyed. The eave supporting the front porch roof and the elm tree limbs caught fire. The blaze is out now. My citrus trees are still standing, but all the blankets I'd used to cover them went up in smoke. I can only pray the trees will survive."

"Abby, I'm so very sorry," said Paola. "These terrible things happened because of me staying here tonight."

Lucas said, "Well, I'm staying the night now, too, with your permission, of course, Abby. I'll be standing guard with Sugar. Come dawn, I'll leave."

"Not before I make you one heck of a farmhouse breakfast, Lucas. But are you sure?" Abby said.

"Damn right. Who knows if that nutcase has a partner who might try to finish the job?" Lucas flashed a rare smile. "Okay by you, Abby, if I put Sugar in the shower to wash away the gasoline from her coat? I noticed some Dawn dish soap on the counter by the sink."

Admiration swelled in Abby's heart that Lucas would not only be thinking of her and Paola but also of Sugar. "Of course, Lucas."

Five Ways a Honeybee Hive Can Die

When a honeybee hive loses its queen through old age, disease and death, a failure to mate, or lack of food, and the hive doesn't replace the queen, it spells the death of the hive. There are many other reasons why a hive can die or a colony can collapse, including the following:

1. Pesticides and fungicides harmful to bees

2. Infectious diseases

3. Pathogens (bacterial, fungal, viral, and parasitic)

4. Starvation

5. Hive pests

Chapter 18

The flowers of a future garden are in
the seeds of seasons past.

—*Henny Penny Farmette Almanac*

Pain throbbed through Abby's face, hands, and
shoulder. Her eyelids fluttered open, and she
took stock of where she was—not in her bedroom,
but on the living room sofa bed. Opposite from
where she lay curled in a fetal position, Lucas slept
in the overstuffed chair. Amused and curious, she
watched his chest rise and fall in a quiet rhythm
for a time. *Some watchman, you are, Lucas Crawford.* After slipping out from under the covers, she
tied on her bathrobe and walked out her front
door to survey the damage.

Her heart sank at the sight of the burned-out
Jeep, which had been completely destroyed; the
blackened elm tree, which had been saved; and
the burned roof eave, the only damaged part of

her front porch. They stood as a testament to what a hellish night she'd been through. Her gaze swept from the broken shards of windshield glass strewn about on the ground upward to the bare branches of trees and beyond. The songbirds were singing, the wind had turned gentle, and hungry cows on the hillside bawled. Standing like a beacon of security and calm in the distance was the Crawford Ranch barn with its silver roof. Behind the structure, a blue-gray fog bank hugged the horizon. Already, shafts of orange, lavender, gray, and pink light splintered through the mist. Dawn was about to break.

Watching the gentle movement of the vapor, Abby recalled the previous night's drama. Her attacker had a name—Gary Lynch. Officer de la Cruz had told Lucas the guy was high and had drugs on him. That made it all the more remarkable that Abby had been able to hold her own against the wacko.

Thinking back to her therapy sessions with Olivia, Abby realized that embroiled in trauma—with no place to put her feelings and no time to process through them—she'd become confused and out of step with her own certainties. Strangely, the seeds of anxiety might have taken root deep within her much earlier—during the horrific languishing and loss of her first love, Ian Weir. A few years later, the devastating death of her younger brother had exacted its terrible toll. The anxiety that had plagued her since Jake's death had been debilitating. But even after all of that, awaking a short while ago in the presence of Lucas Crawford,

Abby's body was racked with pain, but the anxiousness and dread that had long plagued her were gone. Perhaps facing down her foe had made it possible for her to begin healing. But there was so much to understand. And for that, she would continue her therapy sessions with Olivia.

Lifting her gaze to the eastern horizon, Abby gave her full attention to the dawn as a new day came into being. Combing through reddish-gold tangles with her fingers, she watched a pair of ravens winging their way across the horizon and then toward her. They landed atop the scorched elm. Her grandmother Rose had instilled in her that there were signs in the natural world for those who would see them. Her grandmother had counseled that it was right to show gratitude when friends linking the visible and invisible worlds brought a message. *Some warning, guys.*

Abby slipped back into the house to retrieve a bag of unshelled peanuts from the cupboard. After returning outside, she tossed them into the driveway. "Here you go . . . with thanks."

"You talking to me?"

Lucas had followed her out onto the porch. He wore an amused expression on his unshaven face. His broad shoulders; long, jeans-clad legs; and worn cowboy boots shaped a sexy, rugged look that Abby found hard to resist. Whatever her future held, she hoped Lucas would be in it.

"Gratitude, yes, Lucas. But stale peanuts, no. I promised you a proper farm-to-fork breakfast. Fresh-squeezed juice is coming right up."

Appraising her with the intensity of a lover, he

closed the distance between them. With a scant foot separating them, he said in his rich baritone voice, "Anyone ever tell you that you're a damn good-looking woman, Abby?"

Abby laughed lightheartedly. Her pulse skittered. Unlike Kat, who had a rapid quip for everyone who uttered a flattering word to her, Abby didn't often get compliments and rarely knew how to respond. And this was one of those times.

He reached out and stroked her hair. "I've got to go. Ranch chores to do."

"What about that stupendous breakfast I was going to make for us?"

Leaning back, he grinned. Amusement flickered in his eyes. "I don't doubt you're up for it, but how about a rain check?" Lucas asked.

For Abby, his strong, unshaven jaw radiated male vitality. She melted under the intense light of his eyes, the color of creek water, and the sensuality of his face. "As you wish."

A silence hung between them like the thick mist on the hills. His eyes moved from the cut on her cheek to her mouth. Abby thought he might kiss her.

"Mind dropping me off?" Lucas asked. "That way you can keep the truck for as long as you need it. I'll have my car to use."

"Oh, gosh, that would be great. I much appreciate it, Lucas. Give me two minutes to change." She was already thinking of Kat's suggestion of meeting under the holiday tree in the downtown park. She fantasized about having breakfast with Lucas sometime during the holidays. Now, wouldn't that be just the perfect thing? And between pulling on her jeans and work shirt and dropping Lucas off at the ranch in his truck, Abby would think of some artful way to invite him.

It was mid-morning before Abby could take Paola home. They'd been through quite an ordeal. Abby felt guilty about that. But Paola's mood had become unexpectedly cheerful.

"I think we should make truffles today," Paola said when Abby had parked in front of the house on Thornhill Way. "But I know you have much to do. Thank you, *mi hermana*. You kept me safe."

"I'm sorry to have put you through such a night," Abby replied. "But, yes, let's make some lovely holiday treats soon. I've got honey."

Paola grinned broadly. "I am counting on it."

An hour after she'd dropped Paola off, Abby began the process of cleaning up her property and dealing with the disposal of the Jeep. If possible, she'd prefer to recycle it; otherwise, she'd contact a demolition company once the insurance company gave her the go-ahead. The shell of her car was a gross reminder of the past. She was ready to move on.

At noon, Kat texted. **How soon can you get to the station? Sinclair wants a face-to-face.**

Abby had hoped that the inevitable sit-down with the lieutenant would take place after she'd had more sleep. But clearly, that wasn't going to happen. Abby texted back. **Be there in an hour.** She might feel tired and beat up, but she didn't have to look that way. Sinclair would have questions. He might take her answers more seriously if she weren't wearing jeans and a flannel.

After taking a hot shower, Abby dried off and dressed in a knee-length black pencil skirt and a crisp white shirt. The fitted waist-length wool jacket, charcoal scarf, and flats made her look more like a lawyer than a farmer, she reckoned. Brushing her hair back and anchoring it with a sparkly clip was all she could manage. Trying to braid it had proven too painful for her shoulder and arm. Abby applied a little makeup—a light foundation, soft plum blush, and a deeper plum lip gloss. She applied a new bandage to the wound on her cheek and used a bit of mascara to darken her lashes before reaching for her phone and purse and heading to the downtown in Lucas's truck.

Sinclair said, "In here." He'd chosen the briefing room rather than the confines of his office or the tiny interview rooms. Otto, Kat, and Chief Bob Allen walked in. Abby assumed Nettie must be handling patrol, while a cadet worked the desk. It was weird to see the team assembled together like this when Abby was no longer serving on the force.

Once they were all seated, Sinclair thanked Abby for coming in. "On Thanksgiving Day, Ms. Mackenzie, you gave two of my officers a phone number that, as it turns out, belongs to Trevor Massey. Massey is the cousin of Gary Lynch, the man arrested last night on your property." Sinclair slightly loosened the knot of his tie.

"I'd like you to help us plug the holes in the

case we're building against Lynch for the murders of Jake Winston and Dori Langston." Sinclair cleared his throat. "So, let's start at the winery the night you and Officer Petrovsky went to the vow renewal party for Jake Winston and his wife. You okay with that?"

Abby nodded.

A car alarm went off outside. Otto glanced over at the window and said in a dry drawl, "Oh, dang. Someone's stealing my Ford Pinto."

Everyone broke into laughter.

"Like they even make those anymore," said Kat.

Abby appreciated Otto's timing. Levity at the right moment was always a good thing.

"You want coffee or a glass of water or anything before we start?" asked Sinclair.

"No, thanks." Abby just wanted to give them the information they wanted and be done with the case.

"On the night Jake Winston was killed, you stated you heard a shot and then a car engine started up. You described that car as a light-colored sedan. It drove toward you. You dove to hide behind a truck. The car in question slowed and flashed a light through the passenger window. Is that right?"

"Yes."

"Why would the driver be flashing the light out the passenger window?"

"All I can think is that the driver had only the car headlights and his flashlight to find me. If that creep had just murdered someone, he wouldn't want to dally by getting out of his vehicle to go looking for a possible witness. Yet he saw me. He knew I was somewhere in the parking lot and used whatever was handy that might help him locate my hiding place. If he'd found me, I'd be dead, too."

"How many occupants were in the car?"

"I didn't see the driver or occupants. The light through the passenger window appeared to me to be that of a flashlight. It shined briefly in my direction. And then the car took off."

"So you never saw the driver?"

"No."

"And you don't know the make or model of the car?"

"No," Abby said. "Why? Have you found a suspect vehicle?"

"We believe the car you saw was a nineteen-ninety-five silver Honda Accord."

"Means nothing to me."

"Do you know anyone who might drive or have access to that type of car?"

Abby turned slightly in her chair. "No. Should I?"

Sinclair said nothing but looked at her, as if waiting for her to figure out if she did or didn't.

"Like I said, I noticed the car was a sedan, light colored, with the passenger-side lens broken or missing from the taillight. I'm certain that it was the same car that picked up Dori Langston from the Pantry Hut. That was about a week after Halloween. The car had a broken or missing lens cover. On that night, the driver wore a slouchy multi-colored beanie. And recently, when I visited Jake Winston's widow, Paola, in the hospital, I saw the same man in the corridor on the wing where she was recovering. That's when I worried that she might be in danger. I asked Chief Bob Allen here to put a guard on her."

Glancing over at her old boss, Abby noticed his jaw tense.

Sinclair looked over at Chief Bob Allen and tapped his pencil on the table. "The man you saw in the car at the Pantry Hut . . . what did he look like?"

Abby inhaled a deep breath and let it go. "I couldn't see him very well. Like I said, he wore a stocking cap or beanie over his ponytail. It looked to me like the kind of floppy hat a granny would crochet with leftover yarn. Lots of colors."

"So, Lynch wore his hair in a ponytail, but you saw him last night with a shaved head."

"That's right," said Abby. "Changed his appearance . . . It's not uncommon for a criminal to do that if he wants to evade detection."

"We think we can link him through forensics to the knit cap found in the winery parking lot."

"So did he kill Jake Winston?" asked Abby.

"We think so," said Sinclair. "He's the one guy on our radar that had a motive, the means, and an opportunity." Sinclair pulled on his ear and stared thoughtfully at the table surface. "We now believe that Dori Langston provided Gary Lynch with the murder weapon after having stolen the gun from Emilio Varela during the time she stayed with him in August."

Abby now realized that Kat and Otto had taken her theory to Sinclair, and he'd adopted it as his own. She suppressed a smile. "You said he had a motive. Was it money?" asked Abby.

Sinclair nodded. "Two thousand dollars. That's the amount Dori had saved from money Jake had given her."

"Wow. Seems like a paltry sum, although no amount could equal the value of a human life," said Abby.

Kat chimed in. "According to Trevor, who has been singing to us like a songbird, Dori was going to use the money to furnish an apartment that Jake was going to set up for her. She thought he'd move in with her, too, but he renewed his vows with his wife. That infuriated her. And making matters worse, she thought Jake would fire Emilio and promote her to head up the wine club's special events program. But Jake had no such intention."

Sinclair opened his water bottle and took a sip. He screwed the cap back onto his bottle and set it on the table. "The woman was obsessed," he said. "The winery workers thought she was an ambitious control freak. She couldn't control or hang on to a relationship with Jake Winston. In a plot of revenge that was driven by thwarted ambition and jealousy, she hired Gary Lynch to kill Jake. In a twist of irony, Winston was a poor sucker who paid for his own hit, not realizing what Dori Langston would do with the two thousand dollars he gave her."

Kat looked out over the heads in the room thoughtfully. "Who knows what Jake was thinking when he gave Dori the money for the new place? The winery workers and Jake's wife agree that his behavior changed after his last trip to South America. Caught some kind of a brain fever. He was treated for it, but still. . . ."

"Paola worried that the illness injured his brain and altered his behavior," Abby said.

"Well, she would, wouldn't she? It's what she told us, too," said Kat. "She thinks it explains his lack of impulse control and strong desires for the ladies. But the doctors we talked with think that is unlikely. The wife might just need to explain away his bad boy behavior."

"We're not here to discuss the victim, just the perpetrator," Sinclair reminded them.

"And as perpetrators go, Lynch is intriguing," said Otto. He had been sitting back and listening but now leaned forward and put his elbows on the table. "Gary Lynch just got out of the slammer," he said. "Like most ex-cons, he needed money. Lynch was finding it difficult to land a job with his long rap sheet. Father Joseph had cut him loose at the Church of the Holy Names, so he went to his cousin Trevor Massey for help. His cousin tried to get him hired to work at the winery. The company didn't outright hire him, but Jake Winston would call him in to do odd jobs. Winston paid Lynch in cash on the same day he completed the work assigned."

"So," said Kat, "the night Jake Winston died, Lynch had been doing some cleanup around the place. Usually, he'd wait to be paid by Jake, but on that night, he told the sous-chef he was leaving when Trevor came on duty and would collect his moola the next day."

"That's why Lynch's name didn't show up on

the employee roster or sign-in sheet for the day. His deal was strictly an under-the-table arrangement with Jake Winston," Sinclair said.

"Wow," Abby said. "So you think Gary Lynch lay in wait in his car until Jake and Paola arrived?"

"It's plausible," said Sinclair. "And then Dori Langston demanded Lynch return the gun. He, in turn, demanded more money. She refused."

"So her refusal sealed her fate?" asked Abby.

Sinclair nodded. "We found Dori's purse and cell phone hidden on the winery property where he admitted to stashing them. That phone had Jake's private number stored in its contacts. We know from the last three numbers called from it that Lynch made those calls to terrorize Jake's wife," said Sinclair.

"His plan was all rather tidy," said Kat, "until he heard about possible witnesses. You had been nosing around, asking questions of Trevor Massey's girlfriend—Charlotte over at the Pantry Hut. At some point, Gary Lynch believed that it was just a matter of time until you figured out that he and Trevor were cousins and that they both had a great-aunt who owned a light-colored sedan with a broken taillight lens."

"Recently deceased aunt," Otto clarified.

"Lina Sutton," said Kat, "remembered seeing Massey and Lynch at the hospital the night their great-aunt passed away after the nursing home staff had her transported to the emergency room. Lina said she'd seen Lynch on other occasions lurking around the hospital. He didn't seem to have a purpose for being there. She said it was weird the way he just hung out in the corridors or waiting areas. Maybe he was looking for an easy way to score some drugs."

"Well," said Otto, "thanks to your rancher neighbor Lucas Crawford, who got a partial ID of the license plate of the old lady's car that Lynch was using, we were then able to narrow our search field and track down the owner registration to her. Finding her last known address was easy."

"Wait . . . what do you mean Lucas gave you a partial? When?" Abby asked.

"Last night he noticed a suspicious car in the vicinity of your house. He reported it."

"You don't say." Abby suppressed a smile at the thought of Lucas patrolling her neighborhood. "I have always believed that the car was the key. And that if we could find it, we could locate the killer," Abby said. "He must have kept the vehicle hidden. Do you know where?"

"In the garage of his great-aunt's house," said Sinclair. "The old lady broke her hip in a fall and was in a nursing home until she developed pneumonia. Lynch has been living in her house. The team went out there this morning and located the crime scene in the garage. It's where he killed Dori Langston. He apparently transported her body by car to the reservoir where he dumped it."

Kat leaned in and said, "You remember mentioning to me that old church up there that now has a communications tower on its steeple? On the night Dori went for a drink with a friend, she got a call," said Kat. "You remember telling Otto and me about that?"

"Sure do," said Abby.

"Well, Lynch's cell phone call pinged off that

church tower. He called her while she was out drinking that night."

"Who was Dori's drinking friend?" asked Abby. "Did you check the Black Witch's CCTV?"

"Uh-huh," said Otto. "She met with Don Winston. We've learned that her purpose was to convince Winston to fire Emilio and move her into the head chef position. But Winston wasn't convinced it was in the best interest of the winery. He told Dori that he'd decided to keep Emilio Varela employed, that he liked the chef's ideas. Winston said Dori's phone rang as she threw her drink at him. She took her phone call while walking out of the bar." Otto leaned back in his chair and clasped his hands behind his head. "According to Winston, she never returned."

"Let me guess. So the caller was Gary Lynch?" asked Abby.

"Exactly," Sinclair said. "Lynch picked her up in that sedan of his great-aunt and took Dori to the aunt's house and killed her execution-style. Trevor Massey will testify that his cousin Gary began to obsess over whether or not you and Paola Varela might finger him for the murders. Likely high on drugs, Lynch went to Paola and Jake's home. He used Dori's phone to call Jake's private number. Paola wasn't alone, but he wanted to break in, but then Officer de la Cruz and the cadet showed up. You arrived shortly after that."

Sinclair splayed his fingers on the table. He leaned forward and looked directly at Abby. "Gary Lynch followed you and Paola Varela to your place, with the intent to burn the house down with you both in it. Of course, Lynch was high on drugs, so he torched everything around the house first. Drug use was what Lynch and Scott Thompson had in common. Scott depended on drugs that he got from Lynch and didn't want Chef Emilio Varela to expose that. Through his criminal connections, Lynch facilitated Thompson getting the drugs he needed to support his addiction."

Chief Bob Allen stood up. He faced Abby. "The important thing to take away from all this is that Lynch underestimated your courage, Mackenzie." Stroking the sparse mustache he'd grown, the police chief exchanged a look with Sinclair and then again addressed Abby. "So you know how these citizen merit awards work, don't you? Sinclair, here, thinks we ought to give you one."

Abby sat stunned. Her hands, covered in adhesive bandages, remained folded in her lap. "Seriously?" She shot a surprised look at her former boss. Dumbfounded, she glanced at Kat, who was clearly trying not to smile. Then at Otto, who'd leaned over to pick something up off the floor.

Turning to leave, Chief Bob Allen said, "Don't hold your breath, Mackenzie."

Abby struggled to sort through conflicting feelings. "Well . . . thanks," she called out, but the chief had already stepped through the door into the hallway.

Lieutenant Sinclair pushed back from the chair and stood. "We're done here." He stretched out his hand. "Thanks for coming in."

Abby extended her bandaged hands. Her thoughts flashed on Lieutenant Sinclair's stolen service revolver. Abby had seen Gary Lynch casing cars in the hospital parking lot. Should she tell

Sinclair or not? Most assuredly, he'd search Gary Lynch's great-aunt's house and the local pawn shops for his missing service revolver. A thought intruded. *When a cop thinks you are trying to tell him how to do his job, the prudent thing to do is keep your mouth shut.* Abby decided this was one of those times. She waited until Otto had left behind Sinclair, and then she and Kat tarried a moment longer.

"Your leads and theories helped us put this all together, Abby. But it was Chief Bob Allen's idea to give you the award. He has his reasons, I guess, for putting it on Sinclair, but that'll be our little secret. So . . . the holiday tree lighting happens just after dark today. Then the whole downtown flips the switch on the streetlights and decorations. Otto and I are going for a slice of pizza over at the Black Witch. Join us?"

Abby checked the wall clock for the time and thought about Kat's proposition. "Well, that's just an hour or so from now. I guess I could stick around." Mentally, she thought of things to do to kill a little time. "I suppose I could fetch my business mail from the post office box and stop in at the Pantry Hut to look around at their holiday offerings."

"Wait until I sign out," said Kat. "I'll go with you. The walking will do us good."

Abby's expression brightened. "Deal."

At five o'clock, Abby and Kat, already in a holiday mood thanks to a couple of glasses of champagne they'd had at Kat's house after hitting the post office, stood admiring the hand-painted dinner plates featuring nostalgic holiday images in shades of green and red and gold that the Pantry Hut had on display.

"Oh, how lovely," Abby said, drawing Kat to her side. "Wouldn't these look stunning on a buffet table, especially under candlelight or by a blazing fireplace?"

"Hello, Abby. Fancy meeting you here," a female voice called out.

Abby spun around to face Olivia. Standing next to her was Lucas. Gripped by giddiness, Abby reminded herself to breathe. Under Lucas's steady gaze, she was relieved to be dressed in the professional attire that she'd worn for her meeting with Sinclair, instead of her usual flannel and jeans. Then, realizing Kat and Olivia had never met, Abby introduced them.

"And, of course, Lucas and Kat already know each other," said Abby, secretly pleased that her gorgeous girlfriend hadn't claimed Lucas as one of her conquests.

"Our civic leaders always light a holiday tree on the first weekend after Thanksgiving. We're just heading over to the downtown park to meet a friend of ours and watch the festivities," said Kat. "Why don't you all join us?"

"Oh, I'm just here to pick up a trifle bowl I ordered," said Olivia. "And then I've got a little gathering to attend. Maybe Lucas will."

Abby watched as Lucas eyed Olivia before he looked at Kat. Then he turned his attention to Abby, gazing intently at her. "Wouldn't miss it," he said.

"We'd better get going, or Otto will think we've bailed on him," said Kat.

Moments later, after walking to the police station, where Otto was waiting, the foursome joined the crowd that had gathered in the nearby park, under the decorated blue spruce. It towered forty-five feet into the night sky, under a sliver of the moon, which shined a pale light over the town. The crowd listened as a choral group from the Church of the Holy Names sang in four-part harmony "O Come, O Come, Emmanuel."

Kat's waiter friend from the Root Cellar also showed up. He found them near the edge of the park, next to the street where several horses and buggies waited with drivers at the ready. Everyone awaited the flip of the switch that would mark the start of the holiday shopping season in their small town. With the anticipation of a good season before them, the downtown merchants would welcome all comers into their shops this night with markdowns that they served up along with cups of spiced cider and cookies, candy canes, and hot pretzels.

Abby felt Lucas's hand slip around hers. "Shall we take a ride, Abby?"

Her impulse was to hold back, protest that the lights would be turned on in a moment, that the festivities would soon start. But then again, why was she hesitating? What was she afraid of? When had Lucas ever asked her to do something so spontaneous and romantic? She heard herself say, "Why not?"

At the carriage, Abby realized there was no dignified way to step up into it in a pencil skirt. Without a word, Lucas lifted her up into the seat. He then mounted the step to take his place beside her. The driver, dressed in a top hat and tails and looking as though he'd stepped from the cover of a Currier and Ives holiday card, spread a blanket over them. After taking his position in the driver's seat, he soon gave a shake to the reins. The horse pulled forward into an easy clip-clop, clip-clop.

They had just passed Cineflicks, the Black Witch, and Edna Mae's quilt and antique shop when Lucas whispered, "You're shivering. Come close." He slid his arm around her and scooted her closer. "Not hurting you, am I?"

"No." Abby's pulse quickened. Butterflies stirred in her stomach. Breathing in the scent of his body, perfumed by a woodsy spice and leather cologne, Abby felt her senses reeling. She leaned into his body's warmth and grasped the blanket trim.

Putting his hand over hers, Lucas said, "I've thought about this for a long time. . . ." His voice trailed off, as though he needed time to collect his thoughts. Filling the silence were the jingling bells on the horse's harness and the clip-clop of its hooves. Then, in a gentle tone barely above a whisper, he said, "We've let too many seasons pass, you and I. And not a word between us about how we feel."

Abby took in a ragged breath. A warm glow of anticipation spread through her. Such a serious tone. Where was he going with this?

"I've got a confession. Since my wife died, I've filled the void with ranch work. But these places we love—well, a house . . . a barn . . . a field—there's a certain longing inside that they can't fill. Agree?" He impaled her with his eyes.

"Yes, I know what you mean, Lucas," said Abby. "I feel the same." Excitement mounted within her. Something told her if she made a move right now, he'd kiss her. Heart skipping wildly, Abby squeezed his hand. Lucas gathered her into his arms. His lips caressed her forehead, and then he moved his mouth over hers. The touch of his lips was slow and gentle, until it was smoldering. He held her close to his heart. Abby savored the dreamy, intimate silence until the horse jostled them slightly apart when it made a turn to head back up Main Street.

Lucas pointed out the tree in the park. It shimmered in holiday splendor. High above the tree in the night sky, Abby saw a shooting star, a predictor her grandmother Rose would have said of a seasonal shift and good things to come. She and Lucas were on the threshold of something new and exciting and unknown. This was new ground to furrow, new seeds to plant for the seasons to come. And for what it was worth, her Scots-Irish grandmother was almost always right.

"Come for breakfast," she blurted out.

"Thought you'd never ask," he said with a grin.

Acknowledgments

First and foremost, I must thank my fantastic agent, Paula Munier, without whom my Henny Penny Farmette series would not have found its wonderful home at Kensington Publishing. To my brilliant editor Michaela Hamilton, whose unwavering enthusiasm and insights in shaping the books are always spot on, I will forever be grateful. Thanks also to Rosemary Silva and Robin Cook for the excellent copyediting work and incredible attention to detail on the manuscript and galleys. Thanks also to the hardworking publicity team: Karen Auerbach, Morgan Elwell, Lauren Jernigan, and everyone else at Kensington who has contributed to making my Henny Penny Farmette mystery series a success.

I'm blessed to have a phenomenal group of professional writers in my critique group. Writing a novel a year means that for many months at a time, I face the blank page alone. But I know that there is an invisible cord connecting me to my Scribe Tribe, and I have only to tug on it for help. For your tremendous support, insights, and feedback, I owe huge thanks to Mardeene Burr Mitchell, Paula Munier, Susan Reynolds, John Waters, and Indi Zeleny.

Thanks to Katerina Lorenzatos Makris for a lifelong friendship, as well as valuable tips and insights about dogs. I don't know anyone who knows more about rescuing our four-legged, furry friends.

I am deeply grateful to Thomas O'Neill, a forensic anthropologist and (ret.) San Francisco Police Department captain, who helped me understand the world of bullets and bones. A big hug and thanks to Sergeant Aaron Pomeroy, who continues to provide me with an invaluable lens for viewing law enforcement issues in my stories. You answered my every text as fast as I could send it. To both Tom and Aaron, know that I sincerely appreciate your help, and if, inadvertently, I have made any mistakes involving the workings of a small-town police department, procedural elements, or other law enforcement aspects, they are all mine.

Thanks to my daughter, Heather Pomeroy, for sharing stories about her life as a paramedic and evidence technician in a small-town police department. As always, these stories provide a plethora of ideas. Thanks also to Madison and Savannah for their suggestions, story ideas, and infectious laughter, which kept me going in times of fatigue. I'm thrilled you both are such avid readers.

A big thanks to my beekeeper neighbors Botros (Peter) Kemel and Wajiha (Jill) Nasrallah. Your encyclopedic knowledge about honeybees is what provided me with the impetus and confidence to start my own apiary. And your praise and promotion of my homemade jams is opening doors to new opportunities, for which I am grateful.

A hug of appreciation goes to my son Joshua for all the tech support needed for maintenance of my Web sites and social media platforms.

A big hug to my Dominican-born architect husband, Carlos J. Carvajal, for aspects of my stories that involve buildings and for the Spanish language translations. You deserve credit also for being one of my recipe taste testers.

For her wonderful ideas and support for recycling, gardening, jam making, fine wine, world travel, and all things home crafted, I offer my heartfelt thanks to Jeanne Lederer, heir and owner of the property behind the real Henny Penny Farmette.

A huge thank-you goes to talented writer, editor, and friend A. Bronwyn Llewellyn, who gifted me her mother's collection of mysteries and an unfinished quilt in an orange box (a mystery in itself), which started me down the path into this story.

In case you missed the first delightful Henny Penny Farmette Mystery, keep reading to enjoy an excerpt from *A Beeline to Murder*!

Chapter 1

A drone (male honeybee) must be able
to fly fifty feet straight up, or he will
miss the chance to mate with the
queen; it is nature's way of ensuring a
robust gene pool.

—*Henny Penny Farmette Almanac*

Abigail Mackenzie pushed the trowel deep into
the soft, loamy earth where she had been
planting lavender from gallon pots. She rocked
back on her heels and cocked her head to one
side, listening intently. The low-pitched drone
could mean only one thing. Removing her gloves,
Abby pushed a tangle of reddish-gold hair off her
face and yanked up a hemmed corner of her faded
work shirt to wipe the perspiration from her forehead. Squinting up into the dappled sunlit branches,
she spotted them: thousands of honeybees writhing in a toffee-colored mass in the crotch of the
apricot tree.

"Arghh," Abby groaned. "Would it have killed you to wait another day?"

The sound of honeybees swarming ordinarily would have lifted Abby's spirits; it meant an additional hive for her growing colony of bees. But today that buzzing pushed her stress level as high as the cloudless May sky. The queen and her entourage had left the hive en masse, and unless Abby acted quickly, they would follow their winged scouts to a suitable new home, even if that home was five to eight miles away. To rescue the bees, she would have to don her beekeeper's suit, position a hive beneath the swarm, tie a rope around the apricot limb, and shake it with enough force to dislodge the bees into the open box—all adding up to precious minutes that she would have to shave from her already over-scheduled morning.

Watching the bees coalesce into a thickening corpus, Abby pondered the remote possibility that the bees might also hang around. But, for certain, the lavender wasn't going to plant itself. More importantly, she couldn't postpone delivering that file to the district attorney's office before noon if she expected to get paid for her part-time investigative work. And, of course, she had better get those ten jars of honey to the chef at the Las Flores Patisserie by eight thirty or risk another dressing-down, although the chef's cursing in French somehow rendered it less offensive.

Blowing a puff of air between her lips in exasperation, Abby threw down the trowel. The lavender and the bees would have to wait. Chef Jean-Louis Bonheur could be a tyrant or a charmer, and his moods seemed to swing without warning. She could only hope that today he'd be happy to see her. He was paying her well—twenty-two dollars for a sixteen-ounce jar. With her first delivery of lavender-flavored honey, the chef had convinced her to also sample his delectable pastries and had even invited her to watch him work. Abby recalled how she had enjoyed the role of observer—he was definitely eye candy, with thick brown hair, large brown eyes, and a buffed physique. It didn't hurt that he oozed personality. What woman wouldn't fall for that combination? But Jean-Louis was gay, and his hair-trigger temper had already become legendary along Main Street. So she vowed today to skip the banter and just deliver her honey, get paid, and stick to her schedule.

After guiding the Jeep into the parking space at number three Lemon Lane, the alley behind the patisserie, which faced Main Street, Abby checked her watch and smiled. Five minutes early. Not like last time, when she'd arrived late because of a flat tire to find Chef Jean-Louis in his kitchen, pacing and swearing under his breath. He'd shocked her by throwing a pastry bag of batter that he'd been piping onto a parchment-lined baking sheet with such force, it knocked over a bowl of chocolate ganache. And later, while counting out cash to pay her for the delivery, he'd launched into another tirade, punctuating his French exclamations with incredulous glares, his hands wildly gesticulating in the air. As she hurriedly pocketed the money and made her way to the back door, he'd called out an apology, or so she'd thought. His words stuck with her. "It is not you, AHbee." She'd never get used to his pronunciation of her name. "Non, c'est Etienne. Il est en retard." Apparently, she hadn't been the only person that day to violate the chef's obsession with punctuality.

Now with minutes to spare, Abby hoisted the box containing the sixteen-ounce jars of honey into her arms and scampered to the pastry shop back door, which stood slightly open.

"Chef?" Abby called cheerfully through the crack. "Chef Jean-Louis. It's Abigail Mackenzie. I've got your honey order here."

Abby pushed the box against the door. It swung open. Inside, the sudden hum of the motor of the chef's commercial-size, stainless-steel refrigerator kicked on. The sound pierced the silence of the empty kitchen. On the long center island, metal sheets of pastries on cooling racks awaited icing, filling, and drizzling. Cream horn and madeleine molds, pastry slabs, baking liners, mats, and cannoli tubes littered the counter space. Next to a large mixing bowl of royal icing lay a pastry bag filled with icing that had hardened from its wide tip. The ovens were still on, and the burnt smell of cake permeated the room.

Abby frowned. Something was terribly wrong with this scene. Setting the box of honey on the island, she instinctively grabbed a pot holder and turned off the oven. The law enforcement training she had gone through while at the academy and during her seven years with the Las Flores Police Department had honed her senses. Now, like back in the day, when she was often the first at the scene of a crime, her stomach knotted in that old familiar way. Why would the chef leave the premises with the back door open? Why was the CD player not on, when the chef, a fan of opera, always listened to his favorite arias while he worked? And why was his workstation so messy, when the chef took great pride in keeping his kitchen clean and organized to be as efficient as possible? Where was Chef Jean-Louis?

Abby's pulse quickened. Her muscles tightened. *What's going on here?* Abby tensed as she looked around. "Jean-Louis," she called. And then again more loudly, "Hello, Chef. Are you here?"

No answer.

Abby moved the box of honey in jars over to the cupboard where the chef usually stored them, since his pantry was often overflowing with supplies. Turning back, she walked slowly to the other side of the large island and rounded the corner. Her breath caught in her throat. There lay the chef, near the pantry door—eyes open, body not moving.

"Oh, my God in heaven!" Abby knelt and felt his wrist. No pulse. She leaned against his chest, desperately hoping to detect a breath. His open eyes were dull and cloudy. The ashen pallor of his skin, the bluish-colored lips, and the nonreactive and dilated pupils told Abby he was gone. She looked for signs that would tell her *how* he'd died. Instinctively, she peered at his neck and the narrow ligature mark it bore. Her senses flew into high alert.

Scanning the room for any sign of movement, Abby slowly rose. So what happened here? Had he killed himself? Or had he been the victim of foul play? She glanced at the pantry door, which was not completely closed. Could a killer be hiding on the premises? Heart pounding, adrenaline racing, Abby took out her cell and tapped the speed dial for her old boss.

"Chief Bob Allen, please," Abby said in a low voice. When he answered, she replied softly, "It's Abigail Mackenzie. I want to report a death. It's Chef Jean-Louis Bonheur . . . and it looks suspicious. You might want to send a unit to his pastry shop on Main. I entered through the rear, facing Lemon Lane."

Abby stared at the pantry door. Spotting a box of latex gloves on the counter, which the staff used to handle pastries, Abby took two and slipped her hands into them. She slowly, firmly grasped the pantry doorknob. Held her breath and yanked hard. She flipped on the light switch. Seeing no one, she exhaled in relief and pivoted slightly and noticed a length of knotted twine tied to the inside knob. The loose end had been cleanly cut and lay on the tile floor. An icy shiver ran up her spine. It looked like suicide, but who'd cut down the body?

Abby understood that she'd unwittingly stumbled into a crime scene. She knew how quickly the officers could respond to a call, especially to the pastry shop, which was located just ten blocks from the police station. Police headquarters occupied the first floor of the Dillingham Dairy Building, a century-old, two-story brick building situated at the end of Main Street, next to the city offices of the mayor, the town council, and the district attorney. Abby didn't want to contaminate the scene in any way, but her instincts told her to take in the details.

Gazing down upon the chef's dim, unanimated eyes, their once snappy brilliance forever quelled,

Abby felt a twinge of sadness. She noted that the sleeves of his chef's jacket were rolled almost to the elbows and that his left forearm was tattooed with what looked to be an interlocked nine and six. Siren screams ended Abby's observations. She quickly peeled off the gloves and tucked them into her jeans pockets.

A tall, blond-haired uniformed officer, her gun and nightstick holstered on her duty belt and her black boots shining, apparently from a recent polishing, stepped in through the back door. Abby relaxed and grinned. So the police chief had sent Officer Katerina Petrovsky to investigate. Kat had been Abby's best friend since they met at the Napa Police Academy. Abby had been invited as a guest speaker when Kat was still a cadet. Finding themselves seated together during the lunch that preceded Abby's talk and again afterward, Abby and Kat had promised to stay in touch. Later, after Kat had been hired by the Las Flores Police Department, Abby had served as her field training officer.

Before the two friends could say hello, a malnourished woman with matted gray hair and bright blue eyes banged her metal shopping cart filled with stuffed plastic bags against the wall before shuffling in through the open back door. Abby instantly recognized Dora; she was one of Las Flores's more colorful eccentrics.

"Where's my coffee?" she asked. "The chef always gives me coffee."

"Not today, Dora," Kat replied.

Abby watched Dora try to undo the covered button of her once stylish, threadbare gray sweater—

the task made more difficult since Dora seemed intent on not removing her 1940s-style cotton gloves. Abby remembered meeting a much younger Dora years ago at the historical cemetery, when the nearby, newly constructed crematorium had caught fire. That was before Shadyside Funeral Home was built; before the Las Flores Creek had flooded, prompting the town council to prohibit the building of any new cemetery within city limits; and long before Dora's chestnut-colored hair had turned gray and she had taken to sleeping at the homeless encampment beneath the bridge by the creek.

"I want my coffee."

"The chef can't give you coffee today," Kat explained. "You have to leave."

"No, he told me, 'Later. Come back later.' "

"When did he tell you that?" asked Kat.

"He always tells me that."

"Okay, well, there is no coffee today. So out you go." The officer took Dora by the arm and escorted her through the back door.

"You should talk to her. She gets around," Abby said when Kat had reentered the kitchen. Abby pulled another pair of gloves from the box on the counter and slipped them on.

Kat looked at her with a wary eye. "Yeah, but *usually* her conversations are with those voices inside her head, so I'll get right on that, girlfriend, but I'd like to see the body first."

"Over there." Abby pointed to the opposite side of the island.

"And why, may I ask, were *you* here?"

"Delivering my honey. What else? When I got

here, Kat, he was already dead, lying just like that. I swear."

"Uh-huh. And of course you didn't touch anything, did you?"

Abby had anticipated the question. "I promise you won't find my fingerprints on anything here except my honey jars."

"Good." Kat walked over to view the body more closely. She scanned the scene, taking special note of the area where the chef lay on the black-and-white tile floor.

"No blood, no splatter, unless you count stipples of frosting," Abby observed.

"So how did he die?" Kat asked. Unsnapping the fastener on the small pouch of her duty belt, Kat removed a pair of latex gloves. Sliding her hands into them, she knelt to look closely at the body. She leaned in to see the ligature marks on the neck. "What could he have possibly done to anyone to get himself killed?"

"Well, he could have killed himself. Take a look at the pantry doorknob . . . on the inside."

Kat stood and walked to the pantry. "I see what you mean. So if he hung himself, who took the ligature from around his neck and laid out his body on the floor? And what did he use to stand on?"

"All good questions I've been asking myself," said Abby. "Since the only chair in here holds a ten-pound bag of meringue powder, I'm guessing he didn't use it to stand on. Maybe a café chair from the other room?"

"Yeah," Kat said with a peculiar look. "And I

guess after he hung himself, he got up and moved it back?"

"Well, someone else was here. When I arrived, the back door was ajar. Perhaps someone he knew."

Kat's expression grew more incredulous. "Would that be the someone who couldn't bear to see him hanging? Or the someone who wanted to tidy up after murdering him?"

Abby chuckled. "I see you haven't lost your sense of humor. Clearly, if he was murdered, there would have to be a motive."

"Pretty much everyone on Main Street has experienced the chef's temper."

"Yeah," admitted Abby. "Even I have felt the brunt of his temper. But he was also generous to a fault. I mean, he doled out coffee and sweets to unemployed vets and the homeless." Abby watched as Kat surveyed the kitchen before strolling into the adjacent room, where glass display cases and small wooden café tables and chairs filled the cramped space. Fleur-de-lis wallpaper above dark wainscoting was partially obscured by the numerous black-and-white posters of Parisian scenes. Above the cash register a memento board hung slightly askew. Its crisscrossed red ribbon secured photographs of customers and friends posing with the chef.

Kat leaned in for a closer look.

"I've come through that door many a morning while his ovens were still on and the smell of freshly baked dough permeated the place," said Abby. "People would line up outside, all the way down to the antique store. Well, you know, he always had free coffee and fresh pastries for us cops. He liked having law enforcement around."

"For being in such a small space and open for only two and a half years, his business seemed to be booming."

"True, but you and I both know that things aren't always as they appear."

"Uh-huh." Kat walked toward the restroom, which was tucked off the kitchen, and flicked on the overhead light to look around.

"Is his apron in there?" Abby asked. "He never worked without one."

"You don't say. Now, what made you think of a detail like that?"

"Lest you forget, I notice little things like that."

"Does anything else come to mind?"

"Not really. I just remember how he always tucked a towel into his apron strings. Makes sense if you're wiping your hands often. You'll notice he doesn't have dough or icing or flour on his clothes, so he must have worn an apron if he worked all night in the kitchen. And I don't see it."

Kat looked behind the restroom door. "Not here." She walked back to the body, where she halted, finger against her radio call button. She pushed the button, and dispatch answered. "We've got a DOA at number three Lemon Lane. Notify the coroner and get me backup."

"Need help documenting this?" Abby asked.

"I ain't sayin' no. Just me and Otto working the streets this week."

"I thought Chief Bob Allen had hired some new recruits."

"Yeah, but three are in San Francisco for defensive tactics training, two are getting recertified at the firearm range, and our crime-scene photographer is in L.A. all week."

Abby winced. She knew working short staffed could be grueling, what with patrol work, traffic stops, ticket and report writing, court appearances, and the like. God forbid anything more serious, like a robbery or a murder, should happen. When she and Kat had worked together, their beat was the downtown district. They had worked mostly petty crimes, which ranged from the occasional burglary to high school pranks and shoplifting.

Las Flores was ethnically mixed, mirroring Northern California's Bay Area and wine country towns, and without much crime. The outskirts and rural areas were populated by farmers, ranchers, and young, upwardly mobile urbanites who favored family-friendly businesses and all things organic. Like any other town in America, Las Flores had its share of hotheads, rednecks, gangbangers, and retirees. But the vast majority of folks were decent and hardworking. Abby knew that the largest number of traffic tickets went mainly to nonresidents of Las Flores who used Main Street as a shortcut from the cities in the valley to the beach towns on the other side of the coastal mountains. But with a state prison only twenty-five miles to the north of town, just outside the county, Las Flores also got its share of shady characters passing through—convicted felons, parolees, and gang members, who frequented the local watering hole, the Black Witch Bar. Anything could happen on any day, but especially over the weekends, when out-of-towners cruised through.

Abby and Kat had witnessed plenty of public

drunkenness and brawls at the bar, a favorite of bikers, who frequently stopped in for one last cool drink after a long day of riding in the mountains or visiting wineries. The bar and the dead chef's pastry shop shared space in the same building that also housed Cineflicks, the local theater. Occasionally, the business owners along Main Street would complain of the stench of urine, sure that the culprits were bar patrons. Having worked the streets for years, Abby had seen many crimes and criminals during her tenure in the downtown, but homicides—those were few and far between in Las Flores.

Abby sighed, "What about the county sheriff? Couldn't Chief Bob Allen request some extra officers from him?"

Kat shot an incredulous look at her. "Are you kidding? Chief Bob Allen threatened to withhold our uniform-cleaning allowance to reduce departmental spending. That is, until the comptroller told him he couldn't do that. Ask for outside help? No way."

Abby frowned. "Well, what if I take the crime-scene pictures for you . . . ? I've got my camera in the Jeep."

Kat rubbed an earlobe between her thumb and finger as she weighed Abby's offer. "You know the rules. I'm supposed to say no. But seeing as how it's you, I don't think the chief could get too flipped out."

"Just trying to help," Abby said. "I've got to deliver a file to the DA's office by noon and head back to the farmette. If I don't rescue my bee swarm, they'll take off for parts unknown. So if you want pictures, speak up, or I'm out of here."

"Oh, what the heck! Let me grab the crime-scene tape from my cruiser." Kat turned and walked to the back door.

Following her to the parking lot, Abby opened the door of her Jeep and rummaged through the glove compartment until she located her digital camera. She slammed shut the door and, with camera in hand, said, "Just like old times."

"Yep," Kat replied. "Let's start inside and work our way out. I'll bag and tag everything on the countertop."

"I suppose you'll want me to get some shots of the scene, the body, and close-ups of the ligature mark on his neck."

"Uh-huh." Kat's gaze swept the room, as though she was searching for something, anything that could help her understand what had happened here that had resulted in the death of the town's award-winning chef. Once the crime-scene tape had been strung, and evidence collected and labeled, Abby pulled the camera from her shirt pocket. "Besides the interior photos and the body, anything else you want me to shoot?"

Kat motioned toward the kitchen's back door. "In the café, get some shots of the baker's rack and close-ups of items on the shelves like the recipe binders and that box up there, but don't remove anything."

"Okay," Abby replied.

Kat looked around. "I want images of the blue metal Dumpster between the pastry shop and the theater, a shot of the back door of the pastry shop all the way to the biker bar, and a panorama shot of the back of the building, since those two other businesses share common walls with the pastry shop."

"You got it. Are you thinking that somebody from the theater or the bar might have had a run-in with our chef?"

"We can't rule out anything at this point," Kat said. "I think a Dumpster search for a rope or the apron might be in order. The murderer could have tossed them, unless, of course, the chef hung himself, which I'm not buying."

Abby walked across the alley and turned to face the building's back side. She took several shots of the weather-beaten, stucco-covered grand ole lady, which the townsfolk considered a landmark of sorts. Built in the 1930s, it had remained unchanged as businesses emerged and closed while the town evolved into a chic little enclave of stylish shops and restaurants. The old building had endured the October 17, 1989, earthquake in the Bay Area, with only a few horizontal fissures to prove it, but the city engineers had found it stable enough to leave it standing.

Other buildings in town had not been so lucky. Bright red CONDEMNED notices had been tacked or taped to them, indicating they were to be torn down. The replacements, such as the row of small office buildings on the opposite side of the Lemon Lane alleyway behind the pastry shop, provided commercial tenants more functionality, but without any of the charm or character of the older buildings, which reflected the pre– and post–World War II architecture of Las Flores.

Returning to the chef's kitchen, Abby determined the best angles for her shots. She wanted clear and focused images for the investigation. Police chief Bob Allen didn't need another reason to be angry or upset with Kat . . . or her.

To establish the distance and relationship of the back door to the island and the restroom, she positioned herself at the back entrance to the kitchen. Later, she shot images from the opposite direction. Then, climbing on a chair next to a tall wire baker's rack, Abby clicked off a couple more photos. When she leaned into the last one, she nearly lost her balance. Grabbing the top of the baker's rack to steady herself, she knocked over a basket of dusty faux ivy that concealed a small security camera. Dismounting from the chair, she sidestepped the camera until Kat could bag and tag it, tugged a pencil from her pocket, and used it to pick up a plastic cup that had tumbled to the floor. Before setting it aside for Kat, Abby sniffed it and made a mental note to tell Kat about the booze smell in the cup.

Working the room, Abby photographed from every conceivable direction and angle. As she zeroed in on the area occupied by the body, Abby recalled the first homicide she and Kat had worked together. The victim had been a local divorcée who had met a man for drinks at the Black Witch. The man had driven the woman home. The next morning, the woman's boyfriend had found her on the floor of her cottage. She had been strangled and sexually assaulted.

The victim's boyfriend had called police. When his alibi had checked out, he'd been eliminated as a suspect. Strangely, it was the boyfriend who had noticed the woman's colorful patterned rug had gone missing. He gave a description of it to police. Then Kat, a flea market addict, spotted the rug a month later. Las Flores cops began surveillance of their new suspect, a Turkish immigrant whose family had ties to carpet weaving in the old country. He had a good eye and had, apparently, recognized the rug as a Ladik prayer rug from central Anatolia. Abby and Kat arrested him for selling stolen property and, after having the rug tested for trace evidence relating to the homicide, charged him with the woman's murder.

Abby knelt and took some shots of the chef's body. She noticed tiny particles of dough on the cuticles of the first and second fingers on his right hand. She also noted the lividity, or discoloration, from blood pooling in the parts of the body touching the floor. Pressing a gloved finger against the chef's right hand where it rested upon the tile, Abby realized that although the chef's body was not yet cold, it was stiff. She surmised that the corpse was in the early stages of rigor mortis. Abby knew that blanching would not occur after four hours from the time of death, so she deduced that Jean-Louis was probably killed sometime within the past few hours or just before dawn. Her estimate, she knew, was rough; the coroner would give a more accurate time of death.

Putting the camera back into her shirt pocket and removing the gloves, Abby walked outside, to where Kat was leaning against the wall, jotting notes in a spiral notebook. A white van pulled in and stopped just behind the flares. The van sported the blue coroner's department logo and insignia— stalks of wheat curved into a half circle.

"She's new," said Kat as she watched the young woman, in her late twenties and wearing her chestnut hair pulled back in a short ponytail, hop out of the driver's side.

"What happened to Millie?" asked Abby.

"Maternity leave."

"Oh, gotcha." Abby recalled Millie, with whom she had worked over the years. Her chirpy voice and quick smile for first responders—regardless of how grisly the scene was—somehow made the scenes of death more bearable.

"Millie married the son of the fire chief, didn't she?"

"Yep."

"Liked her."

"Me, too," Kat replied. "Dunno about this one."

The young woman slammed the van door and introduced herself in a loud voice. "Dr. Greta Figelson, assistant investigator with the coroner's office." She flipped her hand in a backward motion over her shoulder to a young black man with an Afro, who seemed hesitant to exit the van. "My driver, Virgil . . ." She couldn't seem to recall the rest of the man's name.

"Smith," the driver called out through his open window to finish her sentence.

Abby looked down and suppressed a smile. *Yeah, Smith's so darn hard to remember.* Kat jotted their names in her notebook.

Dr. Figelson marched over. Abby wondered why the coroner's assistant had even bothered to come with such an attitude. Two workers were needed to handle the gurney, although Abby recalled that the newer gurneys had electric controls and could be operated by one person. Maybe one of the workers had called in sick and the doc had to fill in, doing grunt work along with her regular duties today.

"So, where's the body?" Dr. Figelson asked, pulling a yellow mask with white ties from her khaki pants pocket. "I'm just here to pronounce him. Don't have all day."

Kat jerked her thumb in the direction of the kitchen. "In there." She stepped aside to allow Dr. Figelson to pass.

Dr. Figelson disappeared inside the pastry shop.

Finally, Kat's backup arrived. The second cruiser, red light flashing and siren screaming, wheeled into the empty parking space next to Kat's police car.

Kat called out, "Really, Otto? You needed lights and siren? Seriously?"

Otto Nowicki, a hefty, balding man with skin the color of an unbaked pie crust, hoisted himself out of the seat. Once upright, he spent two minutes adjusting and readjusting his gear, guns, and nightstick on his duty belt. Abby knew Otto was always talking about becoming police chief one day. He had a thing about looking and acting official. Both she and Kat believed it was unlikely, since Chief Bob Allen had no plans to leave and would never be pushed out, but Otto kept on acting like *he* was in charge.

"Ya thinkin' pastry shop . . . doughnuts?" Kat winked at Abby.

"Uh, *no*," Otto replied, running his hand across his spare tire of a belly. "I'm on a diet. Wife says I gotta eat more like a caveman and stay away from sugar."

"That right?" Kat quipped. "Does your wife know about the four teaspoons in your coffee at roll call every morning?"

Otto grinned sheepishly. "Jeez, the station's coffee is like drinking turpentine. I've got to put something in it, or it doesn't go down." He hooked his thumbs into his duty belt, sucked in his belly, and stood a little straighter.

Abby noticed Otto had lost a little more hair and had gained a few more pounds from when they had last worked together. His pate was bald except for a few sprigs of gray-brown hair standing up like beleaguered dried grass on the California hills during the dog days of summer.

Kat lifted the yellow crime-scene tape, allowing Otto to enter.

He trained his eyes on Abby. With a deadpan expression and a slow drawl, he greeted her. "Hello, Abby. Seen ya around. You don't drop by the station anymore. Don't you miss us?"

Abby inhaled deeply before answering. "You know, Otto, I kind of do miss the work, but then again, there are some things I don't miss."

"Yeah? Like what?" Otto asked.

"Well . . . for starters, being micromanaged by Chief Bob Allen. In my new life, I'm the boss. I like it that way."

Otto nodded. "Know whatcha mean. So how's the hand?"

Abby winced. Otto never shrank away from asking the direct questions. He was good in the interrogation room. He was the one who made the bad guys squirm.

"Healed. Thank you," she said, sliding her hand into her jacket pocket. Abby turned and walked through the back door. Standing just inside, she let go a deep sigh.

There was no need to share her medical history with Otto. He certainly didn't need to see the scars left by her surgery, which the doctors had hoped would repair the ligaments of her right thumb. The surgery hadn't worked out the way she'd hoped. To shoot her gun, her thumb had to be consistently stable. Hers wasn't. And she didn't want to talk about it anymore to anyone, least of all to Otto, whose tongue had a tendency to wag in gossip about as much as it did when licking doughnut sugar from his thin lips. Still, to his credit, he could also shut down and clam up, especially in matters involving police business.

From where she had been examining the body, Dr. Figelson stood up and untied her mask. "I'm finished."

Abby wasn't wearing a police uniform, and she was pretty sure the assistant investigator to the coroner would resist telling her anything, but she asked, anyway. "Time of death?"

Kat entered through the back door.

Dr. Figelson ignored Abby's question. She said, "Get my driver. Tell him to tag the body with a blue label, wrap the hands, and let him know that I've authorized the removal. You've no knowledge of any infectious diseases here or any involving the deceased, have you?"

Abby looked at her wordlessly. She shrugged. *Now, how would I?*

"Good. See to it, then."

Abby's forehead creased in a frown.

Dr. Figelson addressed Kat. "Obviously, he's dead. Did he have a regular physician I can talk with?"

Kat shrugged. Abby shook her head.

"Our office will do a limited investigation," Dr. Figelson said. After writing on a form, she handed it to Kat. "Here's the release number and my contact information. Now I've got a call to make."

Abby didn't like the assistant's attitude. Generally, the coroner's office and the police adhered to an agreeable level of professionalism. This woman was irritating. When Dr. Figelson brushed past, boot heels in paper covers clicking against the black-and-white porcelain tiles, Abby looked at Kat and shook her head. *What arrogance. Oh, well.* Helping the coroner's driver to remove the body would present an opportunity to take a closer look. On the other hand, Abby wasn't a police detective anymore, but even when she was, her pesky curiosity had gotten her into trouble more times than not. Still, she reached for the box of gloves on the counter, grabbed two more, slipped them on, walked to the door, and motioned for Virgil to come inside.

Virgil slid out of the driver's seat and dropped to the ground. He looked taller perched behind the wheel than standing at full height. Abby guessed he was a head taller than her own five feet three inches. He scampered over.

Abby tapped her watch. "Your partner says it's

time to load and go. Oh, and she said to wrap the hands."

Virgil's blue-black forehead and cheeks glistened with sweat. He glanced furtively at the body lying on the floor next to the counter and swallowed hard. Twice.

"Oh, come on. Don't tell me you're new, too?" Abby asked.

"Uh-huh." His complexion assumed a greenish cast.

"Why don't you go get into your protective gear and bring the sterile sheet, the hand wraps, and a body bag?" Abby said.

He nodded, but then cried out weakly, "Toilet!" His hands flew to his throat. He doubled over.

"No. Do not vomit. Not now. Not here." Abby pushed him in the direction of the restroom. "There." For the next several minutes, Abby clenched her jaw and waited for the disgusting sounds from the restroom to cease. *Newbie.* Another reason why she didn't miss police work.

Tips for Maintaining a Strong, Healthy Beehive

- Plant lavender, sunflowers, and such herbs as basil, thyme, and sage near your honeybee hive. When the food source is close to the hive, the hive tends to grow robustly in less time than if the bees have to fly off in search of food. Also, flowering food sources keep the bees on or near your property, where they will pollinate your garden vegetables, flowers, and fruit trees.

- Avoid using pesticides to control pest infestations on your flowers, as the chemicals will poison your honeybees.

- Place the hive on an elevated stand or platform, and off the damp ground, to aid with air circulation, help prevent frames from molding, and keep marauding animals from molesting your bees. And don't forget to control ants.

- Keep the hive dry, and face it toward the east and southeast for warmth, dryness, and light.

- Use a screened bottom board under the hive. It allows mites (which harm bees) to fall through to the ground, thus ensuring the mites will perish and will not reenter the hive.

- Feed your bees, especially if the autumn and winter seasons have been harsh, to prevent starvation.

Connect with Us

Visit us online at
KensingtonBooks.com
to read more from your favorite authors, see books
by series, view reading group guides, and more.

for sneak peeks, chances to win books and prize packs,
and to share your thoughts with other readers.

facebook.com/kensingtonpublishing
twitter.com/kensingtonbooks

Tell us what you think!

To share your thoughts, submit a review,
or sign up for our eNewsletters, please visit:
KensingtonBooks.com/TellUs.